HER TRUE MATCH

PAIGE TYLER

Published by Sourcebooks Casablanca, an imprint of Sourcebooks, Inc.
P.O. Box 4410, Naperville, Illinois 60567-4410
(630) 961-3900
Fax: (630) 961-2168
www.sourcebooks.com

Printed and bound in Canada.
MBP 10 9 8 7 6 5 4 3 2 1

With special thanks to my extremely patient and understanding husband. Without your help and support, I couldn't have pursued my dream job of becoming a writer. You're my sounding board, my idea man, my critique partner, and the absolute best research assistant a girl could ask for. Love you!

Prologue

Washington, DC, 2008

"WHAT ARE YOU DOING?"

Detective Braden Hayes looked up from his cell phone to see his partner, Tommy Knight, frowning at him from the passenger seat of their unmarked four-door sedan. "Calling in the emergency response team."

Tommy snorted. "So those heavily armed mouth breathers can get all the glory? I don't think so, Rookie. We gave up weeks of off-duty time tracking these low-lifes, not to mention spent our own money to pay off informants. Hell, we've been on stakeout in this car for so long that we stink of the damn pine tree deodorizer hanging from the mirror. We're going in there and taking down these a-holes ourselves."

Braden winced, both at the way Tommy called him a rookie every time he suggested doing something by the book and because he'd known his partner would want to handle this arrest on their own no matter how epic a bad idea he thought it was. Braden had only gotten promoted from investigator to detective level II a few months ago, but he was a fast learner, and he'd quickly figured out how his partner liked to do things.

Simply put, Tommy was a cowboy. Twenty years Braden's senior, Tommy was the most experienced and decorated cop in the robbery section of the Washington

Metropolitan Police Department. He'd made a name for himself by refusing to do things by the book, going balls to the wall on every case, and doing whatever was necessary to take down the bad guys.

Braden ran his hand through his dark hair and turned his attention to the empty warehouse across the street where the suspects were supposedly crashing, wondering what the other cops in his family would think of going into a completely unknown situation like this without a plan or backup. Something told him they wouldn't be too thrilled.

His great-grandfather had been a police officer in DC for thirty-five years, while his granddad still told stories about walking his beat for three days straight without a break during the Washington riots of '68. His father had retired two years ago after twenty-eight years on the force, and his older brother was driving a patrol car over in the Sixth District.

"Every rule in the book is written in a cop's blood," his granddad had told him on more than one occasion. "Do the job the right way every time, and you and your partner will come home alive every time."

To say that his family wouldn't think too much of Tommy's fast and loose way of doing things was an understatement, but he had to admit, his partner's style was starting to grow on him.

"Sometimes you just have to follow your gut," Tommy said as he narrowed his eyes, giving the warehouse a final scan. He turned to Braden, giving him a grin. "My gut's telling me this is solid."

Braden slowly shook his head, wary. "My gut is telling me to call for backup."

Tommy looked at him, frowning. "Sooner or later, you gotta learn to trust your partner. Because at the end of the day, when you go through that door, it's just the two of you."

Braden's mouth tightened. Tommy would never ask him to kick in a door if he didn't think the two of them could handle whatever was on the other side. "I do trust you."

Tommy gave him one last look. "Then let's do this."

They got out of the sedan and made their way across the nearly empty midday street to the abandoned warehouse they'd been casing for three days, trying to seem casual as they chatted about Redskins football and whether the team would regret the decision they'd made at quarterback.

The sign out front said the place had been an electric supply business. If Tommy's informant was right, the building was currently being used to store half a million dollars in cash, jewelry, and art stolen over the past four weeks by a burglary crew who had been hitting the homes of rich socialites and politicians when the owners were out on the town.

Lately, though, the thieves had gotten more brazen and broken in when people were home. Two older couples and a thirty-year-old political consultant had been roughed up pretty good over the past three days, with all the victims ending up in the hospital. It had put the crime spree squarely on the front pages of the local papers.

Braden tensed as he and Tommy headed to the rear of the building. Tommy's informant had said there were only three men in the crew and that even though they'd all flashed weapons during the last break-in, they'd ditched the guns after the job. Braden trusted Tommy with his life, but he'd be lying if he said that part didn't concern the hell out of him. When he'd asked Tommy how the informant knew for sure they didn't have guns and what the guy's connection was to the thieves, his partner refused to answer.

He and Tommy were going to have a long talk about that…later.

The rusted metal door was locked, and Braden did a double take as his partner pulled a small leather case out of his back pocket and unzipped it to expose a lock pick set. Dropping to one knee, Tommy slipped two thin pieces of metal into the face of the lock plate and wiggled them back and forth.

"Where did you learn to do that?" Braden whispered.

Tommy didn't look up. "Another lesson from my misspent youth."

"And how the hell are we going to explain how we got through this locked door?" Braden asked. "It's going to come up when we file our reports."

Tommy stopped what he was doing and gave Braden that patented smart-ass smile of his. Then he twisted the thin piece of metal, and the lock turned with a slight click.

"What locked door? It was open when we got here."

Braden frowned, but there wasn't much he could say about his partner's wavering moral compass. He watched as Tommy stood and slipped his Glock 19 out of the holster at the small of his back, which had been hidden by his T-shirt.

Ignoring his doubts, Braden pulled out his own MPD-issued 9mm from the holster under his leather jacket. At this point, all that mattered was covering his partner, and that was something he didn't have to think about.

The door opened up into a dimly lit room with rows of metal racks and stacks of industrial work bins. As Tommy moved ahead, checking each row they passed, Braden kept his head on a swivel, looking for an ambush from behind.

Voices drifted from the next room, and Braden turned to cover that direction. He was so focused on what he was doing that he almost missed his partner gesturing at the last line of metal racks. He glanced over to see what had caught Tommy's attention and almost laughed. Besides boxes of jewelry, bins full of small art pieces, and piles of rolled-up canvases, there were stacks of cash—lots and lots of cash.

Tommy grinned, and Braden couldn't help smiling back. This bust was going to be frigging huge.

Tommy motioned toward the entrance to the other room, and they moved forward together. Ahead, Braden could hear the sounds of clinking glasses and shuffling cards to go along with the low murmur of voices.

On the other side of the open door, Tommy gave him a silent finger countdown. *Three…two…one…go!*

Braden stepped into the room, taking in the three guys playing cards around a small table in the center of it—and the pistols sitting out in the open beside each of them.

Guess Tommy's informant had gotten the part about them ditching the weapons wrong.

Shit.

"Freeze!" Tommy shouted as one of the men reached for the Colt .45 inches from his hand.

"Metro PD," Braden added. "You reach for that weapon, and you're done."

When the guy hesitated, Braden moved to the side to get a better angle on the men while Tommy went to get their weapons away from them.

The front door of the building was a good twenty feet away on Braden's left, and the only other way out of the room was through one of the two windows on either side of the front door, or through the second door behind a counter directly across from him. The counter might have been tempting for the thieves to use as cover, but to reach it, the men would have to turn their backs on Braden and Tommy. Braden didn't think they were that desperate—or stupid.

Braden didn't like how calm the men seemed, though. It was almost as if they weren't concerned at all by the sudden appearance of two cops in their midst.

Eyes still locked on the three thieves, Braden opened his mouth to warn Tommy that something wasn't right when two men stepped out of the darkness behind the counter and started shooting. So there were five bad guys in the room, not just three.

Something else Tommy's informant got wrong.

Braden dived to the right to avoid the hail of gunfire coming his way. All the advantages they'd had against the three men seconds earlier—no nearby exits, nowhere to run, and no cover—now turned to disadvantages for him and Tommy. They were facing five men who seemed more than willing to kill them to avoid prison.

He rolled onto his left side and raised his weapon, aiming at the three men at the table, since they were closer and the greater threat at the moment. No doubt,

Tommy was doing the same thing with the men behind the counter, but he didn't have the time to check.

As Braden put a bullet in the chest of one man, he felt something hot sting through his right shoulder. It didn't hurt at first, and he was sure he'd just been grazed, but then all at once, holding his weapon up got a lot harder, like he was lifting a thirty-pound weight.

A second man at the table stumbled backward and fell to the floor, obviously hit by a round from Tommy's weapon.

Braden turned his attention to the third guy at the table, but he must have decided he was done standing in the open, blazing away at cops like this was some old west showdown. Instead, he shoved the table over and hid behind it, probably thinking the tabletop would protect him. It wouldn't.

Braden aimed for the center of the table and put three rounds through it. He scrambled to his feet and ran for the table, intending to hide behind it long enough to get a shot off at the men behind the counter. Somewhere along the way, he got hit in his left thigh, and his sprint turned into an awkward stumble. He fell to his knees behind the table, lucky he didn't end up on his face. It alarmed him that he hadn't even felt himself get hit. Was that bad? He didn't know.

Instead, he used the opportunity to drop the clip out of his 9mm and slide in a fresh one. He sure as hell hadn't kept count of the number of rounds he'd fired, but he had to be just about out. He expected the two men behind the counter to send a hail of bullets through the table at any second the same way he'd done earlier, but thankfully, they didn't. It was a good thing, too. The reload maneuver took him a lot longer than it should have. His right shoulder was on fire, and his arm refused to move the way he wanted it to.

Finally slapping in the clip, he transferred his pistol to his left hand and popped his head up for a look-see. Both men behind the counter were too focused on Tommy to notice Braden at first. That quickly changed when he took careful aim at one of the men and put a bullet in the guy's stomach, making him stumble. The shot should have been in the center of the man's chest, but shooting left-handed wasn't something he practiced as much as he probably should. He adjusted his aim and got the second round on target just as the injured thief turned to face him. The guy flew backward, hitting the wall and sliding to the floor.

Braden twisted his body to take aim at the final man, but the man was already tumbling to the floor before Braden could get a shot off. Out of the corner of his eye, he saw Tommy on his knees, his weapon pointing in the direction of the guy who'd just gone down.

Braden pushed himself to his feet, moving as fast as he could to see if the three men who'd been around the table were dead, then hobbling across the room and around the counter to check on the other two. They were dead, too. He took a few extra seconds to clear the room, but the place was empty.

"Clear!" he shouted before heading out to limp around the counter. "Holy shit, Tommy. I can't believe we lived through that. I thought we were screwed for sure."

He reached inside his pocket for his cell phone but froze when he realized his partner was still kneeling on the floor. Both arms hung loosely at his sides, his face pale and etched with pain. There were dark red splotches staining his T-shirt, running down his chest, and covering his stomach. Even as Braden watched, Tommy slowly fell forward.

Braden lunged toward his partner, catching Tommy before he slammed into the concrete floor.

"Don't you die on me, Tommy!" he yelled as he pulled his partner into his lap and tried to press his hands to the gunshot wounds. But there were too many of them. Shit, how many times had he been hit?

Tommy's eyes fluttered.

"Stay with me, Tommy!" he begged, trying hard to keep the panic out of his voice. "Don't give up."

Keeping his arm around Tommy, Braden dug his phone out of his pocket and hit the speed dial button for MPD dispatch. He didn't waste time with details, just giving them his name, badge number, the address of the warehouse, and that there was an officer down and in need of critical care. The dispatcher asked him something, but Braden ignored the woman.

Dropping the phone, he turned his attention to his partner. Blood flecked Tommy's lips. Braden wasn't an EMT, but he knew that was bad.

"Hold on, Tommy," he told him. "I called for an ambulance. Just hold on."

Tears stung Braden's eyes. Since making detective, he'd spent more time with Tommy than he had his own family. The guy was more than his partner. He was like an older brother.

"Did we get them?" Tommy asked in a bubbly whisper that brought up even more blood.

Braden wanted to tell him that none of that shit was

important, but he didn't bother. Because it was important to Tommy. "Yeah. We got them."

Tommy nodded. He opened his mouth to whisper something else, but the words were too soft for Braden to make out.

He leaned forward, putting his ear right next to Tommy's mouth. "I'm right here, partner."

Tommy didn't say anything for a moment, and Braden thought perhaps it was too late.

"Don't be scared…" Tommy finally whispered.

Then he stopped breathing.

Braden ground his teeth and leaned over his partner and friend, hugging his lifeless body. Lesson learned. He'd trust his gut and never break the fucking rules again.

Chapter 1

Washington, DC, Present Day

Dreya Clark climbed on the apartment's balcony railing, then stood straight and tall in the warm night air for a moment to catch her balance before leaping up and out, twisting in the air and snagging the edge of the next floor above her with the curved claws at the ends of her fingers. The needle-sharp tips found the tiny crevices in the brickwork, and she hung there for a moment, her feet swaying slightly above the ten stories of open space below. She tightened her stomach to minimize her swing as much as possible, not wanting to put any more strain on her claws than necessary. She'd ripped out a few of them doing this very same thing when she was seventeen and just learning how to use them. Back when she was still trying to deal with the freak she'd turned into.

Seeing her fingernails turn into long, curved claws for the first time had been hard enough to handle back then. But the fangs, green glowing eyes, and the yowls that slipped out whenever she'd gotten angry, upset, or confused that came along with those claws had been even more disconcerting.

She relaxed the claws of her left hand and pulled them away from the wall, reaching up carefully and finding another set of almost invisible cracks ten inches higher on the wall. She dug in, then released her right hand, pulling her body weight up with her right arm and shoulder at the same time. She hadn't done anything like this in a while and was happy to see her body hadn't forgotten how. Her hands, claws, arms, and shoulders worked in perfect harmony, pulling her up the outside of the building as easily as most people would climb a ladder.

Dreya moved quickly, covering the four floors to the roof in a few minutes. By the time she reached the top, she was breathing a little harder, but it felt exhilarating.

How long had *it been since she'd done this?*

She counted up the weeks as she crested the roof's parapet wall and hopped atop it, then jogged casually along the three-inch-wide edging toward the next corner and realized that it had been more than two months since she'd climbed more than a set of stairs, much less broken into a building and stolen anything. That had to be a record for her.

There was a good reason she'd been out of the game for a while. The last time she'd broken into someone's house and stolen something, Rory Keefe, her mentor and best friend, had died. She'd almost died, too, but that didn't bother her nearly as much as the fact that Rory, the man who'd taught her how to accept her claws and fangs, how to make jewelry, and how to steal it, had been murdered trying to protect her. All because she'd been arrogant enough—and stupid enough—to steal from that rich ex-senator, Thomas Thorn.

Dreya stopped when she reached the corner of the condo and gazed at the apartment complex on the far side of the street. Compared to the dull, boxy concrete structure she stood on now, the other place looked more like a work of modern art than a residence for people with more money than they knew what to do with. It was all glass and steel with a series of arcs and wavy projections sticking out at random angles to break up the outline of the building. She imagined some people staring at the place for hours, wishing they lived there.

Not that Dreya ever did. She liked her small apartment in Foggy Bottom just fine, thank you. The only thing that mattered to her was that those fancy sweeping arches and dramatic exposed trusses required all kinds of structural cables to hold them up and that one of those cables just happened to be attached to the ugly, boxy building on which she stood.

The cable ran at a slight upward angle and was attached to the fourteenth floor of the far building. Being able to access the other apartment complex that far above the ground would allow her to bypass nearly all of the building's security systems, as well as the guards who roamed the lower floors. Once she was across the cable, getting to her target would be almost too easy.

Dismissing the fact that the cable was more than one hundred and twenty feet above the ground and that there was a twenty-five-mile-an-hour wind whipping between the two apartment complexes, Dreya flipped her long, blond braid over her shoulder and hopped off the parapet and onto the cable. She ran up the slight incline at the same fast-paced speed she'd use on a treadmill. As she ran up the cable, her arms outstretched on either side of her to help keep her balance, she thought about Thorn and how lucky she was to be alive.

She'd been stealing stuff since she was eighteen, right after she'd figured out that being a freak with catlike agility, an affinity for climbing really high places, and perfect night vision would be considered a gift to some people. Rory had reluctantly taught her what she needed to know to be a good thief, more so she wouldn't get caught than because he'd ever wanted her to be part of his world. But she'd been good at it—really good. And in time, she'd gained a reputation within their circle for hitting tall buildings, highly secured targets, and filthy-rich people.

Most of her fellow thieves thought she stole stuff for the same reasons they did. But Rory knew she did it for fun and for the thrill it gave to the part of her with claws and fangs. The truth was that most of the stuff she took ended up buried in a landfill somewhere—or in her very private and very well-hidden collection.

She'd been questioned a few dozen times by the cops, even threatened with arrest now and then, but mostly, it had all been a big game. Then she'd stolen that big diamond and the strange black box from Thorn, and her whole life had changed.

After torturing and killing Rory, Thorn's goons had tracked her to a safe house where she'd been hiding until things cooled off. Some big bull of a man had appeared at the last minute to save her life, then a woman with a strangely familiar scent and a certain something that made Dreya instinctively want to trust her had shown up. When the woman told Dreya that she was there to help, Dreya had believed her.

She'd given the woman the diamond—and the strange black box—then took her advice about getting out of town, immediately heading north and crossing the border into Canada. She'd had money and fake identity papers stashed up there—another precaution Rory had insisted on—knowing that if she needed to, she could have disappeared and never come back.

Dreya reached the end of the steel support cable where it connected into one of the big exposed trusses and hopped up on it, then weaved her way through the maze of struts until she came to the place where the truss intersected a large arch made mostly of glass. She gave the nearest section of glass a tentative nudge with her foot to make sure it would hold her weight. Satisfied that it would, she stepped off the truss and onto the arch, careful to keep her weight near the edges as she slowly moved along. It was windy as heck up here, and the last thing she wanted was to get blown off the building by an unexpected gust. Her claws were good at getting a grip on almost any material—except glass. One wrong move, and it was a long way down.

Dreya had assumed Canada would only be a temporary layover. She'd figured Thorn would find her again and she'd have to keep running. But she'd only been hiding out in Quebec City for five days when the articles started showing up in the local news about how the American police and federal authorities had tracked a retired thief named Abbott to a warehouse near the Navy Yards in DC. A shoot-out had ensued, then an explosion had nearly leveled the whole place. Even though there'd been a lot of damage, the authorities had somehow managed to recover Thorn's diamond and had identified Abbott as the man who'd broken into Thorn's home and stolen it. Dreya knew the whole story was a complete fabrication, almost certainly created by the mysterious woman she'd met who'd promised to find a way to divert Thorn's attention away from her.

Dreya had hung around a few more days up in Quebec just to make sure Thorn's goons weren't still looking for her. Getting chased away from her home by that rich a-hole had pissed her off, though, so when it looked like the coast was clear, she'd taken a chance and come back to DC. Even though she was safe now, her experiences with Thorn and everything that had happened in May had shaken her to the core. For a while, she'd seriously considered getting completely out of the business. It had gotten her best friend murdered, along with nearly a half dozen other thieves and fences, and had come damn close to getting her killed as well. If it weren't for the mysterious woman who'd helped her, Dreya would be dead. It seemed a waste to go right out and do the same stuff that had gotten her in trouble before.

But in the end, Dreya hadn't been able to walk away completely. The crazy, freaky animal inside her seemed to need the thrill of the job to stay sane. Within a month of coming home, she'd been bouncing off the walls, designing jewelry and sleeping nearly impossible. She tried running and working out to keep the feelings at bay, but they hadn't worked. The itch was back, and the only way she knew to scratch it was to find a job to do, preferably one that involved some serious heights.

She'd learned one valuable lesson during the fiasco with Thorn, though. No more stealing from people who had a security company on their private payroll or psychos who were willing to kill to get their stuff back. Stick to plain, old-fashioned rich people who had more money than they knew what to do with and kept insurance policies.

That was why tonight's target was a simple thirty-year-old, trust-fund, blue-blood playboy who liked to impress his dates by showing off his private collection of Jeff Koons porcelain art pieces. They were worth a vulgar amount of money, and unlike a lot of the stuff she usually stole, these particular items were something she found attractive. There would be some security stuff to get past once she got inside, but nothing too complicated. The hardest part would be getting into the apartment.

Dreya paused when she reached the end of the glass arch she'd been walking on, eyeing the large balcony and its railing that stuck out from the building fifteen feet away with nothing but open and gusting air in between. The balcony would give her access to the playboy's apartment. Of course, only an insane person would try to get inside it by clambering around the outside of a building on the fourteenth floor.

She'd much rather deal with making a broad jump fourteen floors up than mess around with people like Thorn anymore. Those days were behind her. From now on, she was going to settle for low-risk jobs that wouldn't attract anyone's attention.

"Don't tell me she's going to try to jump all the way from the arch to that balcony," Braden's partner of several weeks said in a hushed tone, as if he didn't want to distract the thief they were watching on their surveillance monitors.

"Okay, I won't tell you," Braden said drily. "She

went to all that work to get within fifteen feet of her goal, and now she's going to turn around and go home."

Mick Radcliff ignored his snarky comment and kept his blue eyes glued to the monitor from the close-up camera. The one that showed every detail of Dreya Clark's face as she seemed to mentally measure the distance she needed to clear. Braden knew why Mick was so tense. They'd been watching her aerial escapades for the past fifteen minutes, and even he had to admit that he'd caught himself holding his breath more than once. He'd known she was good. That was how she'd been able to pull all the jobs he was sure she'd done and never ended up in prison or even in front of a judge for that matter. But he realized now that he'd drastically underestimated just how amazingly talented she was.

He and Mick had nearly fallen off the chairs in the surveillance van when Dreya had climbed onto the balcony of the building on the far side of M Street and jumped off the tenth-story railing like she was stepping off a curb. Then they'd sat stunned as she'd climbed the side of the building without any gear that either could see. And that walk across the cable to the other building had been positively insane. High-wire people in the frigging circus couldn't have moved as fast as she had, not with the way the way the wind was blowing between the buildings.

Braden had been working robbery for more than eight years, and in that time, he'd run across some seriously good second-story thieves who specialized in hitting high-rise targets, but Dreya put them all to shame. The things she did shouldn't have been possible. Flat-out, this woman was the most graceful person he'd ever seen.

"Damn," Mick said as he stared at the monitor. "She's gorgeous. Seems a shame she's a cat burglar."

Braden couldn't argue with him. Dreya was an extremely beautiful woman. With long blond hair, hazel-green eyes, full lips, and an amazing body, she was the complete package. But she was also a thief, and that ended any fascination the woman might have held for him. Okay, maybe that wasn't quite true. If he were being completely honest, he'd have to admit he was more than a little attracted to her. But that wouldn't keep him from doing his job.

He didn't blame his partner for being distracted by the woman's beauty. Mick hadn't been in robbery long enough to read all the files on Dreya, much less feel the frustration of seeing her walk out of the station less than fifteen minutes after she'd been brought in. All because the assistant district attorney refused to drag a woman who looked like her up in front of a judge or jury without an airtight case.

Mick might have changed his opinion of Dreya if he'd been around two months ago when her fellow thieves had been dying left and right because she'd stolen a family heirloom from Thomas Thorn. The former senator had his goons torture and kill six people in an effort to find out who'd taken it. None of them had flipped on Dreya, though. It was harder to think of a person as clean as the driven snow when you knew she was indirectly responsible for those deaths.

Not that he'd ever told anyone in the MPD about her involvement. After he'd realized what lengths Thorn would go to to get his diamond, Braden had purposely left any mention of Dreya out of his report. If her name had shown up in it, Thorn would have come after her, too.

After Thorn had gotten his diamond back, the case had been closed—fast. As far as the MPD was concerned, the other dead thieves who'd turned up, as well as a fence named Rory Keefe, had all been involved in the theft and killed each other so they wouldn't have to share the money they got from selling the diamond. Braden had tried to convince his bosses there had been more going on than a stolen diamond and a half dozen dead thieves. In fact, he'd gone all the way to his division and bureau brass, insisting Thorn was responsible for the murders instead of Abbott. They'd thought Braden was crazy. Nobody went after a man like Thorn unless they had career suicide in mind.

He'd tried to find Landon Donovan and Ivy Halliwell, the agents from Homeland Security he'd worked with, hoping they'd corroborate his story, but he hadn't been able to find them, much less talk to them. It was like they didn't exist, at least not within any DHS list he could find.

When he hadn't found Dreya either, there was a part of him that figured she was dead. A lot of people who tangled with Thorn ended up that way. The thought of her being tortured and killed had made him feel ill. The whole pathological burglary thing notwithstanding, he'd always believed Dreya was a smart, intriguing woman who could have had a bright future ahead of her if she'd only stop stealing other people's stuff.

Not liking to dwell on the image of Dreya ending up like the other thieves they'd found, he'd preferred to think she'd smartened up and gotten out of the game.

The idea that he wouldn't have to arrest her was appealing, even if it meant he'd never get to see her again.

That make-believe bubble had popped four days ago when one of his more trustworthy confidential informants had told him Dreya was back in town and scoping out her next job. Braden hadn't wanted to believe it. Why the hell would she go right back to doing the thing that had almost gotten her killed?

He and Mick had only needed to tail her for a couple of days before he realized his CI might be right. He had hoped the guy was wrong. That maybe she was simply looking for a new place to live instead of casing upscale condo apartments in West End. But now as she stood on the outside of a building fourteen stories about the ground getting ready to jump onto the balcony of an apartment owned by some rich art collector type, Braden had his answer. Up until now, all she'd been guilty of was trespassing and reckless behavior. The moment Dreya made the jump and entered the apartment, it officially signaled she was back in business. And with Braden here to catch her in the act, it meant that, this time, she was finally going to end up in jail.

In the blink of an eye, Dreya went from standing statue-still on the arch to leaping across the distance without even taking a running start. Braden doubted he could have jumped half that distance with one.

Beside him, Mick's eyes widened as she grabbed the balcony railing and vaulted over it easily. "Holy crap, she's good."

"Unfortunately," Braden muttered as she made extremely short work of the lock on the apartment's sliding glass door and walked inside.

There was no room left for doubt. Dreya Clark was going to jail tonight.

Mick glanced at him as he grabbed the radio. Eight years younger than Braden, he had dark blond hair and the wiry build of a wide receiver. "Do we call in the cavalry and move in now?"

Braden shook his head. "No. Tell them to stay on the perimeter unless they see her coming their way."

Mick frowned. "We going to take her by ourselves? I thought you said she was slippery."

He nodded. "She *is* slippery. That's why I want you to stay here and keep an eye on the monitors. Tell me if you see anything strange."

"Where are you going?" Mick asked, but Braden was already out of the surveillance van and closing the door behind him.

Braden crossed M Street and walked toward the fancy apartment complex Dreya had broken into. She'd just slipped through the sliding glass door and would need a few minutes to disable the security system. After that, she'd move fast, but he instinctively knew where she'd come out, so there wasn't any need to go up to the condo when he could wait for her here.

He strode over the perfectly manicured lawn until he was directly under the apartment Dreya was in, then hid in the shadows of the hedges and waited. Mick would think Braden was insane for thinking he could outwit Dreya and claim to know which way she'd choose to flee from the scene of one of her crimes. But after all these years studying her file and verbally jousting with her over an interview table, he had a pretty good feel for exactly who she was and what she'd do in any given situation.

Maybe it was arrogance talking, or maybe he was just listening to what his gut was telling him. He almost laughed. Listening to his gut and doing things by instinct weren't things he was too familiar with these days, but somewhere out there, Tommy was probably smiling down at him.

Braden was still thinking fondly of his old partner when he heard a buzzing sound above him. He looked up and saw Dreya zipping down the side of the building so fast that he thought for a moment she was falling. But then the buzzing sound grew louder, and her descent began to slow. That's when he caught sight of the ultra-thin cable trailing the side of the building. Dreya was using a descender that mountain climbers used, albeit ten times faster than any sane climber would have tried.

A split second later, Dreya touched down on the ground with barely a sound. She stood there, glancing around cautiously. Even though West End was one of the busier parts of DC at night, it was still after three in the morning. The chances of someone seeing her—other than him, of course—were slim to none. As he watched, Dreya tilted her face to the sky, as if she was sniffing the air. That would be silly, but that's what it seemed like.

After a moment, she disengaged the descender handle from the steel line with quick, confident movements. She was dressed all in black, from her snug-fitting cat-suit to her soft ballet-like slippers and gloves, making it easy for her to blend in with the shadows. Whenever he'd brought her to the station for questioning, she'd been wearing some trendy pantsuit or pretty dress. He'd figured that was because she'd known he was going to bring her in and she wanted to look all professional and respectable to throw off the ADA.

Now, Braden realized she'd been dressed like that before to hide the fact that she had a body that would put a gymnast to shame. If someone saw how incredibly fit she really was, they might seriously think she was a woman who climbed buildings for a living. Then again, maybe she dressed like that while at the police station because she didn't want every man in the place tripping over their tongues when they looked at her.

Then he caught sight of the canvas bag she had slung over her shoulder. It looked fuller than it had been before she'd entered the apartment, reminding him once again that Dreya was much more than just a beautiful woman.

Braden stepped out from the shadows of the hedge where he'd been waiting. "Nice night for a break-in, Ms. Clark. But wouldn't it have been easier to take the elevator like everyone else?"

Dreya didn't need to turn around to know it was Braden Hayes behind her, but she spun anyway. She'd talked to the detective enough times to recognize that deep, sexy voice. Damn, he was even more handsome than she remembered.

Why the hell hadn't she heard or smelled him? Even the tingle she usually felt along the back of her neck whenever someone was behind her had been strangely absent. Her freaky senses were always on high alert during a job. Why hadn't they warned her that he was there?

She tensed, waiting for him to pull his gun, but he didn't. He wasn't backed by a squad of uniformed police officers either. Her heart still pounded. Hayes had been after her for a long time but had never gotten close to pinning anything on her, not even when she'd stolen that diamond from Thorn. Now he was standing five feet away, and she was carrying a stolen piece in her bag.

She was so screwed.

Her gums suddenly ached, like her fangs were trying to come out. A second later, her fingertips tingled as her claws tried to extend. She sure as hell couldn't let that happen, not in front of Hayes.

Biting back a growl, she whirled around and took off running.

When she didn't have to worry about anyone seeing her run, she could make Usain Bolt look like a sloth. And right then, she sure as heck wasn't concerned about Hayes seeing how fast she was. It wasn't like he'd be able to get anyone to believe she could accelerate faster than a Ferrari. Hell, he'd be too embarrassed to tell anyone he couldn't catch her.

She ran around the side of the apartment building she'd just broken into, then turned onto the sidewalk that ran along M Street, slowing as she headed toward Twenty-Sixth Street. There were a few cars out even at this hour of the night, and she didn't want to freak them out, seeing her blaze past them like a cheetah.

She hadn't planned on this being her escape route. She'd parked her bike in the parking lot of a big grocery chain a block from her target in the other direction. She could have headed straight for it and made it there in less than a minute, but if she had, Hayes would have seen what she was driving and had every cop in the city after her in minutes.

Instead, she'd run in the opposite direction, hoping Hayes would direct all police pursuit this way. All she would have to do is make a left on Twenty-Sixth, another left on Pennsylvania, then veer onto L Street, making a great big square and bringing her almost to the same place she'd started. It would take a few minutes longer, but it would be worth it.

On the downside, she wouldn't be able to go to her apartment, which meant that everything in it, as well as all the stuff at her jewelry shop over in Foggy Bottom, were lost to her forever. That sucked, but after running off to Canada a couple of months ago, she'd finally realized that all the *stuff* she had surrounded herself with for years didn't mean nearly as much to her as it once had.

Her canvas bag thumped rhythmically against her back as she ran down Pennsylvania, reminding her of the fragile piece of Jeff Koons art. If she were smart, she would have tossed the *Balloon Dog (Blue)* piece before she got caught with it. But she couldn't dump it. The thing was too beautiful. And it wasn't like she could climb a building and tuck it in a corner somewhere, not without being seen. So she took the risk and held onto it.

She was still running all her escape plans through her head as she reached the grocery store parking lot and found her bike where she'd left it, leaning on its kickstand in the shadows beside the store. She didn't waste a lot of time looking around. If the cops had been there, the area would have been awash in flashing blue lights.

Dreya climbed on her Ninja, ignoring the helmet attached to the rear seat as she straddled the powerful engine and leaned forward to slip the key into the ignition switch between the handle bars. Being on her bike always relaxed her. Once she was moving on this thing, nobody was catching her.

She reached out with her right hand and thumbed the start switch, but instead of the aggressive growl she was used to hearing when she cranked her bike, she didn't hear anything at all. She frowned at the ignition, checking to make sure she'd turned the switch all the way to the on position. She had. She thumbed the start switch again, but still nothing.

She was leaning over to see if maybe a cable had been pulled off one of the spark plugs when she felt a tingling sensation run up her spine and settle at the base of her neck. It wasn't exactly the sensation she got when she was in serious danger, but her freaky side was definitely trying to tell her something.

Dreya heard a crunching sound and turned her head to see Braden Hayes standing beside her. Crap, this was the second time tonight she hadn't smelled him coming. Could she have been that distracted, or was it that those two months on the run in Canada had dulled her senses so much she'd completely missed him? Twice!

The thought of running again entered her mind, but she quickly dismissed it. Braden was so close that any sudden move on her part was sure to prompt an immediate response on his, and while she might be fast, even she couldn't outrun a bullet.

Dreya was still thinking about him shooting her when he held out his hand, palm up, fingers closed. When he didn't open them, she looked at him. His features were bathed in shadows from the store but still clearly visible. Braden Hayes had dark hair, dark eyes, and a sculpted chin and jawline that looked like they belonged more on a leading man in Hollywood than on a burglary cop in DC. It had always struck her as unfair that a guy this attractive was only interested in taking her to jail instead of to bed.

Braden slowly opened his hand to reveal four small electrical fuses, like the ones used in cars—or motorcycles.

She was still staring at the fifty-cent widgets Braden had pulled out of her bike when he reached out his other hand and gently snapped a handcuff on her right wrist.

"Dreya Clark, you're under arrest."

Chapter 2

"How do you know I wasn't testing the security system?" Dreya asked, her lips curving into a coy smile.

Braden sat across from the beautiful thief in one of the burglary section's interrogation rooms, working hard to keep from smiling back at her. Even though he knew her record backward and forward, he was still having a hell of a time maintaining a professional detachment.

He was good in the interrogation room, but Dreya was better. She charmed, she flirted, and she controlled where she wanted the conversation to go. Braden had already been forced to toss Mick out of the room. His partner had come damn close to asking their suspect out on a date, even though she was sitting at the table wearing a pair of handcuffs.

Though Braden had to admit she made the cuffs look good.

Even now, she was sitting at the table with her long, blond hair cascading around her shoulders, talking animatedly with her hands as if the heavy stainless steel cuffs were a fashion accessory. He wasn't even sure when she'd gotten her hair out of the braid it had been in before, but he had the crazy urge to run his fingers through it. He resisted—barely.

Dreya had been saying since they'd brought her in that this was all a big misunderstanding and that she could straighten this out if she could talk privately with the owner of the art piece they seemed to think she'd stolen. Like that was going to happen. Something told Braden that putting her in the same room with some rich playboy would be an incredibly bad idea. All she had to do was bat those hazel-green eyes at him a few times and tousle her hair with her fingers, and the guy would agree with anything she said. Hell, the guy would probably give her the silly blue balloon dog thing sitting on the table between them as a gift.

"If we're going to talk about security systems, Dreya, let's start with how you managed to climb the wall of that apartment on the south side of M Street. Because I gotta tell you, that was damn impressive."

He expected her to deny it had been her—or beam with pride at the compliment—but her eyes widened in shock. For the first time that night, there was fear on her face.

"You saw that?" She darted a nervous glance at the one-way glass mirror to her left, the one Mick was standing behind.

He nodded. "Sure did. In fact, we have it all on video. The climb, the walk across the cable, the jump you made to the balcony."

On the other side of the table, her face went pale. Shit, was she starting to hyperventilate?

"How many people have seen the video?" she demanded.

Braden frowned. Why the hell was a second-story thief worried about how many cops had seen her display her talents? That made no sense.

"Just my partner and me," he assured her. "But while the video is amazing, it doesn't explain how you were able to scale that wall. Were you using something on your hands to get a grip? I searched your bag but didn't find anything."

Dreya swallowed hard. In all of the previous occasions he'd questioned her, she'd been confident and posed, but suddenly it was like she'd been hit by lightning. She seemed off balance…lost.

"You can't let anyone else see the video," she said.

He shrugged. "That's not really up to me."

She stared at her cuffed wrists, her shoulders slumping in a defeat he hadn't seen coming. "What if I confess?"

She said it so softly he wasn't sure he'd heard her correctly.

"What?"

Dreya lifted her head to look at him, that usual glimmer missing from her eyes now. "If I confess right now, will you destroy the video?"

Braden hoped to hell his mouth wasn't hanging open. Being interrogated by the cops could make people say strange stuff, but Dreya had to know that even with the evidence they had on her, a woman with her background and clean record could likely get a case like this whittled down from the standard five to seven to less than two years. Why would she agree to a written confession? What the hell was on that video she was so terrified of letting anyone see?

He knew he needed to be careful, but right then it was hard to think of Dreya as the hardened criminal he'd always believed. He was smart enough to know she wasn't a saint, but there was something going on here. She was so terrified she was on the verge of tears.

The sudden aura of vulnerability had his heart beating

hard and fast. The urge to protect her from whatever was freaking her out was impossible to ignore. Part of the reason he'd become a cop was to help people in trouble, and Dreya definitely seemed to be in trouble.

Even as he turned to look at the one-way mirror, giving the signal to Mick to stop the video recording of this interrogation, he reminded himself that this might all be an act. This could simply be another weapon she had at her disposal, something she pulled out when she wanted people to underestimate her or cut her a break.

But somewhere, Tommy was pointing out that maybe Dreya wasn't acting. Maybe she really was in trouble.

There was a knock on the glass—Mick letting him know the camera had been turned off. This was something Tommy would have typically done, not him. Braden rarely broke department standard operating procedure on something so fundamental, but he'd found himself doing it more than ever since that insanity with Thorn. And now that he had Dreya in custody, he seemed to be doing it again.

He turned around in his chair, taking in her tense expression and fear-filled eyes. "What's going on, Dreya? Why do you want that video destroyed?"

She threw another glance at the one-way mirror. "If people see that video—especially the wrong people—my life is over."

He leaned forward, lowering his voice. "Does this have something to do with what happened with Thomas Thorn? Are you worried about him seeing the tape?"

Dreya opened her mouth, then closed it again. Finally she nodded.

Braden wanted to ask how she'd gotten involved with Thorn, but a loud commotion outside the door interrupted him. It was five thirty in the morning. Who'd be making a racket at this hour?

Then he heard Mick's voice.

What the hell?

Frowning, Braden pushed back his chair and headed for the door as it burst open. The dude standing there was at least six four with shoulders so damn wide they practically filled the doorway. He was dressed in jeans, a T-shirt, and biker boots, and he looked like he broke kneecaps for a living. If Braden had his gun on him, he probably would have pulled it, but cops weren't allowed to carry weapons in the interrogation rooms. So he did the next best thing. He stepped forward to block the guy.

"Who the hell are you?" he demanded at the same time Mick said, "I told you that you can't go in there!"

The guy ignored Mick, instead regarding Braden with a look that made him think the man blamed him for everything from the national debt to the Redskins losing their quarterback to free agency in the off-season. Then again, it was possible the pissed-off expression Mr. Grumpy wore was normal for him. Like the male version of resting bitch face.

Regardless, Braden wasn't impressed. He wasn't backing down no matter how huge the guy was. "In case you didn't figure it out, this room is in use right now."

Mr. Grumpy glared at Braden. "Do I look like the kind of guy who gives a shit about whether the room is in use?"

Braden crossed his arms over his chest. "If you don't

tell me who you are and what the hell you're doing here in the next five seconds, I'll arrest your ass."

Before Mr. Grumpy could answer, a tall, dark-haired woman stepped around him into the room and casually positioned herself between him and Braden. It was like she knew a fight was brewing and believed she could stop it with her mere presence.

"We said we were going to be tactful about this, remember?" she asked, glancing over her shoulder at Mr. Grumpy.

Mr. Grumpy scowled. "*We* didn't say anything. *You* said we should be tactful. *I* tried out the whole tactful thing by not telling you it was a bad plan."

She sighed. "It's a start, I suppose."

Before Braden could ask what the hell was going on, the woman reached into the jacket of her pantsuit and pulled out a badge wallet. Braden got a sinking feeling in the pit of his stomach before she even opened it.

"I'm Special Agent Danica Buchanan from the FBI. This is my partner, Clayne Buchanan from Homeland Security."

Braden couldn't decide what was more bizarre, that the big dude worked for a federal law enforcement agency, that the FBI and DHS had partnered up two of their people, or that the two of them were married. Or simply had the same surname by chance.

He was still trying to wrap his head around the idea that the mouth breather might be married to the attractive FBI agent when he realized that Danica Buchanan was still talking to him.

"…the Department of Homeland Security will be taking custody of your suspect," she said, giving Dreya a pointed look as if she wanted him to know she meant that suspect and not some other suspect he might have hidden in a closet.

Anger began to boil in Braden's gut. He'd expected this from the moment the woman had pulled out her badge. Because there was only one reason the feds would walk in on the middle of his interrogation at five o'clock in the frigging morning.

"And why exactly does DHS want a small-time thief like Dreya Clark?" he asked. "It's not like she stole government secrets. She swiped a glass dog."

"Porcelain," Dreya corrected.

Braden ignored her.

"She stole a paperclip from the federal government," Mr. Grumpy growled. No lie, he actually growled. "We take theft of government property very seriously."

Danica Buchanan ignored Mr. Grumpy the same way Braden had ignored Dreya.

"I'm not really in a position to comment on why the DHS wants Ms. Clark, Detective," she said. "My partner and I were just sent to pick her up."

Braden locked eyes with the FBI agent. "And what if I'm not in the mood to let you have her?"

Danica Buchanan gave him a small smile. "Look, I know how you feel, I really do. I've had the carpet pulled out from under me a few times, and it's never fun. You caught your suspect red-handed, and now a couple of feds walk in and think they can take over. It sucks, I get it. But at the end of the day, there's not a lot you can do about it. This is way above all our pay grades."

Reaching into the inside of her jacket again, she came out with a neatly folded stack of papers and offered them to Braden. He unfolded them, already knowing what they were. He made a living arresting thieves, not handling prisoner transfers, so he didn't see documents like these very often, but the paperwork looked legit. It was signed by what seemed like all the right people, from the commander of the Criminal Investigations Division to the desk sergeant downstairs in addition to a dozen admin and legal people in between.

"You'll notice that there's a form in there requiring you to turn over all surveillance footage related to Ms. Clark's arrest as well," the FBI agent added. "I assume you have the videos here?"

Braden nodded absently, still reading.

"I'll grab them," Mick said, disappearing out the door.

Braden didn't need Tommy's voice whispering in the back of his head to convince him that there was something seriously wrong here. His gut told him to tell the Agents Buchanan to go pound sand. While the idea might make him feel good, he knew that ultimately it would be a waste of time. He could drag his feet and slow down Dreya's release for a little while, but the moment his bosses got to work, they'd order him to release her. To them, she was a small-time collar, a petty thief who'd stolen a silly glass dog. They wouldn't even question why the DHS and FBI wanted someone like her. She'd simply be sacrificed on the altar of interagency cooperation.

Dreya Clark belonged to the feds now, and there wasn't a damn thing he could do about it.

Braden turned and met Dreya's eyes, seeing the fear there. She was probably thinking the same thing he was, that there was an ex-senator named Thomas Thorn out there who still had the connections to make something like this happen. Thorn probably had his goons watching Dreya the moment she got back in town. Which meant they would have seen him and Mick tailing her. That explained how they'd known she was about to be arrested and how they'd had time to arrange her transfer.

Shit.

Mr. Grumpy must have decided he and his partner had given Braden enough time to read the transfer paperwork. He took the stack of surveillance DVDs from Mick, then asked for the keys to the handcuffs Dreya was wearing. Handing his partner the DVDs, he brushed past Braden and motioned for Dreya to stand up. She did so hesitantly, her eyes going from Mr. Grumpy to his FBI partner, then finally to Braden.

"Where are you taking her?" Braden asked, ignoring the guy and turning to focus his full attention on the FBI agent. "What's she being charged with?"

Danica Buchanan regarded him thoughtfully. "I can't comment on those things either."

The thud of metal hitting the table made Braden jerk his head around. Mr. Grumpy had taken off the cuffs and was leading Dreya toward the door, more than ready to escort her out of there with no restraints at all.

If everything else up until now hadn't struck him as strange, that definitely would have.

"Aren't you going to cuff her for the transfer?" Braden asked.

The guy stopped, but instead of turning to look at Braden, he kept his gaze on Dreya. "Our little thief doesn't need any cuffs. Do you?"

The DHS agent's voice came out low and threatening,

and while Braden couldn't see his face, he could sure as hell see Dreya's. Her eyes widened, her face going pale. After a moment, she shook her head.

Mr. Grumpy turned to look at Braden. "There you go. No cuffs necessary."

Something twisted in Braden's gut, those stupid instincts he'd always blamed on Tommy telling him something bad was going to come of all this. The FBI agent gave him a nod, then followed her partner and their suspect out the door.

"What the hell just happened?" Mick asked.

Braden could only shake his head, getting more pissed off—and worried—by the second. Finally, he couldn't take it anymore. He shoved his fingers through his hair in frustration, then headed for the door. He'd gone out of his way in the years since Tommy's death to do the important things in a careful, well-thought-out, and by the book manner, knowing that was the best way to make sure nobody else he cared about ended up dead. What he was considering right now wasn't careful, well-thought-out, or by the book, but he was going to do it anyway. For the first time since Tommy, his gut was telling him something terrible was going on, and it was important enough to break the rules.

"Cover for me, okay?"

"Where are you going?" Mick asked.

"You asked me what the hell just happened," Braden said. "I'm going to find out."

Even though Ivy and her husband, Landon Donovan, had spent a lot of time at the Chadwick-Thorn corporate headquarters over the past few months, she still got a little uneasy when Thomas Thorn called and told them he wanted to see them ASAP. Not only was Thorn the CEO of one of the largest defense companies in the world, he was also the most powerful member of the Committee, the shadowy group that ran the Department of Covert Ops, the organization she and Landon worked for. People who got on Thorn's bad side had a nasty habit of showing up dead. Even though he was no longer a senator, he was still as powerful as he'd ever been, maybe more so.

"What do you think he wants this time?" she asked as Landon drove his F-150 pickup through the security gate of Chadwick-Thorn. Located south of Joint Base Anacostia-Bolling and the Naval Research Laboratory, it was half corporate offices, half defense research facilities, and heavily guarded.

"I have no idea," her husband said. "I just hope it doesn't involve getting dirt on someone so he can use it as blackmail again."

Ivy silently agreed, shuddering at the memory of the most recent job they'd done for Thorn in which they'd followed a Virginia Supreme Court justice around for days until they'd gotten pictures of him taking part in an orgy. Ivy was never going to be able to forget the things she'd seen that night.

Digging up blackmail evidence on a state judge—or anyone else, for that matter—wasn't a typical job for most operatives in the DCO, but especially not for Ivy and Landon. They were trained to track down terrorists, rogue military leaders, and psychotic killers. The stuff Thorn had them doing lately was a far cry from the usual.

She and Landon had gotten on Thorn's good side after the part they'd played in the destruction of a hybrid research lab in Tajikistan back in March and the deaths of the two doctors who were the only people who could tie the former senator to it. Thing was, she and Landon hadn't intended for those doctors to die. As much as Ivy hated them for using science and her DNA to create volatile man-made versions of shifters like her, she'd wanted to take those men in alive so they could testify against Thorn. Before the mission, Thorn had asked Ivy and Landon to make sure the two men never got a chance to talk. When they'd ended up dead, he'd assumed she and Landon had killed them as he'd asked. Nothing got you on a scumbag's Christmas card list like cleaning up his garbage for him.

So at the urging of John Loughlin, the director of the DCO, she and Landon had spent the past few months using his trust to get close enough to find the evidence they needed to put the man in prison for life. But just because you wanted to find something didn't mean you could. Ever since they'd recovered Thorn's fancy hard drive from the thief who'd stolen it, they'd focused all their attention on finding the encryption key and password to access the data inside it.

They'd checked out Thorn's home on Embassy Row as well as the vacation house he had on St. John's and the place he kept in Paris. When they hadn't found anything in those, they'd moved on to the small office he kept near the Capitol to handle Committee business and schmooze with his congressional buddies. That hadn't turned out any better.

The only place they hadn't looked yet was the Chadwick-Thorn corporate offices.

They parked on the second level of the underground garage and took the elevator to the top floor of the main building, where Thorn had his office.

"Are there even more guards than usual around?" Landon asked quietly as they walked down the hall.

Ivy frowned as she took in another pair of security guards coming their way. Neither man was wearing a sign that proclaimed them security, but if their thick necks and broad shoulders weren't giveaways, the distinctive bulges under their jackets certainly would have been.

"Yeah," she said softly, reaching up to smooth the bun she'd put her long, dark hair in. "I've counted six of them since we came off the elevators, and I saw four more roving around the parking garage. But they don't concern me as much as the new cameras."

The worried look Landon threw her way mirrored her own. They'd broken in here several times but hadn't found anything useful. She and Landon had been able to search some parts of the building, but other parts, like the classified storage area, computer server rooms, and Thorn's office, had been too secure. Ivy had no idea how they were going to get in with the extra layers of security now.

Thorn's head of security, Douglas Frasier, met them outside Thorn's office. Ivy's skin crawled the moment she saw him. She'd read enough of the old DCO files to know that Frasier had been one of the earliest members of the DCO. In fact, he'd been paired up with Adam, the first shifter the organization had ever discovered.

She didn't know what had happened between them, but whatever it was, it made Adam go off the grid.

"He's been waiting for over an hour. What took you so long?" Frasier snapped, then glared at her. "And what the hell are you looking at, EVA?"

Beside her, Landon stiffened. Back in Frasier's day in the DCO, shifters weren't even considered human. Instead, they were known as Extremely Valuable Assets—EVAs. Thankfully, things had gotten better at the DCO since Landon had come to work there. People rarely used the demeaning term anymore, at least to Ivy's face. But hearing Frasier use it reminded her what it was like to have people look down on her and every other shifter simply because they were different. It wasn't her fault a latent gene had flipped on in her teens, turning her into a feline shifter.

"What am I looking at?" she asked. "Absolutely nothing."

Letting her eyes flash green, she walked ahead of Landon into Thorn's office, but not before she caught her husband's smirk.

Ivy expected Frasier to follow them. He usually stood in the back of the room during their meetings with Thorn. But this time he pulled the heavy oak doors of the office closed. Ivy listened as his footsteps disappeared down the hall. Today's meeting must be about an unusually sensitive subject if Thorn didn't want his vicious right-hand man in attendance.

Behind his desk, Thorn looked up from his computer. "You're here. Good. Sit."

Did he want them to beg and roll over, too?

As Ivy slipped into one of the chairs in front of

Thorn's desk and Landon took the other, she was once again struck by the older man's powerful presence. The former senator was nearly sixty, but with his athletic build, dark hair, and good looks, he appeared much younger. Dressed in an impeccably tailored suit, he exuded pure charm and charisma. It was hard to believe he was a man whose ego and ambitions had led to the murder and torture of hundreds of people over the years.

Ivy had faced a lot of evil men in her time at the DCO, but Thorn scared her at a gut-deep level that none of the others had ever come close to. Psychos like Johan Klaus and Jean Renard, the doctors who'd tortured her in their hybrid experiments, employed violence because at some level, they enjoyed hurting others. While Thorn was capable of inflicting the same kind of pain and suffering, he did it for business purposes. Killing, maiming, and torturing were simply a means to an end for him. That complete lack of humanity was terrifying.

Thorn handed her and Landon two photos of an older, dark-skinned man wearing a suit and tie. One showed him talking to a younger man in a white lab coat. In the other, he was coming out of a quaint, one-floor home.

"This is Doctor Kamal Mahsood," Thorn said.

Ivy exchanged looks with Landon. His dark eyes filled with surprise. "Isn't that the name of the doctor who headed up the hybrid research team in Costa Rica?" she asked.

Back in November, a DCO team had gotten ambushed and very nearly killed there by a group of ferocious hybrids.

Thorn nodded. "Yes. Based on your previous reports, all that we'd been able to say with any certainty is that the man disappeared at some point before everything fell apart. I've had people looking for him ever since, but we hadn't found him until recently."

Ivy started getting a bad feeling in her stomach. After the deaths of Klaus and Renard in Tajikistan, they'd been sure there was no one left who possessed the knowledge of how to make hybrids. Something that was confirmed when a DCO operative had died a horribly painful death only minutes after being given a hybrid formula created by Chadwick-Thorn a few months ago.

Now it looked like they'd all been wrong. Of course, Dr. Mahsood hadn't been on anyone's radar. Other than knowing he'd been responsible for leading the research team that had developed the wild second generation of hybrids in Costa Rica and that he'd been working for someone on the Committee not named Thomas Thorn, they knew very little about the man.

"Has he started up another hybrid research project?" Landon asked.

Ivy hoped not. She'd had her fill of going toe-to-toe with out-of-control hybrids. It also didn't help that after getting to know Minka Pajari, the hybrid rescued in Tajikistan, Ivy couldn't help but see the man-made shifters in a completely different light.

"We don't know." Thorn shrugged. "I don't have much more than a location and these pictures to go on. I suppose it's possible Mahsood has simply left that part of his life behind and returned to a normal medical practice."

"But you don't think so?" Landon prompted.

"Let's just say I'm not willing to take the risk," Thorn said. "All I can tell you for sure is that Mahsood is working at a private psychiatric facility in Maine near a place called Old Town. We've looked for the usual indications of hybrid research—missing people, unexplained bodies showing up, unusual purchases of high-tech scientific and medical equipment—but nothing like that seems to be occurring in the area. I want the two of you up there to find out for sure."

As far as Ivy was concerned, she and Landon couldn't leave soon enough. A private psychiatric facility in an out of the way place like Old Town, Maine, sounded like the perfect location to conduct hybrid research. People who lived in that part of the country usually weren't the type to stick their noses into other people's business.

The thing that worried her the most was that they were getting this information on Mahsood from Thorn and not John. If Mahsood was out there trying to create more hybrids, why hadn't the director of the DCO known about it? Was John so focused on taking down Thorn that he'd started missing the other bad crap going on in the world?

"So what's our mission if we find out Mahsood is actually taking another run at creating hybrids?" Landon asked. "Do you want everything gone, including Mahsood?"

Thorn shook his head. "No. I only want you to figure out how far along he's gotten and who's backing him, then I want you to pull back without alerting him to your presence. If you can get your hands on anything related to the exact nature of his research, like tissue and blood samples, do it. But only if you can make it happen without tipping him off. This is strictly an observe-and-report mission. Do I make myself clear?"

She and Landon nodded.

"And if he's progressed to the point where he's produced a functional hybrid?" Landon asked. "Does that change anything?"

Thorn regarded them coolly. "If Mahsood has created a functional hybrid and not another psychotic killing machine, I want you to bring it to me—alive. Do whatever you have to do to bring me that hybrid."

The glint in Thorn's eyes made Ivy shiver, and she prayed they didn't find any hybrids in Maine. Fortunately, John had been able to keep Thorn away from the other hybrids the DCO had taken under its wing, like Tanner Howland, Minka Pajari, and that poor anonymous girl they'd rescued in Tajikistan. Ivy shuddered to think what Thorn would do with a hybrid if he got his hands on one.

Chapter 3

Dreya jerked awake, lifting her head from her arms on the table and looking around in confusion. Where the hell was she? Oh yeah, that's right. She was still in federal custody. Although she was fairly certain neither the FBI nor the DHS typically held their prisoners in a classy conference room like this.

She pushed her long hair from her face and glanced at her watch, surprised to see that it was nearly ten o'clock in the morning. She did the math in her head, trying to figure out how long had she been there—which was harder than it should have been thanks to how tired she was. Crap, she'd slept for three hours.

She still didn't know why she'd been brought here or what was going on, and that freaked her out worse than getting arrested. Okay, maybe that was an exaggeration. Getting arrested was definitely near the top of her list of bad experiences, especially considering that this time, they'd caught her with the goods.

She pushed away the rolling chair and stood, stretching and working out the kinks that came with sleeping in a chair. Wandering over to the door, she opened it and took a quick peek. The two guys in black military uniforms were still stationed right outside, exactly where they'd been before she'd fallen asleep.

She closed the door and leaned against it. The uniforms had no markings on them, so she still had no idea where she was. She was pretty sure it wasn't FBI or DHS offices though. As far she could tell, this one was attached to the Environmental Protection Agency. At least that was what the sign at the entrance to the underground garage they entered earlier had said. Somehow, she couldn't imagine the EPA hiring security guards who looked as intimidating at the men outside the door.

Dreya went back to pacing the room as she tried to wrap her mind around everything that had happened in the past several hours.

First, she'd been arrested. She still couldn't believe Braden Hayes had caught her. Then again, if anyone was ever going to catch her, it would be him. Braden was the one cop who seemed to see the facade she'd carefully erected around her real life. He'd brought her in for questioning almost a dozen times over the past three years, all for burglaries she'd actually committed even though she'd never left a speck of evidence. It was as if he somehow knew her style so well that he could spot which jobs were hers purely by her MO. But that was crazy. A cop would have to spend hours poring over someone's whole life and career to be able to ID a burglar by subtle signs like that.

Fortunately, Braden had never gone much beyond the questioning stage, but that wasn't due to lack of trying on his part. She'd sat in too many MPD interrogation rooms while Braden argued with the ADA in the room on the other side of the one-way mirror, trying to convince them to at least book her and make her sweat a little. Of course, Braden had no way of knowing Dreya could hear everything that was being said, but she doubted he would have changed anything. The man was stubborn to a fault.

Rory had asked her on more than one occasion why she didn't hire a lawyer and file a harassment suit against Braden. The truth was she hated defense lawyers as much as prosecutors. And in some strange way, she appreciated the fact that Braden kept coming after her. It validated her talent in a bizarre way. Besides, for a cop, Braden was cute. She could put up with a little police harassment from a guy like him. If nothing else, she'd always enjoyed their verbal sparring matches in the interrogation rooms.

At least that was what she'd thought until he'd actually snapped the cuffs on. Then her whole outlook on the situation had changed drastically. Suddenly, the game wasn't nearly as fun.

The situation had started to get seriously real as she sat alone in the interrogation room with Braden discussing the evidence he had against her. He didn't gloat, talk down to her, or tell her she was being stupid when she attempted to flirt her way out of the situation. He'd simply laid out how bleak things looked for her.

Having the Jeff Koons piece in her possession was bad. Unless she could get the owner to support her version of events—which was unlikely—she was probably looking at a couple of years right off the bat. More terrifying than that was the video Braden had of her doing things that no normal person should be able to do. So far, only he and his partner had seen the video, but when other people did, her life was screwed.

While she knew she was a complete freak, she didn't broadcast it. The only other person in the world who'd ever glimpsed her circus sideshow attributes was Rory, and she doubted many people like him existed. People would watch the DVD and realize there was something insanely different about her. Then the poking and prodding would start, and it wouldn't stop until they had her stuffed away in a lab somewhere with tubes and wires coming out of every part of her body. Unless they just went straight for the dissection route.

Dreya shuddered.

The thought that Thorn might see the video hadn't even occurred to her until Braden had brought the man up. If there was one thing she feared more than being experimented on, it was Thorn figuring out that she'd been the one who'd stolen his property. She was sure that whatever he'd do to her would be even worse than what a bunch of doctors in lab coats could conjure up.

Then just when she couldn't imagine things getting any worse, the feds had shown up. Not only the FBI, but the Department of Homeland Security, too. Dreya barely knew what the hell the DHS did within the government, but she couldn't imagine what she'd ever done to get on their bad side. The fact that Thorn knew people in federal law enforcement came to mind, though, and scared the hell out of her. She appreciated the way Braden had tried to stick up for her. It would have been really sweet if it weren't for the fact that he'd gotten all possessive simply so he could put her in prison instead of the federal odd couple.

Even though she was nervous about going with them, she figured she could wait for the feds to look the other way, then make a run for it. Well, until the big, mean guy from DHS—Clayne—had smiled, showing off a pair of long fangs at the same time his eyes flashed gold. She'd walked out of the police station on knees so wobbly that she would have fallen if he hadn't been holding her arm.

He must have thought the display in the interrogation room hadn't been scary enough, because he stopped her before they got in the car.

"I'm guessing you're a little freaked out and planning on bolting the first chance you get. I understand that, I really do. Believe it or not, I was in your shoes a while back, so I know how you feel," he said. "But here's the thing. When you run, I'm going to chase you. And now that I have your scent, I can track you through a cattle stampede at the Mall of America during a Black Friday sale. So run as fast as you want. I will catch you."

Something told her the DHS agent hadn't been lying about the tracking thing. Her life was weird these days.

Dreya was still doing laps around the conference table and thinking about the big man with the fangs when the door opened, and an attractive older man walked in. Tall with salt-and-pepper hair, he wore an expensive suit and wire-rimmed glasses. She would have pegged him for a lawyer, if it weren't for the fact that the female FBI agent and her DHS husband came in with him.

The older man smiled and extended his hand. "Nice to finally meet you, Dreya. I'm John Loughlin. I apologize for keeping you waiting so long, but I had an emergency to deal with this morning. Would you like some coffee or perhaps breakfast before we start?"

She'd like both, but she wasn't going to tell this guy that. She regarded his outstretched hand and considered ignoring it. After all, it wasn't like this was a friendly meeting. The feds had dragged her into this conference rooms hours ago with no phone call and no explanation. She'd rather kick the man in his tenders than shake his hand, but she resisted the urge. There was something going on here that she didn't understand, and until she did, she needed to play the game.

"I'm fine. Thank you," she said, returning his smile as she shook his hand.

Rory had taught her a long time ago that a disarming smile could be her best weapon in a tight situation, so she might as well start working this guy now.

"Then let's get started."

He gestured toward one of the chairs at the front of the table, close to the projection screen mounted on the wall, then took a seat opposite her as the FBI agent—Danica—dropped a pile of DVDs on the table and loaded one into the small laptop. The big guy with the fangs took a seat in a chair against the far wall, leaning his head back and closing his eyes.

Dreya's stomach clenched as the DVD loaded. It didn't take a genius to figure out it was one they'd confiscated from Braden.

"I'm sure you have a lot of questions about why we brought you here," Loughlin said while they waited for the projector to warm up. "After we talk, you'll have answers to all of them."

Dreya frowned. She was in the custody of two organizations within the federal government. She'd assumed this would be all about *her* answering *their* questions, not the other way around. She didn't have long to think about what that meant, because the projector screen lit up, and the video of her climbing out onto the balcony of that apartment on M Street started playing.

"Detective Hayes was very thorough with his surveillance," Loughlin said. "Most of the DVDs are snippets of you casing the area around the apartment building, and while I appreciated watching how detailed you were in your preparation, this disk is the only one I'm interested in."

Dreya's hands shook as the video showed her jumping off the tenth-floor railing and catching the stonework with her claws, then scampering up a wall. She cast a surreptitious look in Loughlin's direction, then Danica's and Clayne's. Clayne's eyes were still closed, but the other two were watching the DVD calmly, as if seeing a person pulling a Spider-Woman routine up the side of a building was the most normal thing in the world.

She held her breath, waiting for them to say something, to call her a freak. But Loughlin and Danica made no comment, even as she ran across the steel cable to the other apartment complex and made the long jump to the glass arch.

After watching the whole video, all the way to the point where she descended the side of the building on the thin escape cable and bumped into Braden, Loughlin nodded at Danica. The FBI agent turned off the projector and ejected the disk, then handed it to him.

"Ivy told me that you were impressive, but I think she might have been holding back," he said. "I'm not sure if I have another agent in the DCO who could have done what I just watched you do."

Dreya had no idea who Ivy was, what the DCO was, or what kind of agents this man had if there was even the slightest chance of them being able to do what she did. Before she could ask any of the dozens of questions that popped into her head, Loughlin made a quick motion, snapping the DVD in his hands in half. Then he carefully broke those two pieces in half again before sliding them across the table to her.

She blinked at the four plastic fragments lying there. "What…?"

"Consider that a gesture of trust and goodwill," Loughlin said. "Regardless of what else happens during our conversation, the evidence of your special abilities is off the table. The threat of exposing what you are—and what you can do—isn't something I'll be holding over your head."

Dreya picked up a piece of the broken DVD, still trying to wrap her head around what was happening here. "How do I know you didn't make a copy?"

"You have my word that I didn't, though I doubt that means very much at this moment. Suffice it to say, exposing you—or any of the special people who work for me—isn't in my best interest."

Dreya gave Clayne a sidelong glance. His head was still resting against the wall, but his eyes were open now. He gave her a lazy smile, as if he thought this whole thing was all very amusing. That was when it dawned on her.

"Are you like me?" she asked softly, though she thought she already knew the answer.

Clayne let out a short laugh. "It depends on what you mean. If you're asking whether I have fangs, claws, and glowing eyes, you already know the answer. But if you're suggesting that you'll ever catch my ass climbing the side of a building like you were doing—hell no. In that way, we're completely different."

Just like that, Clayne had given her an answer she'd been waiting to hear for her entire adult life. She wasn't the only freak in the world. This guy was one, too, and he worked for the people who'd taken her out of MPD custody. She found herself smiling at him. Amazingly, he smiled back.

Dreya turned to Loughlin. "Who are you people?"

"We're part of a special organization called the DCO," he explained. "We handle difficult or unusual jobs that would typically be outside the capabilities of your traditional three-letter federal agencies like the CIA, FBI, ATF, etc. Officially, we're part of Homeland Security, but that's a technicality. Few within Homeland even know we exist."

Dreya nodded, even though she wasn't actually sure he'd answered her question. "Why am I here?"

Because it was starting to become obvious that whatever else was going on here, being sent to jail on federal charges wasn't part of it.

"That's simple." Loughlin smiled. "I've brought you here to offer you a job."

She wasn't sure what she expected Loughlin to say, but it hadn't been that. She'd gone on a couple of job interviews, and not one had started with a visit to the police station.

"What kind of job?" she asked, curious despite herself.

Hazel eyes held hers. "A job that will make use of your special skills. To make a difference in the world. To help people instead of stealing from them."

Suddenly, the curiosity that had been there a few seconds ago took a nose dive. Dreya had spent most of her life taking care of herself—and the thing inside her that demanded a constant rush of adrenaline in order to stay quiet. She wasn't the superhero type, even if she had claws and fangs like a comic book character. If this guy thought she was going to go out and be some kind of Catwoman for him, he was dead wrong.

"Are you going to send me to jail if I turn down your job offer?" she asked, the feel-good sensations she'd gotten from finding out she wasn't the only freak in the world fading as she realized what this was truly about.

Loughlin's brow furrowed. "Is the idea of using the unique abilities you have for anything beyond stealing that distasteful to you?"

Considering they were coming from a man she didn't even know, the words hurt a lot more than they should have. She shrugged them off, refusing to let the little stab of pain show.

"I don't like being coerced, regardless of the pretty whitewash a person slaps over the reason," she said. "You drag me here against my will, put armed guards on the door so I can't go anywhere, then think I'm going to be thrilled when you offer me a chance to work for you? I might be a freak, but your people skills suck."

On the other side of the room, Clayne snorted.

Loughlin's mouth tightened. "This wasn't the way I wanted this meeting to go, but I guess you're a bottom-line kind of woman, so here it is. You owe me five days at the DCO complex. You bail before then, and I'll send you to Detective Hayes and the MPD to finish whatever they had planned for you. The video of you climbing the building is gone now, but they still have the art piece you stole, and it'll be their word against yours. If that's enough evidence to put you in jail, then I guess the answer is yes, you'll be going to jail. But if you stick with us for those five days, and give me an honest effort, I'll make the charges disappear, and you'll be free to go."

A low growl came from across the room. Dreya looked over at Clayne to see his eyes flash gold. He seemed pissed, but surprisingly, his anger wasn't directed at her. He was glowering at Loughlin.

"Do you have something you want to add, Agent Buchanan?" the older man asked in a calm, controlled voice.

Clayne didn't respond but instead got up and walked out of the conference room. Danica watched him go, an unreadable expression on her face.

Dreya turned her attention to Loughlin, trying to figure out if she could believe him. He'd said five days. If he'd really wanted to stick it to her, why hadn't he said a month?

She sat back and folded her arms. She hated giving in, but she didn't have a choice. Not unless she wanted to go to jail. "If you think I'm going to help you catch other thieves, you can forget it. I'm not a rat."

"I wouldn't dream of it," he said. "All I expect out of you over the next five days is to take part in a few training exercises with Danica and Clayne, talk to other people at the DCO, and above all, keep an open mind. You might find out that what I'm asking you to do isn't as distasteful as you seem to think it is."

Dreya sighed. It looked like she was going to be stuck with the DCO odd couple for the next five days. She could do worse, she supposed. As prison guards went, they weren't that bad.

"Shall we go?" Danica asked.

Dreya stood and followed her to the door, only to stop as a thought struck her. She turned to see John Loughlin leaning back in his chair, a thoughtful expression on his face.

"What does DCO stand for anyway?" she asked.

Dreya wasn't sure why she cared. It wasn't like she was going to be around the place long enough for it to matter. One hundred and twenty hours, and she was *hasta la vista*, baby.

Loughlin's mouth twitched. "Stay around long enough, and you'll get to find out."

Dreya followed Clayne and Danica out of the DCO offices and over to the four-door sedan parked off to one side of the EPA parking garage. She still couldn't believe that a covert government organization like the DCO was tucked under the EPA building.

"Where are we going?" she asked from the backseat as Clayne pulled out of the garage and turned onto Twelfth Street into traffic.

"To the main DCO training complex near Quantico," Danica said over her shoulder. "It's about an hour or so outside the city."

Clayne must have seen Dreya's less-than-thrilled expression in the rearview mirror, because he laughed.

"Don't worry. We're not doing any training today," he said. "We're going to get your access badge for the compound, then get you set up in one of the dorm rooms. It's already stocked with food, so you can get something to eat and crash."

Her stomach growled at the mention of food. "Can you swing by my apartment first so I can pick up some stuff? If I'm going to be spending the next five days at this compound, I'm going to need some things."

"Clayne and I stopped by your place after we dropped you off at the DCO," Danica said. "I packed you a bag. It's already in the trunk."

Dreya's jaw dropped. As a thief, she'd been through plenty of people's houses when they weren't there, but this was different.

"You broke into my place and went through my stuff?" She sat up in the seat, glaring at the back of Danica's head. "What if I had turned down Loughlin's offer?"

"Then Clayne and I would have gone over and put everything back. We certainly would have had the time, since you would have been in jail." Danica glanced at her. "I wasn't too worried about you turning down John's offer. He can be persuasive when he wants to be."

Dreya flopped in the seat, dazed at how her life suddenly seemed to be spinning out of control. First the arrest, then the job offer she couldn't refuse, and now complete strangers rifling through her panty drawer. Could this day possibly get any worse?

In the front seat, Danica was frowning at Clayne. "What are you looking at?"

Clayne glanced at the driver side mirror. "We have a tail. We picked him up the second we pulled out of the garage."

"Can you tell who it is?" Danica asked, her gaze darting to her side mirror.

Dreya turned in the seat to look behind them, but there were dozens of cars. She had no way of knowing if any were following them.

"Our favorite MPD detective, Braden Hayes. He

must have been so pissed off that we took his collar, he decided to follow us."

Danica laughed softly. "You have to appreciate a determined man."

No, you don't. Dreya turned around, realizing that yes indeed, this day could get worse.

Tommy always said to act like you were supposed to be there when you went someplace you weren't supposed to be, and no one would ever question what you were doing there. With that in mind, Braden walked into the EPA building, flashed his badge to get past security, and worked his way to the parking garage.

He found the fed's black sedan parked off to one side, near a set of unmarked and unremarkable double glass doors. Figuring that was where they must have taken Dreya, he walked in and up to the big U-shaped reception desk. Other than framed photos of historical DC landmarks mounted here and there on the walls, there was nothing that made him think the office belonged to the FBI or DHS, much less give him a clue where they might be holding his hijacked cat burglar.

The attractive blond woman at the desk regarded him curiously. Braden did his best to seem charming as he gave her what he hoped was a warm smile.

She smiled. "Can I help you?"

"I'm here to see Agent Jenkins," he told her, saying the first name that popped into his head. "I have an appointment."

She shook her head. "Sorry, but there's no one here with that name."

"You're kidding." He put on a surprised look. "I'm sure this is the address he gave me. Maybe he's new to the FBI and you don't know him. Could you check?"

"I'd be glad to if this were the FBI, but it isn't."

Braden waited for her to follow up with the next most obvious piece of info, like what kind of office this actually was. When she didn't, he reached into his pocket and pulled out his phone.

"Wonderful," he muttered. "I better call him and tell him I'm lost. Mind telling me where I am, so he can give me directions from here?"

The woman smiled and pointed out the double glass doors with one hand while slipping the other under her desk.

"Why don't you tell him you're in the parking garage of the EPA headquarters on Twelfth? That should do it."

So the blond wasn't simply a receptionist—she was a gatekeeper, too, one who seemed to think he was a gate-crasher. No doubt the hand under her desk was hovering over a button to alert security—if she hadn't pushed it already.

Braden poked a few buttons on his phone, bringing up his contacts and calling the first number on the list—Angelico Pizzeria, best damn delivery in DC. He held the phone to his ear and gave the woman a nod and wave, then headed for the door.

Once outside, he hung up on the poor person at Angelico who answered the phone, left the EPA building, and walked to his car. He shoved some extra change in the parking meter on the curb, then got in his Charger, trying to figure out what the hell was going on.

Three hours later, he was still sitting in his car, his

stomach threatening to gnaw its way out of him and run off down the street looking for breakfast, when the black four-door sedan rolled out of the parking garage and turned onto Twelfth Street. The big guy was driving, the woman who'd claimed to be an FBI agent was in the passenger seat, and Dreya was sitting in the rear. He was relieved to see that she looked okay.

Shit, what did he think, that those people had tortured her in there?

Braden started the car, giving the sedan a two-block head start before pulling out onto the street after them. He followed as it weaved through a few turns, then the 395 connector, and finally I-95. The big guy drove fast, so Braden was forced to move closer so he wouldn't lose them.

His phone rang while he was changing lanes. It took him a few seconds to get it out of his pocket and see that it was his partner. He hit the speaker button.

"What's up, Mick?"

"Since you answered the phone, that must mean the feds haven't arrested you yet," Mick said drily.

Braden chuckled. "Not yet, but the morning's still young."

He gave Mick a recap of what happened at the EPA building, but instead of being as baffled as he was, his partner had a completely different perspective.

"A prisoner transfer request approved before the arrest was even made, an unmarked office located in an underground garage, and a receptionist who's obviously there to keep people out. You ever think maybe these two feds who came in to grab Clark are with the CIA?"

Braden frowned. He hadn't thought about it, but he

supposed Mick's idea made sense. If he disregarded the whole Thomas Thorn angle. He wasn't yet ready to talk to Mick about the former senator.

"It's a possibility, I suppose," Braden agreed. "Though what the hell the CIA would want with Dreya is beyond me."

"Maybe they need her to break into some Russian military complex or skyscraper in Dubai," his partner ventured.

Braden snorted. "I'm pretty sure that's the plot of some—if not all—of the *Mission: Impossible* movies. You really need to stop confusing Hollywood with real life."

"Go ahead and laugh if you want, but we both saw how easily Dreya slipped into that apartment complex last night. I've spent the whole morning reading your files on her, and if you're right about even half of the stuff you think she did, then climbing a skyscraper would be a piece of cake for her. You're telling me the CIA or some other covert organization like that wouldn't love to get their hands on a person who can break into any building in the world?"

When he put it that way, Braden couldn't disagree.

"Where do you think they're heading now?" Mick asked.

Braden glanced at an exit sign. "No clue. I'm just south of exit 160. No sign that they're planning to get off I-95 yet."

Mick was silent a moment. "You know, rumor has it that the secretive CIA Farm is near Williamsburg, hidden on a DOD training base at Camp Peary. Then farther south, just over the border in Hertford, North

Carolina, there's the Point, where they conduct all kinds of cool counterterrorist training and test out new spy gear. They might be taking her to one of those places."

Braden first thought was to pray that his partner was wrong. His bladder—and his empty stomach—couldn't hold out all the way to North Carolina. His second thought was how the hell did Mick know this shit?

"When I get back, we're going to sit down and talk about how much time you spend in front of your TV, Mick. We might need to cancel your Netflix account."

"Yeah, like that's going to happen," Mick said with a snort. "What would I do then? Live the job like you?"

"Ouch," Braden muttered.

He supposed his partner was pretty spot-on. He did spend a lot of time on the job, a shocking amount of it without getting paid. It was something he'd always done. Yet another habit picked up from Tommy. It had been nine years since Tommy's death, and it still hurt like hell to think about. Braden hadn't stopped blaming himself for what happened that night. If he'd insisted on calling for backup instead of going in guns blazing, Tommy might be alive right now.

"Do the job the right way every time, and you and your partner will come home alive every time."

His grandfather's words echoed in his head, mocking him.

Braden's hand tightened on his phone. "Anybody asking about where I am?"

"I told the lieutenant that you were worn out and needed to go crash for a while. He seemed to buy it," Mick said. "That's only going to work for so long, though. You know that, right?"

Braden exhaled loudly. "Yeah. Just keep them off me for as long as you can, then I'll deal with it after that."

"You mind if I ask you something?"

Braden was surprised his partner bothered to ask permission. Though he was pretty new in the robbery division, Mick was never shy.

"Go ahead."

"What exactly are you after with all this? Look, you've probably forgotten more about being a cop than I'll ever know, but I have to admit, I don't understand what you're doing. Is this about being pissed off that the feds came walking in here all bold as brass and snagged your suspect out from under you? Or is there something else going on? What was all that stuff I heard you and Dreya saying about the video needing to be destroyed…and Thomas Thorn? What the hell does a thief like her have to do with a man like him? Is he the reason you're doing this?"

Braden didn't answer right away. He was the last one to ask about why he was doing anything. All he could say for sure was that his instincts were telling him to follow the black sedan.

"Truthfully, Mick, I'm not sure what the hell I'm doing," he finally admitted. "I'm making this shit up as I go along."

On the other end of the line, his partner sighed. "Okay, I can respect that. But try to text now and then, huh? Just so I know you're not dead or anything."

Braden promised he would, hanging up in time to realize that the sedan had suddenly moved from the left lane to the middle, as if they were getting ready to exit the freeway soon. He did the same, trying to figure out where they were, and saw the sign for Quantico.

After the conversation with the receptionist, he'd been sure the people who had Dreya weren't connected to the FBI regardless of what Danica Buchanan said. But Quantico was the home of the FBI Academy, and it couldn't be a coincidence that they were slowing as they approached the exit for the place. Maybe those two were legit feds. Then again, didn't the CIA have a presence in Quantico? Hell, he didn't know. Maybe he should ask Mick.

Braden was sure they'd pull off at the main Quantico exit, so he was surprised when the sedan suddenly veered into the right-hand lane and took the next exit instead of the one another mile or two up the road. He hit the brakes hard, knowing that if he overshot the exit, he'd never catch up before Dreya and the vehicle disappeared.

He knocked up a few loose rocks as he cut across the edge of the off-ramp, praying the feds didn't see him. He merged with the smaller state road, barely able to see the sedan ahead of him as it took a curve in the road. Had he been made?

He cursed, but it didn't matter now. He had to figure out where they were taking Dreya.

Braden steered into the oncoming lane and floored it, watching the needle of the speedometer shoot higher as he passed the line of cars in front of him. His gut told him that if he didn't reach Dreya soon, something really bad was going to happen.

He pulled in before the next curve, catching sight of the sedan disappearing around another bend. He sped up, the trees and buildings whipping past as he drove as fast as the curvy road and traffic would allow.

He was so intent on closing the gap that he almost spun

out when the road took a sharp turn to the right. He got his car under control just in time to see the sedan parked on the side of the road, the Agents Buchanan leaning casually against the side of their car, waiting for him.

Braden slammed on the brakes, the whole car shuddering and shaking as the ABS kicked in. He ended up coming to a stop a few feet from the feds and their sedan.

Shit.

"Detective Hayes, are you following us?" Danica asked as he got out and walked over to them.

Braden ignored her and Clayne, focusing his attention on the back window of their car. Dreya had turned slightly in the seat to look over her shoulder at him. She seemed fine. What the hell was he going to do now? That would have been easier to answer if he knew why he'd followed her and the feds in the first place. A sane cop didn't drive miles outside his police jurisdiction… just because. There had to be a reason he was doing this. Either he was pissed the feds had taken custody of Dreya, and he followed them so he could apprehend her when she escaped—which she would. Or he was worried that Dreya was in trouble, and he wanted to be there to save her ass when things went bad. Both reasons seemed equally implausible—and equally insane.

He dragged his gaze away from Dreya to look at the two feds. "What makes you think I was following you? Maybe I was just out for a drive."

Clayne snorted. "Bullshit. You followed us from DC. You still would have been tailing us if we hadn't seen you. What were you planning to do, stealth your way into a federal facility in the middle of the night and steal Dreya Clark away?"

Braden couldn't help chuckling.

"What so funny?" Danica asked.

"Nothing. It's obvious you two don't know Dreya very well. I wouldn't have to sneak onto federal property to get her away from you, because she's going to bolt all on her own, probably tonight."

Clayne arched a brow. "You think she'll be able to give us the slip that easily?"

"Hell, yeah. Unless you're willing to lock her in a cell and watch her 24/7." Braden shrugged. "Don't get me wrong. She simply hates people in authority positions—like the two of you—telling her what to do, even if it's in her best interest. You say go left, she'll go right. It's this instinctive urge she has to piss certain people off."

Clayne glanced over his shoulder at Dreya, then looked at his partner before finally turning to Braden. "I can appreciate that. But you don't have to worry about it. I'm good at tracking people. If she runs, I'd find her."

Braden nodded, considering that. "The first time maybe. Then she'd run again, and this time, she'd have the benefit of knowing how you found her. You might even catch her a second time, but sooner or later, she'll come up with a way to get away from you. Mostly just to show you she could."

"You don't seem to have a problem keeping track of her," Danica said. "In fact, your files seem to indicate you can find her pretty much any time you want. How exactly is that?"

Braden knew he shouldn't be surprised the feds had seen his case files on Dreya. These two seemed to have all kinds of access to information they probably shouldn't. Another indication they were CIA? Shit, this was bad enough to make his head spin.

"I've been watching Dreya for a very long time," he admitted. "I guess you could say that I get her."

Danica regarded him thoughtfully. "Is that why you've been following us? Because you get Dreya and you don't think we do?"

Braden looked from Danica to Clayne and back again. "Lady, I'm not even sure I know who you two are. But I can promise you that I understand the woman in the backseat of your car far better than you ever will."

Danica exchanged looks with her partner.

"You thinking what I'm thinking?" Clayne asked.

She smiled and nodded. "Yeah. I think they'd work great together. I'll call John and he'll make it happen."

Braden opened his mouth to ask them what the hell they were talking about when Danica stabbed him with a look.

"Here's the deal," she said. "You agree to help keep an eye on Dreya, and we'll pull you into this operation. Most of what's going on is classified, so access to certain parts will be purely on a need-to-know basis. There will be some things we won't be able to tell you until we feel you're ready to handle it, but if you play the game like we ask, you can keep your eye on Dreya."

Braden should have told them to pound sand. He had no desire to be part of any federal operation, be it FBI, DHS, CIA, DIA, NSA—you name it—especially since they weren't going to tell him what was really going on. But then he got a grip. This deal gave him the ability to keep an eye on Dreya—whether to drag her to jail or save her life. What the hell else could he ask for at this point?

Then he decided that there was one thing.

"Before I agree, you have to tell me one detail."

Danica's brow rose. "What's that?"

"What federal charges are you bringing against Dreya?"

Danica smiled. "We aren't charging Dreya with anything. We recruited her to work for us."

Before Braden could say anything, she turned and walked around to the passenger side of the car, then looked at him over the top.

"Don't worry, Clayne will drive a little slower this time," she said. "There'll be a guarded gate a few miles up the road with a visitor parking lot. Hang tight for a bit while we get some paperwork filled out."

Braden frowned, feeling like he'd lost the thread of the conversation somewhere along the way. "Wait a second. I have another question. Which agency is recruiting Dreya?"

Danica smiled. "That's one of those need-to-know parts I mentioned. Right now, you don't need to know."

Braden was still standing there as Clayne started the car and pulled onto the road. In the backseat, Dreya gazed over her shoulder at him, and she didn't look happy at all.

Chapter 4

"The kitchen's stocked with the basics, there's soda and beer in the fridge and some extra towels in the linen closet, so you two should be set for the night," Danica said.

Dreya looked around the dorm room. In addition to the small eat-in kitchen, there was a living room with a big TV and video game console as well as two bedrooms and a jack-and-jill bathroom. As a temporary place to crash, it wasn't too bad—if it weren't for the company.

She glanced at Braden where he stood a few feet away. Instead of a weekender like her, all he had was a plastic bag from the shoppette they'd stopped at after getting their security badges. It was kind of unfair how little a guy could get away with needing when you thought about it.

She still couldn't believe Danica and Clayne had invited him to come along on this five-day, fun-filled vacation slash recruitment pitch. If she didn't know better, she'd think they didn't trust her.

"We'll be back around eight in the morning," Clayne added.

"What are we going to be doing tomorrow?" Braden asked.

No doubt that was his way of trying to figure out what the hell was going on. They had yet to see a single sign with the letters DCO on them, so Braden didn't know who was trying to recruit her, and it was obviously driving him nuts. For some reason, that made her happier than it should have.

"Not much," Danica said. "We'll issue you some gear and introduce you to a few people, maybe do a little basic assessment testing, see what kind of things Dreya is comfortable doing."

Dreya already knew what kind of things she was comfortable doing. Making jewelry, climbing ridiculously tall buildings, stealing stuff...and irritating Braden. She couldn't imagine the DCO paying her for those skills. Well, maybe stealing stuff. She could see how that might be a valuable talent for the government.

The two feds turned and walked out into the hallway that led to the stairs and another set of dorm rooms at the other end of the third floor.

Before he closed the door, Clayne poked his head in. "Training goes on here 24/7, but it can get pretty intense at night. You're probably going to hear shooting and some explosions. Since you haven't had a chance to get a feel for the lay of the land yet, I'd suggest you don't go out tonight. I'd hate for you to wander into a training area and get shot by accident."

Then the big fanged freak was gone, leaving her and Braden looking at each other.

"Did he just threaten us?" Braden asked.

Dreya shrugged and headed for one of the bedrooms to drop off her bag. She was used to people threatening her. If it wasn't cops like Braden telling her they'd arrest her and put her in jail for life, it was other thieves—or guys like Thorn trying to track her down and kill her over something they thought she'd stolen.

She dumped her bag on the floor. There was a full-sized bed, a dresser, two nightstands, and a closet. She walked over to look out the window, but there wasn't much to see. Just a grassy lawn with some thick woods beyond it. She gave the latch on the window a little wiggle, checking to see if it would slide up easily. It did. That was nice to know.

She heard footsteps behind her and turned in time to see Braden standing in the doorway, a knowing expression on his handsome face.

"You hungry?" he asked.

Dreya wasn't thrilled at the idea of eating with the cop who'd been planning to put her in prison twelve hours ago, but she was starving. Besides, it wasn't like she had a lot of other options. She nodded and followed him into the kitchen. Braden tossed his leather jacket over the chair and began rifling through the cabinets with her.

"Found appetizers," he called out from behind her.

She turned at the rustle of cellophane to see him holding out a bag of Oreos, one of which he popped into his mouth. She couldn't help but smile as she took a handful of the heavenly things and bit into one. She hadn't eaten anything since eight o'clock last night, and she'd always loved Oreos.

Braden set the bag down, then took two glasses out before opening the fridge. She was worried he was going to grab a couple of beers—not a good pairing with Oreos—but instead, he came out holding two cartons of milk, one regular and the other fat-free. When he lifted a brow, she pointed at the fat-free carton, figuring she could eat more cookies that way. He poured a glass of skim for her and regular for him.

"Anything on the menu besides cookies?" he asked.

Dreya looked into the cabinet she'd been peeking in before being tempted with the Oreos and saw a jar of spaghetti sauce and a box of pasta. She pulled them out and held them up.

Braden nodded. "That'll work."

Dreya opened the jar and box while he dug out the pots and utensils. When she measured out the pasta in normal serving sizes, Braden reached around from behind her and dumped the rest of the box in the water.

"If they meant for it to be more than one serving, they would have created a better way to seal the box," he pointed out, tossing the empty carton in the garbage.

She didn't bother to argue as he dumped the whole jar of sauce into another pot and cranked up the heat.

They sat at the kitchen table eating Oreos and ruining their appetites as they waited for dinner to cook.

"So," he said casually as he dug another cookie out of the bag. "Are you planning to tell me who the hell these people are? Because I still haven't figured it out."

For a moment, Dreya thought about keeping that to herself. He'd been planning to send her to jail after all. That by itself took him off her Christmas card list—permanently. If he wasn't worthy of a Christmas card, should she really be telling him classified information about the secret organization that wanted to hire her, even if she didn't want the job?

But then she remembered the way Braden had stopped the videotape in the MPD interrogation room and the look he'd gotten on his face when Danica and Clayne had shown up out of the blue to snag her away. Now that she thought about it, he hadn't looked angry about the feds swooping in to take credit for his work. Instead, he'd seemed like he was worried about her—as completely insane as that sounded.

Telling him what she knew was the least she could do. Besides, what harm could it do? It wasn't like she was planning to stay around here that long anyway.

"They told me this place is called the DCO," she said. "Don't ask me what it stands for, because I don't know. It's some covert operations gig, like the CIA, I guess. They seem to think my talents could be useful to them."

"You mean your ability to climb buildings and break into places?" he asked softly, biting into another cookie.

Clearly, the man had never learned the concept of serving size. She got the feeling that if she didn't take the bag away from him soon, he'd eat the whole thing.

"Of course my ability to climb buildings and break into places," she said as she picked up her glass. "It's not like I have any other talents they'd be interested in."

"I don't know about that." His mouth quirked. "I'm betting you have all kinds of talents that no one knows about."

She didn't rise to the bait, not sure if he was fishing for evidence to use against her the next time he hauled her in for questioning or if he was trying to be charming. With cops, it could be hard to tell the difference.

Across from her, Braden downed half his glass of milk, then got up and went over to check the pasta.

"Do you trust them?" he asked. "More important, do you want the job they're offering?"

Dreya sipped her milk while she considered that. "I don't know," she finally admitted. "The guy who offered me the job—John Loughlin—seemed okay. I mean, he was nice enough to destroy the DVD you had of me climbing that apartment wall and running across the cable. So there's that."

She almost laughed at the grimace on Braden's face at learning that his best piece of evidence against her was gone. When he didn't say anything, she continued.

"It's hard not to appreciate a job that allows me to use my natural talents. I'd like to think I'm a good thief."

"I can vouch for that." He glanced over his shoulder at her as he stirred the pasta. "Though exceptional is the word I'd go with."

She took it as a compliment, even if she was pretty sure he hadn't intended it that way. "Plus, there's one particular aspect of the job offer that makes it intriguing."

"What's that?" he asked as he used a fork to fish a piece of the spaghetti out and casually dropped it in his mouth.

She smiled as he made funny faces, trying to keep the hot pasta from burning him as he nibbled, and completely unconcerned that she was watching his antics. Oddly enough, Braden reminded her of Rory in some ways. Her friend used to be oblivious to what people around him thought, too.

"It's not something I can talk about," she said.

"Because it's classified?"

"No, just personal." There was no way she was ever going to mention her *special* attributes around him. "Suffice it to say, there are reasons to think I might actually fit in here."

The fact that the DCO apparently had other people like her working here—and weren't freaked out about it—was important to her. Or at least made her curious.

She'd always wondered if there were others like her in the world.

Dreya waited for Braden to point out that a thief like her wouldn't fit in anywhere, but he didn't. Instead, he took the pasta off the stove and drained off the water using the lid. She would have needed a strainer—or at least oven mitts—to do something like that without burning herself.

"I'm hearing all kinds of reasons why this is a good deal, so what's holding you back?" He set the pot on the stove again. "It must be serious. I've been watching you worry over it ever since we got here."

She hadn't realized she was so transparent. Then again, maybe it was just Braden. She'd overheard him tell Danica and Clayne that he understood her better than anyone. As crazy as that was considering he was a cop, now that Rory was gone, that was probably true.

Dreya watched as he divided the spaghetti onto two plates in a sixty/forty split. She opened her mouth to tell him that was way more than she could eat, but he'd already dumped half a pot of the sauce onto each plate and was carrying the whole steaming mound of carbs over to her. Guess it was too late to complain now.

She stared in fascination as he twirled the pasta around his fork with gusto, wondering if he was going to eat all of that.

He looked up when he realized she wasn't doing the same. "Do you need more milk? Or would you rather have a beer?"

She shook her head. Beer with spaghetti would actually be worse than beer with Oreos. "I'm good."

"So?" he prompted as she slowly twirled pasta onto

her fork. "Why aren't you jumping at a chance to work for these people?"

Dreya chewed slowly. She was hungrier than she'd thought. Maybe she could eat this whole plate full of empty carbs. "It's a little hard to get psyched about working for a group of people who threaten to send you to jail if you don't at least entertain their job offer."

Braden lifted a brow. "They said that?"

"Yeah. If I don't give them an honest effort—whatever the hell that means—for five days, John said the DCO will hand me over to you and the MPD, and off to prison I go."

"And if you hang around for five days?"

She shrugged, twirling more pasta around her fork. "Then I'm free to go on my merry way with a clean record."

Braden frowned but didn't ask how the DCO could manage something like that. "So, I guess you'll be staying then?"

She didn't answer, mostly because she still wasn't sure herself.

"You aren't thinking about doing anything stupid, are you?" Braden demanded. "Like getting arrested again."

She stabbed him with a murderous look. "What's it to you? I thought you'd be thrilled at the idea of sending me to prison."

He put down his fork, scowling at her. "This isn't about me, Dreya. You almost got yourself killed two months ago when you decided to steal from Thorn. Hell, when you disappeared, I thought he had killed you. But then you showed up in town, and I figured that maybe, just maybe, you'd finally smartened up and gotten out of the life. And you want to know something funny? I was damn glad to hear it. Because that meant I wasn't going to have to see you end up in prison or find you in the Potomac like I did your friend Rory."

If she hadn't been so exhausted and mentally drained, she would have torn into him about having the gall to utter Rory's name. Like any cop cared what about happened to a fence like her friend. She wasn't so tired that she wasn't curious about exactly how much Braden had figured out about the whole thing.

"You know about what happened to Rory?" she asked. "And about Thorn?"

"Not everything." He loaded his fork with spaghetti. "If I did, I would have arrested Thorn already. But I know you're the one who stole that diamond from him and that a lot of innocent people died before he got it back—including your best friend."

She swallowed hard. Part of her wanted to admit that he was right, that Rory and those other people had died because of her. But she couldn't, not without Braden using it against her the next time he arrested her.

"Look, I know this isn't anything you're ever going to talk about, and I didn't bring it up assuming you would," he said. "It's just that even after all the crap that went down with Thorn and Rory, you're right back in the same crap. You're like a broken record, stealing a silly-ass glass dog for no frigging good reason that I can see."

"It was porcelain," she pointed out.

"Whatever." His mouth tightened. "You were on your way to prison, and a gift called the DCO falls out of the sky and right into your hands. I have my doubts as to whether this gig is even legit or not. Hell, it might be a case of moving from the frying pan into the fire. For all we know, you could be better off in jail than here. But the least you can do is stay around long enough to figure it out. As a bonus, you might even get yourself out of a prison term in the process."

Dreya stared at him. She was having a hard time keeping her finger on the pulse of Braden's motivation. This morning, he couldn't wait to put her in jail. Now, it was like he wanted her to get away with the crime he'd arrested her for. Why were men so confusing?

She loaded more pasta on her fork. "That's not the kind of advice I'd expect to hear from your typical, everyday cop."

"Who said I'm your typical, everyday cop?" he asked as he went back to eating, too.

She regarded him thoughtfully. "I can't argue with that. I've never met anyone who could keep up with me like you can, that's for sure."

It made her wonder why *he* could. Sometimes it seemed like he knew what she was going to do before she did, which was kind of scary.

Braden's mouth twitched. "Yeah. That's my special talent. Catching you."

She snorted.

As they ate, they batted around ideas about what the acronym DCO stood for.

"Department of Covert Ops?" she suggested.

"Nah," Braden said. "Too obvious."

After that, they went back and forth about what kind of training they'd ask her to do. She had to admit, Braden could be fun to talk to when he stopped acting like a cop—or at least when she stopped thinking of him as one.

It was after eight o'clock in the evening by the time they finished dinner. That wasn't late by any stretch of the imagination, but they were both exhausted.

Dreya was halfway to her bedroom when she realized sleeping naked like she usually did wasn't going to work now that she had a roomie. She figured she might have to wear her tank top and panties when she realized Danica had packed a sleepshirt. Yes, it was a silly Betty Boop one that made her feel like she was sixteen years old again, but that was better than traipsing around in her underwear. She could just imagine how the very reserved Detective Hayes would react if she tried something like that.

It didn't matter, though, since Braden was busy looking at something on his phone when she slipped into the bathroom for a quick shower, then scampered into her bedroom again.

Dreya was lying in bed a little while later waiting for sleep to come when she heard the shower turn on. With her keen hearing, she could easily hear Braden moving around. She didn't intend for her mind to go there, but before she knew it, she was thinking about the fact that he was naked in the next room, probably covered from head to toe in warm, sudsy soap lather.

She bit her lip to stifle a moan. She had no idea why she cared that he was naked in there. Okay, that wasn't true. She cared because he was a very fit, good-looking guy with lots of muscles. And because she'd been attracted to him since meeting him for the first time when he'd brought her into the police station for questioning all those years ago. If she listened carefully now, she could hear his hands moving across his skin.

It wasn't too hard imagining exactly which part of his body his big hands might be touching at any particular moment. It also wasn't difficult imagining her hands touching him in those same places. Wouldn't want him to miss any soap or anything.

That only reminded her of how long it'd been since she'd gotten busy with a guy. Between her legitimate jewelry design business and late-night break-ins, her love life had taken a serious nosedive.

She was still thinking about that when his scent hit her nose. She'd smelled it before, of course, during all those long, flirty interrogation sessions. But this was different. The scent was stronger now…more intense. Not to mention a little arousing.

Dreya almost groaned in disappointment when the shower turned off. How the hell could a man wash himself so fast? It seemed unfair.

There was a rustle of a towel, a mix of fast and slow movements as he dried his hair and his body. A moment later, he walked into the living room and past her partially open door wearing nothing but a towel wrapped around his waist.

As he walked around turning off the lights, she caught flashes of skin and scents of delicious yummy goodness. When the living room plunged into darkness, she had to stop her eyes from slipping into that freaky night-vision mode like they always did when she wanted to see well. Not that she would have minded the view. But Rory had told her that her eyes took on a bright green glow during the transformation. It would be impossible to miss if Braden saw it.

Dreya's breath hitched when he stopped outside her

half-open door on the way to his room. He rested one hand on his hip and the other casually on the doorframe. Even without switching on her enhanced night vision, she had no problem seeing every line and bulge of the muscles on his chest, shoulders, abs, and arms. Clearly, he worked out a lot.

"You going to be here in the morning?" he asked softly.

"Maybe," she said. "I guess we'll both find out when the sun comes up."

He seemed to consider that but didn't say anything. Instead, he gave her a nod, then started toward his room.

"Hey, Braden," she called. "Mind if I ask you something?"

He stuck his head in again. "Shoot."

"Why'd you come after me today?"

He was silent for so long, she thought he wasn't going to answer. Then his mouth edged up in a smile. "Maybe I'll tell you. If you're here in the morning."

Chapter 5

"So, Mrs. Miller, how did you hear about our facility again?" Dr. Peter Brand asked. "I must admit, I don't think I've ever had a referral come from so far away. Washington isn't exactly a stone's throw from Maine."

Ivy had been so busy sorting through the myriad of scents, trying to find out if there might be hybrids in the building, that she almost forgot Miller was the fake surname she and Landon were using for this mission. She looked up from the pamphlets highlighting the mental health therapies at the Stillwater Psychiatric Center to see the attractive, middle-aged blond doctor regarding her and Landon curiously, if not a little suspiciously.

"My brother's psychiatrist in Woodbridge—Gail Meadows—recommended you and your center," Ivy explained. "She said that you've done some amazing work with patients who seem resistant to traditional treatment methods and thought you may be able to help my brother."

Brand looked confused for a moment, but then he smiled. "Gail Meadows? God, I haven't heard her name in years. We went to school together in Boston. I had no idea she was the one who referred you to me."

Ivy almost sighed in relief. Score one for the DCO analyst who'd figured out there was a psychiatrist in the DC area who'd gone to medical school with Brand.

"Gail assured us she emailed you copies of my

brother's records," she said, sounding suitably concerned. "Didn't you get them?"

From where he sat in the chair beside her, Landon reached over and took her hand in a show of support.

"I haven't seen anything yet. Let me check again." Frowning, Brand put on his reading glasses and gave the computer mouse on his desk a little wiggle, then clicked it a few times. "Ah, here we go. They just showed up a few minutes ago."

Probably because it had taken that long for Gail Meadows to fabricate a completely believable medical record for a person who didn't exist. Considering that she and Landon hadn't called John with the idea until well after two in the morning, Ivy was surprised they'd gotten the records here at all.

"Does that mean we need to come back later?" Landon asked.

"I don't think that will be necessary, Mr. Miller," Brand said. "As long as you don't mind sitting here while I skim your brother-in-law's record?"

"We don't mind at all. We're willing to sit here as long as necessary if it will help."

Ivy only hoped the records were good enough to pass a detailed review. Walking in for an appointment like this had never been part of the original plan. After filling John in on their meeting with Thorn, they'd caught a flight up to Bangor, rented a car, then come straight to Stillwater. The plan had been to break into the facility after nightfall and confirm whether the place was conducting hybrid research.

But after getting a look at the huge four-story brick and clapboard building and the stone wall that surrounded it, she and Landon realized getting inside was going to be more complicated than they'd thought. Not simply because Stillwater was so large, but because the place had a security system that was better suited to Fort Knox than a private mental facility. Every window on every floor had wrought iron bars, and every door had at least one orderly and a camera posted on it. They weren't sure if all the security was to keep people out or in. Based on the list of patients they'd been able to get their hands on before coming here, Ivy got the feeling Stillwater was the kind of facility where people with large amounts of money parked family members who suffered from embarrassing little mental health issues. At least it wasn't the kind that housed the criminally insane, even if the security said otherwise. Regardless, there was no way to get into the place without being seen.

As plans went, pretending to be a concerned couple looking to commit Ivy's brother wasn't as good as snooping around under the cover of darkness while no one was the wiser, but at least Ivy could still use her nose to sniff around.

"I can see why Gail referred you to our facility," Brand said without looking up from his computer. "Your brother seems to have gotten himself into quite a lot of bad situations."

Ivy nodded, trying to remember what backstory the DCO had created for her fictitious brother. "I used to think that Miles was simply rebellious. He always seemed to be getting into trouble with someone—our parents, the neighbors, the police. But lately..."

"Lately, it's getting worse," Landon finished when she deliberately let her voice trail off. "He's been committed to four different treatment facilities in the past two years. When he started working with Gail after getting out of the last one, we thought he was on the right path, but then he walked out of one of his sessions with her and right into another civil commitment."

Brand nodded. "If you don't mind me asking, why are you the one taking such an active role in your older brother's mental health, Mrs. Miller?"

Ivy started to answer, then stopped as if she couldn't continue.

"Grace's parents passed away a little while ago," Landon said quietly. "Now it's all on her to try to protect Miles from himself."

Brand gave her a sympathetic look. "I'm so very sorry to hear that. How long ago did your parents pass away?"

Ivy nodded. "Thank you. Just over a year ago. Their death was quite sudden, and now all of the Walker family responsibilities have been left to me—including Miles."

The doctor turned his attention to his computer, his fingers clicking rapidly over his keyboard. "I see. I'm very sorry for your loss."

Brand's eyes narrowed as he scanned something on his computer, and Ivy doubted it was her brother's medical records. More likely he was checking out the Walker family name on the Internet and had discovered that she—or rather Grace—was loaded.

The DCO was very good at creating well-rounded and believable backgrounds for the undercover agents. In addition to a slew of high-society photos and stories featuring Grace and her parents, there would be articles about her mother and father's deaths, some pictures from the funeral, and maybe even a few of James—Landon—marrying into the family shortly before the tragic events.

Brand fixed his gaze on her. "Has your brother's lack of impulse control gotten worse since your parents' passing?"

"Some, I guess," Ivy admitted. "In reality, he's been a little out of control since he turned seventeen. It was like a switch flipped. I barely recognize him as the same person he used to be when we were kids."

Brand nodded. "I'm not going to try and make any firm diagnosis without meeting your brother, but based on what I've read in his charts and Gail has already tried, it seems likely we're dealing with a chemical imbalance brought on by the changes Miles went through as he was moving into adulthood. If that's the case, I think I might be able to help him."

Ivy let hope dawn on her face. "You do?"

"No promises, but I'd like a chance to spend time with Miles so I can put him through some of my therapy sessions and drug protocols."

Landon gave Ivy's hand a squeeze, his eyes bright with excitement. "We could have him here tomorrow."

Ivy nodded enthusiastically.

"That would be fine." Brand gave her an apologetic look. "I hate to discuss topics like this when it's your brother's health that's really important, but I'm sure you understand that this is a private facility. Treatment here can be very expensive, and Miles would need to spend a considerable amount of time with us."

"Money isn't an issue. If you can help my brother, I'll pay whatever it takes," Ivy said. "But before I commit my brother, I want to make sure he'll be well taken care of. I'd like to have a tour of the facility."

Brand hesitated for a moment, then smiled. "Of course. I can take you on a tour of the facility myself."

"Are you sure you smelled hybrids in there?" Landon asked Ivy.

They'd come from the tour of Stillwater and were sitting in their rental car outside the front entrance.

She nodded. "I'm sure. Just outside the big metal door Brand claimed led to the isolation ward. It wasn't very strong, and the scent was completely different from any other hybrid I've smelled before, but it's definitely a hybrid of some kind. Unfortunately, we have more problems than just a new variant of hybrid we've never gone up against."

Landon snorted. "You mean beyond the fact that there's no way in hell we're ever going to be able to break into that damn isolation ward without a SWAT team?"

"Yeah, beyond that," she said drily. "There's a shifter in there, too. And while I couldn't tell for sure, I think it's a woman."

The memory of what another set of twisted doctors looking to make hybrids had done to her—and a sweet Tajik girl named Minka Pajari-soon-to-be-Rios they'd captured—made Ivy want to go into Stillwater right now and tear apart Mahsood and whoever else was working with him. But giving in to her inner shifter and storming the place without a plan would be reckless and stupid.

Landon cursed. "Shit. Now we not only have to get

into the isolation ward to see if Mahsood is behind the research but to get that shifter out of there, too."

Ivy chewed on her lip. "It's not the orderlies on guard duty I'm worried about. It's the patients outside the isolation ward. Brand said some of them are allowed to wander freely around the common areas, even at night. How do we get past them?"

She'd expected Brand to show them one or two rooms on the tour, maybe let them poke their heads in on a group session, then quickly shuffle them out the door. But outside of the scary-sounding isolation ward, which he claimed was set aside for patients who needed to be protected from unnecessary external stimuli, he'd taken them anywhere they'd wanted to go. They'd spent almost an hour in there, and Ivy was sure they hadn't seen even a quarter of the place. But what they had seen scared the hell out of her. There was something unsettling about seeing all those patients with no expression on their faces. It was like they were robots.

"We're going to have to put someone on the inside," Landon said. "And with Brand eagerly waiting for you to decide if this place is right for your brother, that gives us the perfect opportunity."

Ivy's first instinct was to say hell no. The thought of putting anyone into that environment freaked her out. Who knew what kind of drugs or medical treatments their operative might have to endure once they went undercover?

But what choice did they have? A shifter was in there, one who was almost certainly in trouble. There was nothing to say the hybrid with her wasn't in trouble, too.

Besides, they had to figure out exactly what Mahsood was doing and whom he was working for, because it sure as hell wasn't Thorn. Was it Rebecca Brannon or Xavier Danes, or some new player on the Committee they didn't know about yet?

"So who do we send in?" she asked Landon. "Whoever it is has to be able to pull off the part of my brother. And have experience working undercover."

Landon drummed the steering wheel with his fingers. "How about Clayne?"

Ivy gave her husband a look.

"What?" he said. "Clayne could definitely pull off unstable and completely lacking in impulse control."

She couldn't argue with that. "Did you miss the part where I said whoever we send in there needs to be good undercover? I love Clayne like crazy, but he'd start a scene five minutes after we sent him in there. Some doctor would want to take his blood pressure, and Clayne would end up wrapping the arm cuff around the guy's throat and pumping the bulb until he passed out. That or go into full shifter mode in front of a group session of precariously balanced people, thereby ensuring they stayed in therapy for the rest of their lives."

Landon chuckled. "Yeah, you're right. Subtle investigation has never been his strong suit. How about Angelo? I'd rather send a shifter in there, but I know he can keep his cool under pressure."

Ivy shook her head. "He and Minka are in London doing some kind of hostage rescue training. Besides, I don't think Minka is ready for him to go undercover on a mission like this yet. She'd freak out when she figured out what kind of place it is."

"Good point. Any suggestions on your part, or should I just keep throwing names out there?"

"Trevor could do it," she said, thinking of the DCO's resident coyote shifter. "He works counterespionage, so we know he's good undercover. He could definitely pull off a guy who doesn't like to play by the rules."

Landon grinned. "He was going to be my third choice."

Ivy snorted. "Sure he was."

Landon pulled out his phone. "I'll call John and bring him up to speed, see how fast he can make this happen."

Ivy turned to look out the side window at the big, scary building and caught sight of a woman with wild curly hair and pale skin gazing down at her through the window and the bars covering it with big, brown eyes that didn't blink. As Ivy watched, a man's hand reached out and rested on the woman's shoulder, tugging her away from the window. That's when Ivy realized the window was in the isolation ward.

Nope, that wasn't creepy at all.

Chapter 6

DREYA FELT LIKE A COMPLETE DOOFUS SITTING IN THE DCO cafeteria wearing the black military-style uniform and combat boots. When Danica and Clayne had taken her and Braden to pick up training equipment before breakfast, she'd thought it would be some cool spy gear that would make her a better thief, like glasses that would give her X-ray vision or a grappling hook and rappelling line hidden in an ink pen. It hadn't been anything so sweet. Instead, it had been heavy, uncomfortable, butt-ugly clothing. She hated the uniform on sight.

But she'd felt a whole hell of a lot better about it when she realized they'd given Braden the same thing to wear. Unlike her, though, he didn't put up nearly as much fuss about the uniform. Probably because he made the damn thing look so good.

As she ate her French toast, she looked around the room at the insane mix of people. Some wore suits while others were rocking the business casual look, but most of them wore the same black uniform she and Braden did.

Beside her, Braden was all but inhaling his scrambled eggs and bacon as he talked to Danica about cop stuff. Dreya was too busy trying to identify all the strange scents her nose was picking up to pay attention to what they were saying. Across from her, she caught Clayne watching her with a slight smile on his face. He tapped his nose in a covert gesture before pointing at a tall man across the room with a wild mane of hair, then at a big blond guy a few tables away, before finally gesturing at a wiry guy standing in the omelet line waiting for his order.

It took her a moment to figure out what Clayne had been trying to tell her, but then she realized the strange scents she'd been picking up were coming from the three men he'd pointed out. They were like Clayne—and like her. The DCO really did have other freaks working here.

She looked around again and noticed that no one seemed bothered by it. Freaks with claws and fangs eating breakfast with the normal people. Who would have thought it?

"You look beat, Dreya," Danica said, interrupting her thoughts. "Did the shooting at the gun ranges keep you awake?"

Dreya gave Braden a sidelong glance, expecting him to say something, but he didn't look up from his bacon and eggs.

"No, it didn't keep me awake," she said. "I guess I was just geeked up about what I'd be doing today."

She was only half lying. She was so tired because she spent most of the night staring at the ceiling debating whether to skip out on the whole DCO thing or not. She couldn't say why she'd finally decided to leave. Maybe it was simply because her life was complicated enough already, and she didn't want it to get any worse.

Regardless, a little before five, she'd thrown her weekender over her shoulder and climbed out the window only to find Braden leaning against a tree, waiting for her. She had no idea how the heck he'd known she'd bolt. It was almost like he could read her mind.

"I guess this answers my question about whether you're going to be here in the morning," he said drily.

She could have run, but why bother when he'd catch her at some point? So instead, she sighed and walked over to him.

"It's morning, and I'm still here," she pointed out.

"Pure technicality," he said. "If I hadn't been waiting here, you'd already be long gone."

"How'd you know I'd try to run?"

He shrugged. "I could see it in your eyes last night. It was that squirrelly look people get when they're scared and overwhelmed. The look they get when they think running is a better answer than staying around and dealing with a tough situation."

She frowned. "You think that's what I'm doing?"

"That's exactly what I think you're doing. You don't even have a clue where you're running to or why. Your instinct says to bail, so you're bailing."

The blunt words sounded like something Rory would have said. "Do you think I should stay?"

"I think you need to figure that out for yourself," Braden had told her. "But you can't keep running. You either need to go back into that dorm room and make the most of the DCO's offer, or you let me take you to the MPD—and jail. There isn't a third option."

Neither of them had said anything for a long time after that. Finally realizing Braden was right, she'd gone upstairs to their dorm room. She expected Braden to say something pithy about her making the right decision, but he didn't utter a word, other than to tell her to have a good night before closing his bedroom door. Then this morning, he'd acted like nothing had ever happened. She didn't get him.

"You ready?" Danica asked when Dreya and Braden had finished breakfast. "There's someone I want you to meet before we get to work."

Once outside, she and Braden fell into step behind Danica and Clayne as the couple led them along a series of sidewalks. As they walked, Danica kept up a steady narration, pointing out various admin, operations, IT, and training buildings. In the distance, Dreya could hear shooting followed by what sounded like a boom of thunder that reverberated in the air around them. But the crystal clear sky and the sharp jerk of Braden's head in that direction convinced her it wasn't thunder but something blowing up. Okay, she was definitely not having anything to do with explosives. She didn't care if Braden threw her in jail.

When they got to a big building with lots of windows, Danica and Clayne turned onto the walkway. Inside, there was a maze of cubicles, but the couple walked past them to an office where an extremely pregnant blond was talking with two other women. Before Danica could make the introductions, Clayne tapped Braden on the shoulder and motioned toward the door.

"Come on," he said. "If this is like normal, they'll spend the first fifteen minutes talking about pregnancy stuff. Since we're not qualified to hear that, let's leave them to it and go talk about sports, or shooting people, or...well anything but that."

Braden must have been in complete agreement with

that idea, because he turned and walked out of the office like a scalded cat.

"If Kendra attempts to convince you that we should have kids too, run," Clayne told his wife. "Sacrifice Dreya if you have to, but run."

Danica laughed, waiting for the two men to leave before turning and gesturing toward the pregnant woman. "Dreya Clark, this is Kendra MacBride. She's the battery that makes this place go."

Kendra waved her hand as she got up to come around the desk. Dreya hurried forward to meet her halfway. Kendra wasn't simply pregnant—she was get-this-woman-to-a-hospital-right-now pregnant.

"Don't listen to Danica. I'm just a behavioral scientist who helps out wherever I can," Kendra said with a smile. "It's so nice to finally meet you. I've heard so much about you, it almost seems like I already know you."

Dreya wasn't sure she was comfortable with someone she'd never met before knowing so much about her, but Kendra was already turning to introduce the other two women. Skye Durant was also a behavioral scientist, while Sabrina Erickson was a training officer and handler, whatever the heck that was. They'd be filling in for Kendra while the other woman was on maternity leave. Regardless of what Kendra said, she must be a pretty big deal around here if it took two people to replace her.

Skye and Sabrina bailed right after the introductions, saying they had some work to do. As Dreya sat in the chair in front of the desk, she noted the photos around the room of Kendra with different people, including the mountain of a man she'd seen in the cafeteria. Since it was obviously a wedding picture, it didn't take a genius to figure out the guy was Kendra's husband.

Then a thought struck her. If Dreya's nose was right, the big guy was a freak like her. Which meant that Kendra was not only married to him but having his kids. Was everyone here that cool with being around freaks?

She turned to see Kendra regarding her curiously.

"I understand you're not sure you want to become the DCO's newest feline shifter," Kendra said. "I hope you decide to stay. We need good people here."

"Feline shifter?" Dreya frowned. "What's that?"

Kendra smiled. "Shifter is the word that people with your special attributes and abilities use to refer to themselves. As in the ability to shift between your typical, everyday appearance, then flash your claws and fangs."

Not a freak or a monster, but a shifter. It was such a simple thing and so amazing at the same time.

"What about the feline part?" she asked.

Kendra lifted a brow. "You never noticed that your claws are curved like a cat's? That you can climb anything and that you're not afraid of heights at all? That your face takes on an almost catlike appearance when you shift all the way?"

Dreya shook her head. "I've never really given it much thought. I've never looked at my face when my fangs were out." She wasn't going to admit it, but she'd always been too scared to see her face, too afraid to see how freaky she looked. "When you say part cat, do you mean like a werecat? Isn't that…I don't know…impossible?"

"Apparently not." Kendra smiled again. "There's a doctor here named Zarina Sokolov who can explain the science behind all this, but the basic theory is that every person on the planet has a little random animal DNA floating around in their genetic Crock-Pot. For most of us, that DNA might as well not even exist. But shifters can access their animal DNA and take on certain traits and abilities of that particular animal. In your case, you're accessing feline DNA, thus the sharp, curved claws, the delicate fangs, the climbing ability—everything. You may not realize this, but you were born to be a cat burglar. It's in your DNA, you could say."

Dreya was amazed that none of that had ever occurred to her. "Wait a second. If I'm a feline shifter, does that mean there are other kinds of shifters out there?"

Kendra and Danica exchanged smiles.

"Clayne's a wolf shifter," Danica said. "He's about as far away from a cat shifter as a person can get."

"And my husband, Declan, is a grizzly bear." Kendra pointed to the wedding picture Dreya had seen earlier. "There are other kinds of shifters out there, some of them very unique, but the majority of the known shifters are in the feline or canid families."

Dreya's eyes widened. "So there are others who are exactly like me?"

"Not exactly," Kendra said. "Like any other human, every shifter is slightly different, even in the feline class. We have several who work here, and they're all unique and special and do things their own way."

Dreya listened in amazement as Kendra explained what it meant to be a shifter, how the change had been triggered when Dreya was a teen, and how the DNA changes affected different people in different ways.

"The DCO tries to help shifters get the most out of

their talents," Danica added as Kendra told her about all the crazy things shifters could do.

That sounded a little creepy to Dreya, not to mention manipulative. "What do you mean?"

It was Kendra who answered. "You've been living with these abilities since you were a teenager, and even with everything you can do, you're only scratching the surface. With training, you can do so much more."

"Like what?" she asked, curious despite herself.

"I have a friend who's a cat shifter like you," Kendra said. "Ivy's so dialed in to her abilities that she can practically smell when people are lying to her, open a safe based on which keys on the pad get touched more often, and can even figure out when something bad is about to happen based purely from her kitty senses. Plus, she can kick butt like nobody's business."

Kendra made Ivy sound like a freaking superhero. "Can I meet her?"

"Ivy and her partner are on a mission in Maine, but I know she'll be psyched to see you the second she gets back," Kendra said. "There are other feline shifters in the DCO besides Ivy, but both of them are out of the country doing training. Lucy Kwan is here, though."

Dreya sat up straighter. "She's in this building?"

Last night, she'd been afraid to let herself get too caught up in what John and the DCO had to offer, but she'd learned more about her freaky—no, her shifter—nature in the last thirty minutes than she had in the entire rest of her adult life. She was so geeked, she was practically squirming in her seat.

"No." Kendra grabbed her computer mouse and

clicked on it. "According to the training schedule, she's supposed to be in the gym doing some aero training. Want to meet her?"

Dreya nodded eagerly.

She had to force herself to walk slowly as she and the others followed Kendra to a gym. The pregnant woman couldn't move very fast, and Dreya felt like a kid on Christmas who'd been told she had to wait to open her presents until she ate her oatmeal.

"What did you guys talk about?" Braden said as he strolled beside her. He and Clayne had met up with them outside Kendra's office.

Dreya shrugged. "Nothing much. Mostly about Kendra and when her kid is due. A little about what it's like to work for the DCO."

Braden didn't look like he believed her, but what was she going to say?

"I just found out I'm not a complete freak after all. I'm a feline shifter, which means I share DNA with a primitive feline. So you can relax. The claws and fangs are completely normal."

Dreya almost laughed. Braden seemed like he was so stubbornly stuck in the real world that discovering something like that would probably send him straight into cow-birthing mode.

Proof of that came the moment they walked into the big gym and saw a petite woman flipping and climbing her way through a two-story collection of horizontal bars and vertical poles that looked like something out of Cirque du Soleil. The woman was moving so fast, even Dreya could barely track her. And the woman was doing it with a blindfold on.

"You've got to be effing kidding me," Braden murmured.

At first, Dreya couldn't focus her attention on anything but the woman and the hypnotic way she weaved and spun through the obstacles, her long black ponytail bouncing behind her. The only sound in the whole spacious gym was the creak and rattle of the bars, the slap of skin on metal, and the occasional small grunt of effort.

Movement below the bars caught Dreya's eye, and she looked down to see a big, dark-haired guy precisely following the woman. The man's gaze was locked on her, his hands poised as if to catch her. He was clearly worried the woman was going to fall and seemed determined to make sure he'd be in position to catch her if she did.

"Is that Lucy's partner?" Dreya asked Kendra softly.

Kendra's eyes never left the woman. "No. Lucy doesn't work with any one team. She's something of a free agent, meaning she works with whichever team most needs her talents. The guy with her is Jaxson West. He runs security for the DCO. He's here spotting her for this exercise. They've never worked together in the field."

Dreya wondered what talents Lucy possessed that allowed her to be a free agent. She liked the sound of that.

She watched in fascination as Lucy finished up her work on the obstacle course and took a swan dive off the last horizontal bar, flipping in midair so Jaxson could catch her before she hit the ground. Once in his arms, Lucy pulled off her blindfold, revealing exotic Asian features. She smiled at Jaxson, who chuckled and shook his head as he set her on the floor.

It was only when Lucy stood next to the big man that Dreya realized how small the woman was. Then Dreya noticed something else. Jaxson's hand was still resting on Lucy's back, gently moving back and forth.

Dreya glanced at Kendra out of the corner of her eye, wondering if the woman was aware that while Lucy and Jaxson might not be anything other than coworkers at the moment, they would like to be more—if they weren't already.

Finally noticing them standing there, Lucy and Jaxson came over.

"Dreya is considering joining the DCO," Kendra told them after she made the introductions. "I was hoping you might have a few minutes to talk privately with her, Lucy. She has a lot of questions that I think only someone like you can answer."

Jaxson chuckled. "I'm not sure, but I think that was Kendra's subtle way of saying she wants the rest of us to make ourselves scarce."

"Yeah, I'm getting used to that," Braden said, his voice laced with amusement.

Braden wandered over to the far side of the room with everyone else, leaving Dreya alone with Lucy. The other woman regarded her thoughtfully as she removed the fabric wrappings that were weaved around her fingers. They looked a lot like the kind boxers use to protect their hands. Dreya couldn't help but notice the multitude of small scars across the woman's knuckles and the back of her hands.

Dreya was so busy trying to figure out how the scars had gotten there that she almost missed the scent rolling off Lucy. It reminded Dreya of the woman who'd come to her apartment a couple of months ago, saying she could protect her from Thorn.

"So, you're a thief?" Lucy asked.

Dreya's first instinct was to deny it, but then she changed her mind. "I steal stuff, yeah. How did you know?"

"I heard John talking to Kendra about you." Lucy smiled. "I've stolen a few things in my life. There are worse ways to make a living."

Dreya couldn't help returning the smile. "Kendra says you're like me."

Lucy lifted a brow. "Like you?"

Dreya felt her face color. She was so embarrassed, she felt like curling up into a ball like some kind of armadillo shifter, if such a thing existed. "You know—a freak. I mean, a feline shifter."

Lucy laughed. "Oh. Well, then yes, I'm very much like you. After I first went through my change, I considered myself a freak, too. It took me a long time to accept that I wasn't."

Dreya hesitated, then took the plunge. "Please don't take this the wrong way, but could you show me?"

"Show you?"

"Yeah. I don't mean to be rude, but I never knew there was anyone else like me until today."

Lucy smiled again. "Ah."

Lifting one of her small, delicate hands, she held it up, palm toward herself. One moment, Dreya was looking at slim fingers with their fine scars and their carefully trimmed fingernails. The next, they lengthened, and five curved claws slid out. Dreya gasped at how similar Lucy's claws were to her own, right down to color and size. Without even realizing what she was doing, she reached out to touch them. They felt like hers did, too.

Tears welled in her eyes. For the first time, she had

visual evidence that she wasn't as messed up and strange as she'd always thought. She wasn't alone with this thing.

Lucy's claws retracted, and she motioned Dreya to follow her to a workout bench a few feet away. Lucy sat astride the bench cross-legged, motioning for Dreya to join her.

"How long have you worked at the DCO?" Dreya asked as she sat.

"Since I went through my first change twelve years ago," Lucy said. "I was in a bad situation when John found me. I would have died if he hadn't gotten me out. He risked a lot for someone he didn't even know, and I'll never forget that. I owe him everything."

Dreya tried imagining trusting someone that much but couldn't. "Kendra said you work with a lot of different teams, particularly ones who need your special skills, but she didn't actually say what kind of work you do for the DCO."

Lucy shrugged. "It's complicated. Suffice it to say I provide simple solutions to extremely complex problems."

Dreya waited for Lucy to elaborate, but she didn't. Dreya didn't push. Something told her that was the only answer she was likely to get out of the other shifter.

"Do you like it here?" she asked.

Lucy smiled. "Yeah, I do. I won't lie and say that everything here is perfect and that there aren't people who look down on me because I'm a shifter. But there isn't another place in the world that allows people like us to be who we are or values us because of it. It's the only place where I've ever fit in."

Lucy was telling her what it was like spending time with people who were fully aware that you had fangs and claws when the other shifter suddenly stiffened, her eyes locked on something over Dreya's shoulder.

Dreya turned to see that an older man in a pricey-looking suit had joined Braden and the others. She turned to Lucy.

"Who's that?"

"Dick Coleman," Lucy practically growled. "He's the deputy director of the DCO, and as his name implies, he's a dick. Not only does he hate shifters, but he's dangerous. Stay away from him."

Dreya looked over her shoulder again, wondering if it was a coincidence that a man who hated shifters just happened to stop by the gym at the same time as the DCO's newest recruit.

Just her luck.

Chapter 7

"You have to trust your partner," Danica yelled.

Standing on the wooden deck that ran along two sides of the training area, Braden winced. Poor Dreya was spattered with so much paintball dye, she was starting to look like a piece of modern art. Dreya scowled at the curly-haired guy on her left, as if the latest splash of color on her uniform was his fault.

"Don't blame Michael," Danica said. "He was covering your right side just fine, but you didn't trust him, so you turned around to make sure. That means your left side was open, and that's how Clayne was able to get you so easily. It's how he and Tanner have been beating you all day."

Dreya turned and slowly stomped back to the start of the fire and maneuver course, checking her paintball rifle as she went. Danica and Clayne had been pushing Dreya hard since leaving the gym, and she looked beat.

The morning had started off easy enough with a small obstacle course, which had ended up being a flat-out joke. Dreya had maneuvered around the low walls, run along the balance beams, and navigated the monkey bars like they weren't even there. When she was finished, they gave her a heavy backpack to wear and had her do it again. The pack had slowed her down a little bit, but it wasn't until they paired her up with another person on the course that she'd truly started having problems.

Dreya simply had no idea how to work with a partner. She'd climb up and over a seven-foot-high wall, then take off running for the next obstacle. That's when Danica or Sabrina would yell at her to go back and get her partner. And when she couldn't make it work with one guy, they brought in another. Her latest partner—Michael—was the fourth they'd tried to pair her up with, and he wasn't working out any better than the others.

It was getting hard to watch.

From all the second-story jobs she'd been able to pull over the years, Braden had always known Dreya was in great shape, and seeing her climb that apartment building the other night had only convinced him she was even stronger than he'd thought. But this kind of sustained, grinding effort wasn't something Dreya was built for. She was born to be a cheetah, not a bull.

Braden was surprised Dreya hadn't tossed her paintball rifle into the woods and said the hell with it already. She made a living designing jewelry and stealing stuff, not playing war games, but his little thief was turning out to be a lot tougher than he'd given her credit for.

"Move through the course like you did before," Danica instructed when Dreya and Michael were in position. "Cover each other's blind spots, then get to the tower at the far end of the lane without Clayne or Tanner hitting you again."

Danica made it sound easy, as if getting through the course of berms, walls, trees, and culverts was a stroll in the park. But strolls in the park didn't normally include two guys like Clayne and Tanner taking pot shots at you with paintball guns. Clayne was intimidating, but with that wild mane of hair and those intense eyes, Tanner looked even scarier. And they were both fast as hell. The two of them could probably run down Olympic sprinters if they wanted to—then eat them.

"You're going to have to move faster this time, Dreya," Danica added. "Michael can cover your back, but you need to be the one figuring where Clayne and Tanner are coming from. You're going to have to use those instincts we both know you have."

Braden frowned. What kind of instincts did Danica think Dreya had? The woman was a thief, not a cop. Or a soldier. But after casting a quick glance at Braden, Dreya took a deep breath and nodded.

When Danica shouted for them to start, Dreya darted for the protection of the nearest dirt berm faster than he'd ever seen her move, then threw herself to the ground behind it so hard, Braden could hear her hit the dirt. She got up, motioning Michael to the right as she swung wide left to cover him and most of the open real estate between her and the tower at the end of the course.

Braden's jaw dropped open as Dreya hurtled first over a five-foot-high wall, then a ditch that had to be four feet across. She kept her head on a swivel the whole time, keeping track of Michael while at the same time looking out for Clayne and Tanner.

Out of the corner of his eye, Braden saw a flash of movement to his left. Dreya saw it, too, and immediately turned to run in that direction. Tanner came out from behind the trees where he'd been hiding, sprinting toward her, his lips pulled back in a snarl.

Braden gripped the wood railing, holding onto it so tightly, his knuckles turned white. He expected Dreya to take cover so she could protect herself while still getting a clean shot off, but instead, she attacked.

He wasn't sure who was more surprised when she charged forward with a growl of her own, him or Tanner. The guy dropped to his knees and slid along the rough ground as he brought his rifle up to his shoulder and fired.

Braden couldn't imagine how the guy could possibly miss her, but Dreya threw herself sideways at the last minute so that the paintball zipped past her by mere inches. He wasn't sure how she did it, but Dreya kept her balance when she landed, then snapped her weapon up and stitched a line of green dye spots all the way up the front of Tanner's chest from crotch to collar.

Damn.

Dreya didn't have time to celebrate, because Michael called out for backup. She spun on a dime and raced toward her partner, where Clayne had him trapped behind a waist-high wall. Michael was trying to reload his weapon even as Clayne moved around the wall to get into position for the kill shot. There was no way Dreya would be able to get there in time to do anything about it. She'd finally taken out one of the opposition, but her partner was going to get taken out anyway.

Braden knew exactly how much that sucked.

Dreya clearly wasn't ready to accept defeat. She sprinted across the width of the course, leaping over walls and ditches, moving faster than he would have ever imagined possible. Even so, she was still fifty feet away when Clayne stepped around the wall and took aim at Michael.

Then Dreya did something impossible—and

completely insane. Instead of running around the dirt berm that separated her from the two men, she ran right up the side of it at full speed and launched herself off the top.

Clayne spun at the last second and tried to hit her on the fly, but Dreya twisted in the air again, avoiding the paintballs and getting off three shots, catching Clayne square in the center of the chest.

But while Dreya had taken out Clayne, she paid the price for her insane leap off the berm. She smashed into the dirt hip first, and from where he stood, Braden could hear the breath explode out of her body as she tumbled across the ground.

Braden leaped over the railing and was running for Dreya before she'd even slid to a stop.

Shit, this was going to be bad.

Dreya pushed herself to her knees with a groan.

"Don't move!" he said urgently, sliding to the ground beside her.

Braden couldn't believe she was even up and moving after a tumble like that. She should have been unconscious at the very least.

"Careful," he warned as he reached for the arm she'd landed on. "You might have broken something."

Dreya let him check her arm and ribs, but when he moved lower, running his hands over her ass and hip, she shot him a look that backed him off quick.

"I didn't break anything but my pride," she insisted, then gave him a sheepish look. "I was hoping you hadn't seen that."

"Why?" He stayed close as she got to her feet, wanting to make sure she could stand on her own. "I never would have pegged you for the tactical type, but that was impressive as hell."

His words seemed to catch Dreya more off balance than the fall had, and he couldn't help smiling as she blushed. Dreya could handle a hard impact with the ground, but a compliment from him was too much for her.

"Not bad that time," Danica called from the walkway. "But Michael is lucky to be alive, and you still never reached the tower at the other end of the course. Let's set up to go again."

Dreya groaned. "Again? I'm not sure how many more times I can handle."

Braden put his hands on her shoulders, angling his head to see into her eyes. "Then don't worry about how many more times you can do it. Worry about getting through this next one." When she looked dubious, he gave her a smile. "Besides, if it provides any motivation, you could always imagine how dreadful you'd look in prison orange. Trust me, it's not your color."

Dreya snorted, her eyes dancing. "I look good in any color, Detective."

He was about to tell her that no one looked good in orange, but Clayne interrupted him.

"Come on. We're wasting daylight."

Braden smirked. "What was that? That bright green paint on your shirt is so loud, I couldn't hear a word you were saying."

Clayne let out a sound that sounded suspiciously like a growl and headed for the far end of the course. Tanner was already out of sight, and Michael was at the starting point.

Braden grinned at Dreya. Even though she was exhausted and probably sore as hell, she smiled.

"You get through this, and I'll make dinner tonight," he promised.

She regarded him thoughtfully as she slowly backed her way toward the start. "Can you cook anything besides spaghetti?"

"Sure. I can cook lots of things. Popcorn, for example. And soup, and those frozen burrito things. Give me pretty much anything that can be cooked in the microwave, and I'm your man."

Dreya laughed, then turned and hurried over to rejoin Michael. Braden stood and watched her. He'd heard her laugh before, but this was the first time it sounded genuine. And damn, if it wasn't beautiful.

"I feel like I'm a hundred years old," Dreya complained as she slowly walked up the stairs to the third-floor dorm room she and Braden shared.

Behind her, Braden snorted. "Trust me, you don't look a day over eighty."

She was so exhausted, she couldn't even work up the energy for a snappy comeback. "Gee, thanks," she said as she unlocked the door to their dorm room.

She'd always thought she was in good shape, but Danica and Clayne had pushed her harder than she'd ever been pushed in her life. Between the pure physical exertion and the repeated impact with the ground, she was seriously beat. There were some things about today's training that bothered her a lot more than how sore she was, though.

Like the way Danica and Clayne had kept pairing

her up with random DCO operatives. Dreya wasn't stupid. They were putting her with different people to see who they might be able to partner her up with. That was crazy. As a thief, she'd always worked alone. If she was going to work here—and that sure as heck wasn't a given—she was going to be like Lucy and occasionally help out other teams on a case-by-case basis.

Then there was the way that Danica seemed to be so casual about revealing what shifters like Dreya could do while Braden was standing right there. Dreya had spent most of the day holding herself back, because she hadn't wanted him to see her do something she shouldn't be able to. At least any more than he'd already seen. But then Clayne and Tanner had started running around like some kind of demented track-and-field freaks during the paintball training. Finally, Dreya said the hell with it and cut loose, too.

If Braden suspected anything, he didn't let on. Which brought Dreya to her next—and biggest—concern. What the hell was up with Braden anyway? The guy was acting like a decent human being all of a sudden. He'd actually seemed worried she'd broken something when she landed awkwardly after taking out Clayne that first time. The terrified way he'd run his hands over her was surprising.

And nice, too—in a completely freaky way that made absolutely no sense to her.

At the time, she'd told herself it was simply a matter of never having someone worry about her like that before. But after thinking about it, she knew it also had something to do with the fact that Braden was a hot guy and that she liked the way his hands felt on her.

She frowned as she walked into her bedroom. It was sad, really. She finally got a sexy man to put his hands on her butt, and it was because he thought she'd hurt herself. Story of her love life.

She grabbed her toiletry bag from the dresser and headed for the bathroom. "I get dibs on the hot water."

Dreya didn't realize how sore she was until she started undoing the buttons of her uniform top. While she could handle the bottom ones, she couldn't lift her arms up high enough to get the upper one without a lot of pain. She gritted her teeth and tried again, but the pain in her forearm, elbow, and shoulder made her groan out loud.

Crap.

"You okay?" Braden asked softly, suddenly at her side and making the small bathroom seem even tinier. "You sure you don't need to go to the hospital?"

She shook her head. According to Clayne, her aches and pains would be gone in a couple of hours, but Braden had no way of knowing that.

"No, I'm good. Just sore," she told him. "Taking a shower will loosen everything up. Go ahead and figure out what you can nuke for dinner."

He smiled as he came around in front of her and gently moved her hands away from the buttons. "Don't worry about dinner. I'll take care of it after I help you get this off."

Dreya opened her mouth to tell him that was completely unnecessary, but Braden already had one button undone and was working on the other. The heck with it. She did need help.

A frown creased his brow as he tossed her uniform top on the floor. She followed his gaze and almost groaned again when she saw the nasty bruise coloring her forearm.

He caught her eye. "You sure you don't need to get that looked at?"

Clayne had assured her any bruises would disappear as fast as the aches and pains. But she couldn't tell Braden that. "Nah, I'm fine. I've hurt myself worse making jewelry."

He shook his head. "If you say so. I have to admit, you're a lot tougher than I ever gave you credit for."

For some stupid reason, the compliment made her smile, though she had no idea why she cared one way or the other what he thought.

"You don't need to do that," she protested when Braden dropped to one knee to untie her boots.

"I know." He didn't look up as he continued to work on the laces. "But you're too proud to ask, so I'm doing it anyway."

In the end, Dreya was glad he helped. She would have had a hard time squatting to get the laces undone. Still, she did most of the work kicking off the boots, but even with that, she needed to steady herself with a hand on Braden's shoulder, or she would have fallen on her butt. Again.

"You good from here?" he asked when he rose to his feet.

She was tempted to tell him yes, that she could get her T-shirt and pants off all on her own. She was a frigging adult after all. But then she thought about how hard it had been to get her arms up, and the idea of pulling her black T-shirt over her head suddenly didn't seem so thrilling.

Braden must have seen the look of capitulation in her eyes, because his mouth curved into a smile. "Word of this will never pass my lips," he promised as he caught the hem of her black T-shirt and eased it out of her pants. "Your street cred will remain totally intact."

His fingers grazed her stomach as he slowly lifted her shirt, making her catch her breath. She was so caught up in the moment of being inches from a hot guy as he pulled off her clothes that she nearly forgot how sore she was, even when he pulled the shirt over her head. That left her standing there wearing nothing but a sports bra and a pair of cargo pants.

Dreya couldn't miss the way Braden's pulse sped up as his gaze casually skimmed her body. She couldn't ignore the sudden scent of sexual arousal suddenly coming off him, either. She inhaled deeply through her nose, her inner shifter practically drooling at how delicious he smelled right then.

All at once, her gums and fingernails started to tingle, like she was about to go full-on fangs and claws. She'd never felt the animal inside her react to a guy like this before. It took everything she had to clamp down on the urge to shift right there in front of him. If she didn't get him out of the bathroom soon, she might not be responsible for what happened.

His gaze holding hers captive, Braden unbuckled her belt. She didn't remember asking for help getting her pants off, but for the life of her, she couldn't come up with any reason at the moment to not accept his assistance.

Could he tell how turned on she was getting? She thought it likely he could, because his dark eyes had one hell of a smolder right then.

Dreya trembled as he hooked his thumbs inside the waistband of her pants and carefully pushed them over her hips. The feel of his warm hands on her skin was almost enough to make her lose the already tenuous control she had over her inner shifter, and she curled her fingers in case the tips of her claws started peeking out.

When her pants finally hit the floor, she automatically stepped out of them and kicked them. They were standing so close now, she could feel the heat coming off him.

She didn't know if it was feminine or feline intuition that told her Braden was going to kiss her. And she was going to let him. Let him? Hell, she was on the verge of jumping him, claws and fangs be damned.

But even though she could hear his heart beating a hundred miles an hour, could smell the hunger pouring off him, the kiss never came. Instead, he took a step back and smiled at her.

"I'm guessing you're good from here?" he asked.

It was then that Dreya realized she really was standing in front of a fully clothed guy, wearing nothing but a black sports bra and a matching pair of panties. She should have been embarrassed, not only by the lack of clothes, but by the fact that she'd been on the verge of kissing a man she had absolutely no reason to even like.

The funny thing was, even now after the wild urge to kiss him had passed, she still felt more comfortable being nearly naked in front of him than she'd ever been with another guy.

"Yeah, I think I can handle the rest," she said. "But I'll give a shout if I need any more help."

He chuckled as he backed out the door. "Any more help, and I might as well just get in the shower with you."

Dreya bit back a moan as she imagined Braden washing her back—and her front. His lazy perusal of all her revealed skin along with a fresh wave of arousal implied he was thinking the same thing.

"I'll get to work on dinner," he said. "Take as long in the shower as you need to."

She stood there long after he closed the door, wondering what the hell had just happened—or almost happened. The two of them had come damn close to kissing, and it probably wouldn't have stopped there. Even as tired and beat up as she was, she'd still been thinking of stripping Braden naked and getting crazy all over him on the bathroom floor.

That didn't make any sense at all.

She reached into the shower and turned on the water, letting it warm up while she took off the rest of her clothes. The situation with the DCO was complicated enough at the moment. She didn't need to make it worse by getting tangled up with Braden. The man was a cop; she was a thief. There was no way she should be having those kinds of thoughts about him.

Even so, she couldn't ignore the evidence when she finally slipped off her panties and found out that she was soaking wet down there. Her head might know Braden was completely wrong for her, but her body—and her inner shifter—didn't seem to agree. She was more aroused than she'd ever been. And that had been with Braden doing nothing more than helping her get undressed.

What the heck would it be like if he'd kissed her or stripped her until she was completely naked? Based on how excited she was, she might have orgasmed right on the spot if things had gone any further.

She stepped into the tub and under the warm water raining from the shower, sighing at how good it felt. Only the sound came out more like a feline yowl. She slapped a hand over her mouth, terrified that Braden would hear her and poke his head in the door, thinking someone had slipped an alley cat in here with her.

When the door didn't open, she relaxed and let the warm water do its magic. After her sore muscles loosened up, she grabbed her body wash from the cradle on the wall and squeezed some into her hand. As she ran her soapy hands over her body, she couldn't help thinking about how different showering would be if Braden had joined her.

Dreya closed her eyes and slipped a hand between her legs. Oh yeah, this wasn't going to take long at all.

She was imagining Braden's naked body pressing up against hers as he reached around to tease her clit with his fingers when her fangs and claws slid out. Suddenly, she was left with fingertips that definitely weren't going to work for what she'd been planning.

"Well, hell," she muttered.

Chapter 8

"So, Miles, tell me. Have you ever tried to kill yourself?" Dr. Brand asked in a conversational tone.

Trevor Maxwell leaned back in the leather armchair and lazily regarded the man on the other side of the desk from him. When Gail Meadows had briefed him for this undercover mission before he'd left DC, she'd told him that question would probably be one of the first things Brand would grill him about. He didn't have nearly as much of a problem with it as he did with the name he was using on this undercover mission.

Miles.

It'd been bad enough reading it in the file, but hearing it out loud? It sounded like something a socially awkward person would call their pet turtle—or maybe a houseplant they were really fond of. Where the hell had Ivy and Landon come up with that name?

"Miles?" Brand prompted.

Trevor still didn't answer. Instead, he deliberately made a show of taking in the exotic wood paneling, expensive antique desk, high-tech computer, and collection of real potted plants that must be an absolute bitch to keep watered, as well as the two huge orderlies who stood off to the side, eyeing him like they were praying he'd give them an excuse to tackle his ass.

He gave Brand a smile. "I suppose that depends on what you mean by *have you ever tried to kill yourself*?"

Meadows had told him the things he needed to avoid to keep the psychiatrist from figuring out he was faking it, just like she'd told him how to walk, talk, and behave to make a professional like Brand think he was looking at a textbook case of schizophrenia with a touch of bipolar disorder thrown in. Her best advice hadn't been related to his supposed psychology disorder though. It had been about the man himself.

"If you hand him textbook responses like you've practiced it, he's going to see right through you," she'd said. "Make him have to figure you out, and you've got him."

Brand returned his smile. "It's not that complicated of a question, Miles. Have you ever intentionally done anything that could result in your death?"

Trevor had to fight to keep from laughing. If this guy knew what he did for a living, not to mention how many times he'd intentionally walked into a situation knowing he was going to get shot to shit, he'd stamp "Medicate Heavily" on his forehead and keep him locked up forever. But of course, Brand didn't know what Trevor did for a living. He didn't even know Trevor existed. He thought he was dealing with a rich guy named Miles Walker, whose very rich sister wanted him to put away.

"If you ask my dear sweet sister, the answer would be yes," Trevor drawled. "But that's because she's a prissy prima donna who can't imagine doing anything her boring socialite friends would disapprove of. When I go rock climbing, she calls me crazy. When I drive my bike a little over the speed limit, she says I'm suicidal and gets me tossed in a padded cell. I'm living my life, and she can't handle it."

Brand nodded and flipped through the pages of Miles's very thick, very fictitious medical record. "I think you'd agree your sister might have a reason to be concerned. That rock climbing session you mentioned was on the U.S. Capitol Building. And that outing on your bike, the one when you were driving a little over the speed limit, was on the I-395 at four o'clock in the morning, and you were clocked doing a hundred and seventy before the police pulled you over. I think most reasonable people would consider both of those actions to be crazy and suicidal."

Trevor shrugged and went back to looking around the room. "I don't see what's so suicidal about climbing around on the Capitol."

Brand raised a brow. "Your file says that a sniper almost shot you. Didn't you think that might be the response to a man climbing around on the Capitol when Congress is in session?"

He tilted his head to the side again—Meadows had said that people with schizophrenia sometimes held themselves in strange positions—before he answered. "Didn't think about it, I guess."

Brand definitely took note of the head tilt thing but didn't comment on it. Instead, he nodded and wrote something on a pad.

"Do you ever hear voices, Miles?"

"I hear your voice, Doctor. Does that count?"

Brand looked up at him over the rim of his reading glasses. "No, actually, it doesn't. I'd like to know if you hear voices when there's no one else in the room."

If Trevor really wanted to screw with this guy, he would have asked if TVs and radios counted, but that might be pushing his luck. The whole purpose of this mission was to get himself put into the facility's general population, or whatever the hell they called the place where most of the people here got to wander around. From there, he needed to get into the isolation ward Ivy and Landon had described and find out what Mahsood was up to and whether there were actually any hybrids around. Saving the shifter Ivy had smelled was pretty high on his list of priorities, too. He couldn't do any of those things if he pissed off Brand so bad, they tossed him out of the place for being a smart-ass—or if they put him in some kind of solitary confinement. So instead, he went with the pat answer that he and Meadows had talked about.

Trevor shrugged. "Sometimes my penis talks to me, but I'm pretty sure that everyone's penis talks to them. Does your penis talk to you, Dr. Brand?"

Brand looked up again, clearly intrigued. "No, Miles, it doesn't. But I'd love to hear what you and your penis talk about."

Braden thought the first day of training had been crazy, but now he was convinced the DCO was trying to get Dreya killed.

"Dreya, stop!" he shouted. "Don't move another step."

She stopped instantly, her body swaying slightly on the narrow metal beam positioned twenty feet above the gym floor. She turned her head his way slightly, as if trying to pinpoint his location by sound, which she probably was, considering the fact that she was wearing a frigging blindfold at the moment.

Braden was running a little late this morning, because he'd been trying to reach Mick to find out what was going on at the MPD and whether anyone was asking questions about where he was yet. His partner hadn't answered the phone, so Braden had left a quick message, then hurried over here to the gym in time to hear Michael convince Dreya that she should jump across ten feet of open air and grab onto one of the horizontal bars in front of her. Thank God, she hadn't been crazy enough to try it.

"Hang tight for a second, Dreya," Braden called as he jogged across the gym.

The jungle gym she was navigating was similar to the one Lucy had been swinging around on the first morning they were here, but some of the bars and beams had been moved around so it wasn't the same configuration.

"Something bothering you, Detective?" Clayne asked, sounding pissed at the interruption.

Like Braden gave a shit. "Yeah, something's bothering me. It's the fact that you people seemed bound and determined to kill Dreya before she has a chance to decide if she even wants to work here."

Clayne stiffened, clearly not liking anyone up in his grill, but Braden didn't back down. He'd held his tongue up to now, because he didn't want to screw up Dreya's chances with the DCO, but he was becoming more and more uneasy with all the bizarre crap they'd been asking her to do, from the outlandish obstacle courses to the combat assault shit. Today, they were trying to get her to jump around a circus contraption while wearing a blindfold. What they had Dreya doing wasn't training; it was insanity. These idiots were going to get her seriously hurt—or worse—and he was putting a stop to it right now.

"We're not trying to kill her," Danica said as she smoothly slipped in between him and Clayne and subtly moved them apart. "This exercise should be easy for someone with her abilities. She just has to trust what Michael is telling her."

Easy? These people were delusional. "Dreya," he called, turning to look up at her. "Do you trust what Michael is telling you enough to leap off that beam?"

Dreya hesitated, but then shook her head. "No, not really," she said, then added, "Sorry."

Braden could tell from Michael's expression that Dreya hadn't said anything the man didn't already know. At Danica's nod, the guy walked over to the door and left the gym.

When the hell was the DCO going to realize that Dreya was a thief who'd worked alone her whole career? She didn't have it in her to trust someone enough to throw herself off a beam twenty feet in the air simply because some guy told her to.

"Dreya, would you be able to jump off that beam if Braden were giving you directions?" Danica asked.

Braden snapped his head around to ask Danica what the hell she was messing with, when Dreya's response floated down to him.

"Yeah. I think that would work better."

He blinked. "What? Whoa, wait a second. You want me to lead her through this?"

Danica and Clayne both smiled.

Shit. These two had just manipulated the hell out of him, and he hadn't even seen it coming.

"It's obvious she's more relaxed when you're around," Danica pointed out. "She seems to trust you, and unless I'm missing something, you seem to have made it your business to watch out for her. So what's the problem?"

Braden ground his jaw. Dreya didn't trust anyone but herself. Besides, she was a thief, and he was a cop. He didn't point out either of those things, though. The truth was, he'd known there was some kind of connection developing between them over the past couple of days. He wouldn't go so far as to call it trust exactly, but it was as close as Dreya could get. Moreover, his gut was telling him that if Dreya was going to be doing something dangerous, he didn't want her listening to anyone else but him. He wasn't sure when he'd decided to appoint himself her protector and partner, but he had.

God, he was mental.

On the balance beam, Dreya had her head cocked to the side as if waiting for him to say something.

"You sure about this, Dreya?" he asked.

"Yeah." She let out a tense little laugh, making him think she was still more than a little worried. "But you'd better hurry up before I change my mind."

Danica and Clayne backed away, giving him space. That was when it hit Braden. He was really doing this. If he screwed up, he was going to be the one getting Dreya hurt, not the DCO. He took a deep breath and moved so that he was right underneath her. If she didn't make this jump, at least he could give her something softer than the floor to fall on.

"Okay, Dreya, you ready?" When she nodded, he continued. "The bar you're aiming for is ten feet away, ninety degrees to your right, level with your knees. You don't need to jump out as much as fall forward."

"And you'll catch me if I miss the bar, right?"

"I'll catch you," he promised.

Honestly, he had no idea if he could catch a woman in free fall, but somewhere in the back of his mind, Tommy approved.

"See yourself making it happen, and it'll happen," his old partner had always told him.

Braden expected Dreya to hesitate or at least take a timid leap, but she didn't. She simply tipped forward into a swan dive, then pushed off right before her toes left the beam.

His heart practically stopped beating when he saw her falling, his body automatically moving forward to catch her. But then, when it seemed she was going to miss the bar by a few short inches, the palms of both hands smacked into the metal, and she was swinging from it like a trapeze artist.

It was probably a little thing from Danica and Clayne's perspective, but Braden wanted to cheer when Dreya caught the bar.

"Keep swinging like that," he called out. "There's another bar about eight feet in front of you and four feet up. You need to pop off the bar you're on and gain altitude, like you're on a set of uneven bars in the Olympics."

He had no idea if what he was saying made any sense at all, but at least Dreya didn't look down at him like he was an idiot. Instead, she started swinging harder.

"Say when," she told him.

He watched her move, impressed as hell at her ability to hold on to what had to be a slick-ass piece of metal. When he judged she'd gotten high enough, he let her know.

"Get ready," he said. "Now!"

She let go of the bar she was swinging from with more confidence than he ever could have, her palms smacking right into the next bar like she knew exactly where it was.

"Yeah!" he shouted, not able to contain his excitement this time.

Dreya navigated the rest of the aero-maze, picking up speed as Braden started getting a feel for what she could really do, and she began trusting him more.

"Done," he announced, his hands reaching out to grab her hips and steady her when she hopped off the last beam and stuck a perfect landing on the floor.

"That was amazing." She spun in his arms, yanking the blindfold off with a laugh. "I swear I could almost see the maze as you were describing it to me. I can't believe that was so easy."

Her laugh was infectious, and it was all he could do to keep from picking her up and spinning her around. "Trust me, you're the one who made it look easy. It was insane how fast you finished that course."

"Whoa, control your excitement for a second," Danica said from behind them. "You're done with the hard part, but you still have to get over the last obstacle on the course before you're finished."

They both turned to see what Danica was talking about, and Braden felt the excitement bleed right out of him and drip onto the floor.

The "last obstacle on the course" was a twenty-foot-high wood wall. How the hell did Danica expect Dreya to climb the thing when there was absolutely nothing on it to get a grip on?

From the look she gave Danica, it was clear Dreya knew she was screwed, too. "I can't climb that. Not now."

"Yes, you can," Danica said. "You just have to want to."

Dreya shook her head, fear in her eyes. He'd seen that look before in the integration room when she thought someone was going to see the video of her climbing that apartment building.

"I can't," she said so softly, he could barely hear her.

Danica put gentle hands on Dreya's shoulders. "You're going to have to learn to trust someone with your secret sooner or later, and I think we both know that someone needs to be Braden."

Dreya didn't say anything. She stood there looking at the floor.

Braden frowned. He felt more confused than he'd ever been in his life. "Dreya, what's going on?"

She rounded on him with an angry look on her face. "I'm going to do this, but if you say anything nasty or tell anyone, I'll... You'll be sorry!"

He started to ask what she was talking about, but before he could get the words out, she spun around and ran at the wall. He had about three seconds to wonder what the hell she was doing when she leaped at the wall.

And stuck there.

Braden was pretty sure his jaw bounced off the floor as Dreya scrambled up the wall using nothing but the strength in her arms and shoulders...and the inch-long curved claws that had suddenly sprouted from her fingers.

He shook his head, certain he was seeing things. But no, Dreya was really climbing the wall, just like she'd done a couple of days ago. She wasn't using some cool ninja gear, either. She had frigging claws!

When she reached the top, she vaulted gracefully onto the narrow platform attached there, then turned to look at him. He couldn't help but notice that she wasn't even breathing hard. Or that she had two fangs sticking out over her bottom lip. They were sharp and delicate at the same time, like something a cat would have—or a very genteel vampire.

Holy shit. Dreya had claws…and fangs.

They stared at each other for what seemed like forever before she hopped off the platform and slid down the wall, the claws of one hand digging into the wood to slow her descent. Even after she hit the ground so lightly, it was like a feather had landed, Braden couldn't take his eyes off the wall…and the five deep gouges furrowed into the wood.

Dreya marched up to stand before him, her claws and fangs gone, her eyes shooting daggers at him.

"Well?" she demanded.

Braden glanced at Danica and Clayne to see them regarding him expectantly. When he turned to Dreya, he saw that underneath that anger was a whole lot of fear.

"That was…pretty fucking amazing," he said.

Just like that, the tension in the room evaporated. Dreya smiled, a small, tentative smile. That must mean he'd said the right thing.

"I think getting through a morning of training like this calls for an early lunch," Danica said. "You want to hit the cafeteria, Dreya?"

Dreya gazed at Braden for a moment, then nodded. "Lunch sounds good."

"She probably won't be able to tell you this for a long time, but what you just said to her was important," Clayne said after Dreya and Danica had left. "Since she can't say it right now, I will. Thanks."

With that, Clayne turned and walked out after his wife and Dreya, leaving Braden alone in the middle of the gym, trying to figure out what the hell he'd just seen. One thing he definitely knew for sure. His whole world had been turned upside down, and something told him it wasn't ever going to be the same again.

Chapter 9

Braden was halfway to the cafeteria when his cell phone rang. Stopping, he dug it out of his cargo pocket and checked the call screen, then thumbed the green button and held it to his ear.

"Congratulations," Mick said.

"Congratulations for what?" Braden asked.

He wasn't in the mood for guessing games. He was confused enough already.

"Don't act like you don't know exactly what I'm talking about, you lucky bastard," Mick said. "The lieutenant announced it at roll call this morning. He said you'd been detailed out on a long-term assignment for a joint Homeland/MPD task force. I don't think he has a clue what the hell you're doing on the task force, but he got off on implying he did."

Braden clenched his jaw. "Well, shit."

He didn't know why he was shocked. He'd already figured out that Danica and Clayne had manipulated him. It wasn't that much of a stretch that someone had done something official to make sure he hung around for a while. On the bright side, he could stop worrying about anyone missing him at work.

The really scary part of this whole deal was that someone had figured out he'd be a good partner for Dreya long before he or Dreya had even considered it. To pull off the task force thing, someone with a lot of horsepower in the DCO would have had to start working on the transfer the first day he got here.

He wasn't too sure what he thought about the whole long-term thing, though. Then again, based on his understanding of the deal Dreya had made with the DCO, she only had to play along for two more days, and then she was free to leave. Knowing Dreya like he did, it was hard to imagine her hanging around her beyond that.

He almost laughed as the irony of those words struck him. *Knowing Dreya like he did?* Who the heck was he kidding? He'd just watched the woman sprout claws and fangs. From this point forward, he was going to have to admit he didn't know her as well as he'd thought.

"You knew about this, right?" Mick asked.

"No, not really. Though I'm not surprised to hear it coming from you first. They tend to be big about that need-to-know crap around here, and apparently, there's a lot I don't need to know."

Like the fact that the woman he'd helped get undressed last night had fangs and claws. Then again, knowing she came with her own weapons wouldn't have kept him from helping her…or enjoying it.

"But it's a good gig, right? Working with Homeland," Mick said. "I mean, it has to be cool working with Dreya Clark. She's pretty damn hot."

She was definitely that. Not that he was going to admit it to his partner, who seemed to be going through a high school juvenile phase at the moment.

"Dreya is a thief, Mick," he pointed out.

Mick chuckled. "Yeah, but she's a hot thief. So, what kind of stuff do they have you two doing?"

Braden started to answer, then stopped. What the hell could he say? That he was helping a woman with claws and fangs run through an aerial obstacle course while wearing a blindfold? Yeah, that didn't exactly roll off the tongue smoothly, did it?

"It's complicated," he finally said, and that was the God's honest truth.

"Oh shit, what the hell was I thinking? Of course, you can't tell me what you doing. It's classified, right?"

Braden opened his mouth to tell his partner that it wasn't like that at all and that he seriously needed to cut out watching all those spy flicks, but Mick didn't give him a chance to get the words out.

"Don't say anything else. Just telling me something is classified is probably classified in and of itself."

Braden was still trying to wrap his head around that logic when Mick started talking again.

"I won't keep you; I know you're busy as hell. But tell me one thing. Is Dreya as awesome up close as she was in that video we saw?"

Braden grinned, thinking of the way she'd gone through the aerial obstacle course, then climbed that wall, not to mention the epic slide down. *Awesome* was pretty much an understatement when it came to Dreya.

"Mick, if I told you the truth, you'd call me a flat-out liar. I can promise you what we saw that night was just scratching the surface of how amazing she is. The more I learn about her, the more impressed I am."

"I knew it," Mick said. "She might be a thief, but that doesn't mean she's not special."

Special? Yeah, that was definitely a much better word for Dreya.

"Hey," Braden said before he hung up. "Stop by my place and pick up my mail every few days, would you?"

He stood there on the sidewalk, wondering how Mick would have reacted if he'd been the one to see Dreya sprout claws and climb a wall. Something told him that his normally calm, cool, and collected partner would have lost his mind. Now, Tommy, on the other hand, wouldn't even have batted an eye. He probably would have laughed and cracked a joke about being careful she didn't poke out an eye with those things.

Braden shook his head and started walking again. Now that the initial shock of seeing Dreya sprout claws and fangs was starting to wear off, he reevaluated the last few days. All the things he'd seen made so much more sense. She was fast, agile, strong, and could obviously handle a lot more punishment than an ordinary person. It was like she was some kind of superhero. If the DCO weren't trying to recruit her, he'd think she was some kind of government science project.

He cringed. Any more thoughts like that, and he was going to have to apologize to Mick for those comments he'd made about his partner watching too much TV. Dreya might be amazing, but she wasn't a science project. You couldn't create people like her in a test tube.

Then another thought struck him. The DCO had known how special Dreya was long before they'd ever shown up in his interrogation room. They hadn't simply been training and evaluating her. They'd been putting her in situations where she'd have to expose what she could do, not for their benefit but for his.

They hadn't only been recruiting Dreya; they'd been recruiting him at the same time.

Shit.

Who the hell were these people? And how could they possibly know him so well?

Because they had him pegged to a T. He wasn't turned off by Dreya's animalistic qualities. If anything, he was fascinated by them. And as far as Dreya herself, he was pretty damn intrigued with her, too.

Braden only hoped the DCO didn't know how fast Dreya would get to him. He'd always found her attractive. A man would have to be in serious need of a set of corrective lenses not to see how incredibly beautiful she was. But now that attraction was becoming much more physical. When he'd helped her out of her clothes after the paintball training, he'd come damn close to kissing her. And kissing her was only the start of what he'd been thinking of doing. Sleeping that night had been hard as hell, mostly because he'd been that way, too. How could he not be when he'd spent it fantasizing about what it would be like to have Dreya naked in his arms?

He was still trying to push those cock-stiffening thoughts aside when he realized he'd stopped walking and was standing in the middle of the quad, staring off into the distance like an idiot. And that Dick Coleman, the deputy director of the DCO, was regarding him with obvious amusement.

"You look like a man who's been through a life-changing event," Coleman said. "Tell me, did that event come with claws and fangs?"

Braden nodded. For a guy who probably spent more money on his clothes than Braden did on his car, Coleman seemed like an okay guy.

"Is it that obvious?" Braden asked.

Coleman laughed. "Only because I've seen the look so many times. It can be a shock to the system the first time you see the claws come out."

Braden snorted. "A little bit. You people ever consider maybe giving someone a heads-up first?"

"Not really. Most people wouldn't believe it if we did," Coleman said. "There's a certain value in seeing how a person reacts the first time their prospective partner shifts in front of them. You're more likely to react genuinely when everything is raw and unfiltered. If you can't handle this new reality, it's better to find out now than when you're in the field and lives depend on you trusting each other."

Braden thought back to the scared, vulnerable expression in Dreya's eyes when she'd first come down from that wall. She'd been waiting for him to say something hateful and reject her.

"I can understand that," he said.

"I thought you might." Coleman regarded him thoughtfully. "You strike me as a man who rarely lets his emotions outrun his head. It's part of the reason you were considered such a good match for Dreya Clark. That and your particular police background."

Something about the way Coleman said the words caught Braden's attention. "Particular police background? You mind telling me exactly what you mean by that?"

Coleman shrugged. "Nothing negative, I assure you. It's just that you have a reputation for being a straight shooter, a man who understands what it means to do things the right way."

Where the hell had Coleman picked up that little nugget of intel?

"I'm not going to lie to you, Detective. There are some people at the DCO who tend to think that the gravity of our mission gives them the right to play fast and loose with the rules. Sometimes even break the law when they feel it's necessary."

That wasn't surprising. Everything from the bizarre training to the blatant manipulation made it easy to believe there were some in this organization who liked to live outside the box. Tommy would have loved it here.

"Don't get me wrong," Coleman added. "The real world is a complicated place, and sometimes breaking the rules—even the law—is necessary. But I won't mince words. Putting someone with a criminal background like Dreya's in a place like this could be the equivalent of giving the fox the keys to the henhouse."

Braden's first instinct was to tell Coleman to piss off, which made no sense. Dreya *was* a thief. Didn't a part of him think the same thing? Things might be good right now, but he knew better than anyone that she had a history of falling into old habits. Working in a place like this, how long would it be before she got into more trouble?

"From the look on your face, it's obvious you share my concern," Coleman said. "Dreya has a chance to turn her life around here at the DCO and do something with it—something impressive. But it's going to be up to us to make sure she doesn't mess up that chance. There's a lot I can do to help, but you're going to be the first one to see it if those old instincts of hers start to kick in. If she does anything that makes you suspicious, you need to let me know. It's the only way we can make sure she doesn't sabotage herself."

Somewhere in the back of his mind, Tommy was telling him this wasn't cool, that partners—even if only temporary—didn't go behind each other's backs like this. But Coleman was right. Given the right set of circumstances, he could see Dreya going right back to the one thing she'd always excelled at—stealing stuff. Even if it blew everything else she had that was good in her life at the moment.

He promised himself right then that he wasn't going to let it happen. He had no idea how long he and Dreya would be partners, but as long as they were, he wasn't going to let her screw up, no matter what he had to do.

"Lift your tongue, and show me underneath it," the stern looking nurse ordered Trevor, clearly wanting to make sure he'd swallowed his tiny paper cup full of antipsychotic meds.

Trevor did as he was instructed, not because he was necessarily in a compliant mood, but simply because that seemed to be standard protocol among all the other poor zombielike patients who had taken their meds before him. And blending in with the heavily medicated crowd was the plan at the moment.

It didn't hurt that there were the two beefy orderlies accompanying the red-haired nurse. They looked giddy with anticipation at the idea of getting to force-feed someone their meds. Trevor could easily take them if he had to, but that would probably only get him shipped off to jail.

"Now move your tongue to one side, then the other," the nurse instructed before giving Trevor a curt nod. "Thank you."

"No. Thank *you*, Nurse Ratched," he said warmly.

Gray eyes narrowing, the woman tapped the plain black name tag on her white sweater. "It's Nurse Fletcher."

Trevor almost followed after the woman when she turned and walked away so he could ask her if it was legal to work at a mental health facility if you hadn't seen *One Flew Over the Cuckoo's Nest*. He decided not to bother. Being snarky lost all its appeal if you had to explain it.

He finished the paper cup of water she'd given him, then crumpled it up and tossed it in the trash can against the wall for a perfect three-point-play. He wasn't too worried about the meds. His shifter metabolism burned up any drug he took in pretty short order. He only knew that because someone in the Chinese Ministry of State Security—kind of like their version of the CIA—had tried to poison him a little while ago. He'd come out of that with little more than indigestion.

On the bright side, the antipsychotic prescription meant that apparently the conversation he had with Dr. Brand about his penis had been enough to convince the man he was in need of long-term psychiatric care. Nothing said *you need serious help* like a paper cup full of modern pharmaceuticals.

If Trevor had to put his finger on the one thing that had sealed the deal with Dr. Brand, it had to be the detailed narrative on the disagreement he and his penis frequently got into concerning which TV shows they should watch. His penis preferred reality shows over scripted entertainment. Yeah, that part was inspired.

He scanned the common area, taking in the twenty others patients hanging out, either staring blankly at the television or absently flipping through magazines.

On the surface, there didn't seem to be anything suspicious or strange going on. With its brightly painted walls, big screen TV, shelves full of board games and books, loads of comfy chairs, and big windows that let in the last of the day's light and gave picturesque views of the perfectly maintained grounds around the facility, it was easy to be lulled into thinking this place was some kind of resort. With locks on the outside of the bedroom doors.

But if you looked beyond the obvious, there were some things in this place that should give any sane person pause when it came to parking a family member here.

Trevor hadn't been in many institutions like this, but there was no mistaking the fact that Stillwater was set up and run like a prison. In addition to bars on the windows, there were lots of cameras and orderlies on every set of doors leading in or out of the main residential areas. Patients were free to walk around anywhere they wanted as long as they stayed in the common area or on one of the three floors of patient rooms. If someone wanted to get out of this section of the facility and into the hospital wing, the counseling and therapy wing, or take a walk outside along the walled-in gardens, they had to get past the orderlies.

Getting into the isolation ward was going to be even harder. It was at the end of a hallway he'd wandered down shortly after getting there. But he hadn't gotten any closer than fifteen feet from the big steel doors and the security hulk of an orderly stationed there—barely close enough to catch a scent and confirm there was definitely a shifter and maybe something that might be a hybrid in there—when the orderly had told him to turn around.

Yeah, those orderlies were going to be a problem. Between the two with Nurse Ratched, the ones manning the security checkpoints, and the others roaming randomly about the common area and adjoining residential floors, there were easily more than a dozen in this area alone. They were all big and muscular, and if Trevor didn't miss his guess, they were all carrying Tasers hidden in those pouches on their waists. What kind of psychiatric facility armed their orderlies with Tasers?

He bit back a growl of frustration. He and his two teammates, Jake Basso and Ed Vincent, were the DCO's espionage/counterespionage team. They spied on people, hacked into information systems and made off with the data stored inside, stole industrial secrets when necessary, and then, just for fun, went after bad guy spies to keep them from doing the same things to the good guys.

He and his team spent their time playing a complicated and dangerous game of spy versus spy, and they were very good at it. But John hadn't wanted Jake and Ed involved in this mission. Now Trevor was undercover in this place on his own, without equipment or a plan, playing the part of a mental patient and trying to figure out how to get past a bunch of orderlies into a medical research operation that was probably experimenting on a shifter and making hybrids.

He was man enough to admit he was a little out of his comfort zone.

Trevor was considering heading up to the third floor again to see if he could find an entry point into the attic crawl space, thinking that might let him bypass the orderlies completely, when he spotted something interesting—a flash of clear-eyed intelligence that stuck out around here like a unicorn wearing disco pants.

He watched as the slender teenage girl with her dark hair up in a ponytail casually looked around the room, then covertly took something out of her mouth and put it into the pocket of her pajamas. And she did it while standing in one of the few places in the common room that wasn't covered by a video camera.

Bright kid.

She scanned the room again and this time caught him watching her. Panic flashed in the girl's eyes for half a second, then they took on a calculating look. A moment later, her gaze changed, becoming unfocused like the other patients, and she slowly wandered across the room toward him.

Her back to the cameras, she gave him that sharp, clear-eyed look he'd seen a few minutes ago.

"You don't look like the normal type who gets dumped in here," she said softly. "Who'd you piss off?"

Trevor didn't know what the girl's story was, but she was definitely smart.

"My sister," he said. "She told the doctors that I'm a danger to myself and others, but that's crap. Mostly, she thinks I'm an embarrassment to the family name. By the way, the name's Miles."

"Brooklyn."

"What's your story?"

"Story?" she asked.

"Yeah. You've obviously been here for a while to be able to ditch your meds so smoothly."

Brooklyn's eyes darted around again with an alertness

that would have fit better on a deployed soldier—or a criminal in prison.

"I'm not sure how long I've been here," she said quietly. "Four years, I think. But it could be five."

Damn. The poor kid had been in here so many years, she didn't even remember how long it had been? What kind of place was this?

"That means you were, what, like twelve years old when they put you here?" he asked. "How'd that happen?"

The girl looked out the window for a long time before answering. "My parents died in a car crash when I was twelve. I was in the backseat, so I saw what happened to them." She reached up to play with the end of her ponytail. "I didn't handle it well and did some stupid stuff. My mom and dad were loaded, and since I didn't have any other family, their lawyers were the executors of my parents' estate. They sent me here. For my own good, you know?"

"Are they going to let you go home at some point?"

She turned from the window to eyeball the orderly on the other side of the room before looking at Trevor. "I have a friend in here named Ian who helped me break into Dr. Brand's computer so I could see my record. My parents' law firm is paying nearly forty thousand a month to keep me here. If that's what I'm worth to Stillwater, I don't see Dr. Brand ever letting me leave."

Well, that was just plain shitty.

"It's not a big deal," Brooklyn added. "There're lots of people like me here. Ian's pretty much in the same boat. We're not mentally ill. We're just rich."

Trevor ground his jaw. This mission had been hard enough before when it meant getting into the isolation ward, figuring out what Mahsood was up to, finding the shifter, and coming up with a way to stop any hybrid research, all without making a lot of noise. Now he needed to add a couple more tasks to his to-do list, namely putting Brand and this place out of business and helping Brooklyn and the other people like her get out of here.

But one thing at a time.

"You ever see or hear anything weird going on around here?" he asked.

Brooklyn lifted a brow. "Other than the obvious weird crap you'd expect in a place like this?"

"Yeah, other than that."

Her eyes narrowed. "I've had new people ask me how to duck their meds and where the doctors keep the really good drugs. One guy even asked me which nurse might be willing to get busy with a semistable mental patient. But I've never had anyone ask me a question as strange as that."

He smiled and shrugged. "Maybe I'm a bit strange myself. Humor me. Have you seen or heard anything lately that doesn't fit with the norm in this place?"

Brooklyn's look became even more suspicious. "You're different from the other patients who get dumped in here."

"Yeah, I am."

She was silent, as if weighing his words. Finally, she must have come to some conclusion, because she nodded. "There are a lot more orderlies working here than there used to be. They're bigger and meaner, too."

"Anything else?"

Brooklyn thought a moment. "There's something different happening in the wacky ward. It started about six months ago when these new doctors showed up but has gotten worse in the past few weeks."

Mahsood had been here since December? That meant he must have come straight here when he'd left Costa Rica.

"I'm guessing wacky ward is the isolation ward?" he asked.

She nodded. "Yeah. Some of us old-timers call it that. It's where Dr. Brand takes people when their meds stop working or they're being difficult. People stay in there a few days, sometimes a week, then come back really chill."

She jerked her head at two older men sitting on one of the couches, staring at the TV with unfocused eyes, faces slack.

"They'll be like that for a while until whatever drugs Dr. Frankenbrand gave to them wears off."

Nice. As if he didn't already have enough motive to put Brand out of business.

"That's bad enough, but when those new doctors showed up, they started doing strange stuff with the patients, like taking blood samples and cheek swabs all the time." Brooklyn looked around nervously and lowered her voice. "A little while after that is when we started hearing strange sounds from the wacky ward at night. Like freaky, scary sounds."

She must have thought Trevor didn't believe her, because she held up a hand as if swearing an oath. "I know what you're thinking. All crazy people hear sounds that aren't there, but there's someone screaming like an animal in there. Sometimes more than one person."

"I believe you," he said softly.

One person making sounds could be the shifter. More than one meant Mahsood had already created at least one hybrid.

"Anything else weird going on?" Trevor asked.

Brooklyn began playing with the end of her ponytail again. "About a month ago, they started taking certain people to the ward with no justification at all. And now when people go in there, they don't come back."

"Certain people?" he prompted.

She nodded. "Everyone who's gone there recently has been a patient who didn't get any family visitors. Like my friend Ian."

Trevor had been wondering where the other kid was this whole time they were talking. "They took Ian? When?"

"A week ago." She swallowed hard. "He punched an orderly who was getting all grabby with me, and they said he was being disruptive. I've asked about him every day since, but no one will tell me anything. I'm getting scared as hell that when he comes back, he'll be like those old guys on the couch and won't know who he is, much less who I am."

Shit. Trevor had hoped to have at least a day to sniff around and get the lay of the land, then talk to Ivy and Landon a couple of times when they came to visit him. But if regular people were starting to disappear into a hybrid lab and not being seen again, he didn't have the luxury of moving slowly.

Brooklyn's eyes darted to something behind him. "That's them," she whispered. "The new doctors."

Trevor casually turned to see who she was talking about. He didn't recognize two of the men, but the third was definitely Kamal Mahsood.

As if feeling Trevor's gaze on him, Mahsood looked his way. Trevor's gut clenched. Did Mahsood know he was a DCO agent? Even worse, could Mahsood tell he was a shifter?

Then he realized that Mahsood wasn't looking at him, but rather, Brooklyn. Eyes locked on her, Mahsood leaned over and whispered something to the heavyset doctor with him. Thanks to his exceptional hearing, Trevor heard everything.

Is she the one? Mahsood asked.

The other doctor nodded. *Will she work?*

Mahsood considered that for a moment. *I think the girl will make an excellent test subject, yes.*

Trevor stiffened. *Double shit.* If he thought he'd been under a time crunch before, it just got worse. No way was he letting Mahsood experiment on Brooklyn.

"Any chance you know of a way to sneak into the isolation ward?" he asked her.

Her eyes widened, but then that calculating look was back along with the only smile Trevor had seen in this damn place since he'd gotten there.

"Actually, I might," she said. "Do you think you can get Ian out of there?"

"Maybe," Trevor said noncommittally. "Tell me how to sneak in."

"The place I'm thinking about is kind of hard to get into."

"Don't worry about that," he said. "You give me good enough directions, then let me worry about getting in."

Brooklyn chewed on her lip, considering him with that same devious look he'd seen on the faces of some the female operatives at the DCO.

"What?" he asked slowly, feeling he wasn't going to like whatever Brooklyn was thinking.

"Nothing. It's just now that I think about it, I realize it's easier for me to take you there than give you directions."

He frowned. "That's not a good idea."

She shrugged. "Well, you could always go with Ian's method and get into a fight with an orderly. Though if you want to make sure you end up in the wacky ward, I'd suggest punching one. But if you go that route, they'll probably shoot you up with drugs, and you'll end up being a zombie like everyone else who ends up in there."

Trevor ground his jaw. Damn, this girl was good. This was why he was glad the DCO had never teamed him up with a woman. It always turned into a train wreck.

Chapter 10

"Were you born this way?" Braden asked.

They were sitting at the small kitchen table in their dorm room eating the pizza they'd picked up from the cafeteria. Even though everything was different now that Braden knew her secret, it was still kind of weird hearing him say it out loud.

"You mean was I born a freak?"

Dreya cringed a little at how harshly the words came out, but there was a huge part of her that was still worried about what Braden really thought now that he knew what she was.

He scowled at her over the slice of double pepperoni, double cheese pizza in his hand. "You are not a freak."

She held up her hands so he could see her fingernails, then let her claws extend out to their full length. "You don't think so?"

Setting his pizza down, he reached across the table and took her hand in his, pulling it closer so he could get a good look. He turned her hand this way and that, tracing his fingertips over the claws, seemingly fascinated by the way her human nails molded themselves into her animal claws in one seamless extension at the end of her fingers.

The instinct to pull away so he couldn't stare at her freaky curved claws warred with the bizarre pleasure she took from having him touch her. He had strong hands and fingers, yet he was also amazingly gentle as he touched the sharp tips of her claws.

"No, I still don't think you're a freak," he said softly. "If anything, it's like you're some kind of werekitty. These claws of yours are exactly like what I would expect to see on a person who's part cat."

Dreya snorted. "You're more right than you think. According to Kendra and Lucy, I'm a feline shifter. Somehow, there's cat DNA in my genetic makeup."

He looked up from her hands, regarding her casually. "A shifter, huh?" He grinned. "I like that word better than freak."

Braden didn't let go of her hand but instead gently massaged her fingers and lightly traced her claws. It felt *really* good.

But to her utter disappointment, a moment later, he let go of her hand and went back to his pizza.

"You didn't answer my question," he reminded her. "Were you born like this? Did your mom have to deal with little baby Dreya shredding her blankey and chewing her pacifier to pieces?"

Dreya couldn't help but laugh at the image as she let her claws retract. "No, it doesn't work that way. I was a normal seventeen-year-old girl until, one night, I woke up from a really bad dream and tasted blood on my tongue. I ran to the bathroom and discovered I had a mouth full of fangs, which just happened to perfectly match the claws on my fingers and toes."

Braden did a double take. "Claws on your toes, too? I never thought of that. It must have scared the hell out of you."

Dreya nodded, remembering the night vividly. She'd

been sure she was going insane—or turning into a monster. "Understatement there. I completely lost it. I yowled so loud, I sounded like a cat on crack."

"What happened when your parents saw you like that?"

"Nothing, because they never did."

"They didn't hear you scream?"

"They heard." She took a bite of pizza and chewed. "By the time they came rushing in, the fangs and claws were gone, and I was standing in front of the bathroom mirror with a dazed look in my eyes and gashes on my tongue. My parents were worried less about the blood in my mouth than all the crazy screaming I'd been doing. They were worried I was on drugs and tried to pierce my tongue. It took me an hour to convince them I had a nightmare and bit myself. I left out the part about the claws and fangs, of course." She shook her head at the memory. "I was terrified they were going to pop out the whole time my mom and dad were in my room, and they'd think I was a vampire or something."

He reached into the box for another slice of pizza. "And you never told them? Not even after that first time?"

"No." She sighed. "My parents are conservative. They both come from old money, and they both went to Ivy League schools. They're very comfortable in their routines, whether it's the people they associate with, the foods they eat, or even the kind of books they read. I'm not sure how they would have dealt with finding out that their only child was a freak."

When Braden shot her a sharp look, Dreya shrugged. "At the time, it's how I looked at myself. How would you see yourself if you woke up one day and had claws and stuff? I thought I was living a nightmare."

Braden picked up his bottle of beer and took a swig. "So you kept a secret like that to yourself? Didn't you at least have a sister or brother or a friend you could tell?"

She took a deep breath, transported back to those first weeks. "I don't have any brothers or sisters. There were a couple of girlfriends at school I almost told, but every time I got close to spilling my secret, one of them would start gossiping about something they heard about someone, and I was afraid to trust them with anything this big.

"But then I went into a jewelry shop to pick up a custom necklace my mom had ordered. The owner and I started talking, and the next thing I knew, I was sitting in his office, crying my eyes out and telling him everything."

"Rory," Braden supplied.

"Yeah, Rory." She gave Braden a small smile. "He listened to a teenage girl rant and rave for hours without complaining once. He talked me off the figurative ledge I was standing on at the time and saved my life. Even though he knew nothing about shifters, he figured out how to help me learn to control my abilities."

"How so?"

"Well, for one thing, he taught me relaxation techniques to help keep my claws and fangs from coming out at the wrong time. He coached me on when to shift my eyes so I can see even better in the dark than I normally can and, more importantly, when not to shift them."

Braden lifted a brow. "Your eyes look like a cat's, too? Show me."

Other than Rory, no one else had ever seen her eyes change. Heck, *she'd* never seen them. But instead of being nervous and self-conscious like she'd been in the gym earlier, Dreya was excited by the idea of sharing that part of herself with Braden.

Taking a deep breath, she closed her eyes, then opened them. On the other side of the table, Braden's face filled with wonder.

"Damn," he breathed. "That is so frigging cool."

Dreya wasn't sure, but she might have blushed a little at the compliment. "They glow brighter green in the dark, which is why Rory said I needed to be careful."

"What else did he teach you?"

"How to put a filter on my sense of smell and hearing so I wouldn't go crazy from the overwhelming scents and sounds that most people never even know are there." She let out a wistful sigh. "I think I would have gone insane without him and what he taught me about myself."

"You miss him a lot, don't you?" Braden asked.

She looked away. "Yeah. And I hate that Thorn and the asshole he had murder Rory aren't rotting in jail right now. It's not fair."

"No, it isn't," he agreed. "Unfortunately, life is rarely fair."

Dreya regarded him thoughtfully. "You sound like you're speaking from experience."

Braden swigged his beer before placing the bottle down on the table. "Back when I first made detective, my partner got killed in a shoot-out."

"Did you ever catch the guys who did it?"

He shook his head. "Didn't have to. Tommy and I took out the whole crew. Unfortunately, I never found the piece of crap informant who gave Tommy the bad info that put us in that position in the first place."

There was anger in his voice…and pain. She'd become familiar with both those things lately. "Do you think the guy did it deliberately?"

"Maybe. I don't know. All I know is that Tommy is dead in part because of him."

"In part?"

"Yeah." He sighed. "I've always kind of blamed myself for it, too, because I didn't do anything to stop him from going into that warehouse. People tell me there's nothing I could have done, but I blame myself anyway."

She knew what that felt like. "I spent a lot of time blaming myself for Rory's death, too. If I hadn't pissed off Thorn, or if I left town earlier, Rory would still be alive."

Braden's mouth curved in a sad smile. "Rory might have been the biggest fence along the northeast corridor, but I always liked the guy anyway. I wish he was still around so I could thank him for being there for you."

Dreya felt her eyes tear up, and she blinked. "Yeah, I wish he was still around, too. For a long time, he was the only person who knew my secret. After Rory was killed, I never told another soul."

Braden chuckled. "And yet, here you are, telling your secrets to the cop who arrested you. Is the world a strange place or what?"

She laughed and helped herself to another slice of pizza. If she didn't keep an eye on him, Braden would hog it all. The guy ate like a machine.

The rest of the day's training had taken a slightly different tone after her big reveal and learning that Braden was going to be her partner. It had suddenly turned into less about what she could do and more about what she and Braden could do together. But still, it had been physically exhausting, and she was famished.

After they finished eating, they grabbed a couple of bottles of soda from the fridge and moved into the small living room.

"What do you think Rory would say about you getting recruited by a covert organization for the federal government?" Braden asked. He looked good all stretched out on the couch a mere foot or two away.

She rested her head on her hand with a laugh. "He wasn't a fan of the federal government, but since it's not the FBI, I think he'd be okay with it. As long as it's what I wanted."

"Is it what you want? Tomorrow is day four of your deal. Are you going to stay and give this a shot, or are you going to go back to what you know?"

Dreya considered that. It wasn't a simple question. When she'd first gotten here, she'd planned on bailing immediately, but Braden had talked her out of that. Even then, she'd thought of the DCO as little more than a way to avoid a prison sentence. But since that time, everything had changed. Finding out there were other people like her out in the world was huge. Realizing there were also people who knew how different she was and still wanted her to work here counted for a lot.

"I think I want to stay," she finally told him. "It's hard to put into words, but my instincts are telling tell me there's something here for me. That this is where I'm supposed to be. Does that make any sense at all?"

He grinned. "Yeah, it does actually. And if my opinion matters at all, I think your instincts are right. This place is perfect for you."

She smiled at him, feeling extraordinarily happy knowing Braden agreed with her decision. "Thanks. And your opinion does matter."

"You realize these people are going to keep pushing you," Braden said. "I get the feeling you're going to have to do a lot of dangerous stuff. Are you up for that?"

"I'm up for it," she said softly. "As long as you're my partner."

Dreya cringed the moment the words were out of her mouth. They'd spent the whole even talking about her, and she had no idea if he was planning to stay here even to the end of the week, much less long-term. Danica and Clayne had tricked Braden into being her partner for this training stuff. It wasn't like they were recruiting him into the DCO.

If Braden noticed her misstep, he didn't react to it. Instead, he stretched and got to his feet. "Then I guess we need to get cleaned up and go to bed. Clayne and Danica will be here early as hell tomorrow. They said something about getting you a gun."

Dreya let out a shudder that was only half fake. Rory had hated guns, and she had picked up on that disdain. But if the DCO wanted her to carry a weapon, she supposed she'd have to get used to it. Not that she ever planned on using one, of course.

"I don't mind getting up early," she told him as they headed for their respective bedrooms. "I'm just glad I'm not so sore tonight, I need your help getting my clothes off."

O-kay. That definitely didn't come out the way she intended.

Braden gave her a hurt look as they stopped outside

their rooms. "What? You didn't like the way I undressed you last night?"

"No. I mean yes!" she said. "I loved it. You can help me undress any time you want."

Braden lifted a brow, his dark eyes dancing with amusement.

Dreya felt her face heat. "That didn't come out any better, did it?"

He chuckled. "I know what you meant. If it helps, I have to admit that I enjoyed helping you get out of those clothes. So, if you decide you ever need help getting naked, all you have to do is ask."

Dreya opened her mouth to make some crack about partners being there for each other, but the sexy glint in his eyes robbed her of the words.

He was right there, standing so close she could feel the heat coming off his body. Maybe it was the relief of finally having another person to share her secret with. Or the way Braden didn't run screaming when he saw her claws and fangs. Heck, maybe it was three days of living this close to a really hot guy who liked to take her clothes off. Whatever it was, she was going to kiss him.

Braden must have decided to do the same to her, because his mouth was coming down on hers even as she reached out to tug him against her.

The sensations hit her all at once, eliciting a moan from her throat. The hunger of his lips as he devoured hers, the sweetness of his tongue as it dipped into her mouth, the solid strength of his chest muscles as they pressed against her soft breasts.

She buried her hand in his hair, yanking him down harder, wanting to make sure he didn't go anywhere.

His hand found its way to her lower back, fitting her more tightly against him and letting her know just how excited he was.

When that hand on her back slid lower, firmly caressing her ass, she didn't complain. This was absolutely insane, but she wanted him all the same. She barely knew him. He was a cop who had tried to put her in prison three days ago. On top of that, he was her new partner. Those were all good reasons to avoid any romantic entanglements. But none of that seemed to matter as their kiss burned hotter.

A quiver started to build in the pit of her stomach and then pooled lower. She was so turned on, she was surprised she didn't combust. She only prayed her fangs didn't slip out—she didn't want to bite him.

She pushed that worry aside and focused on something else instead—like the fact that Braden was as turned on as she was. She could smell his arousal in the air, taste it on his tongue, and feel it in the hard-on pressed against her stomach. Sighing, she reached for the buttons on his uniform top, but he broke the kiss and took a step back.

She blinked up at him in confusion. There was no mistaking the same lust she was feeling mirrored in his eyes. He wanted her as badly as she wanted him.

"We have to get up early for training tomorrow," he said in a ragged voice.

She let out a sound that was half growl, half purr and closed the distance between them. "I don't care about tomorrow."

Braden stepped back again, like they were doing a complex dance step. "You need to care. Tomorrow is only day four of the deal you made with the DCO. You can't afford to screw up and blow this chance. Not after everything you've made it through already."

The urge to say the hell with the DCO was overwhelmingly powerful. Dreya had never experienced anything like it. She'd been with guys before, but she could take it or leave it with most of them. With Braden, she was hungrier than she'd ever remembered being.

But he was right, and she knew it. She'd just told him she wanted to be here. She hadn't proven anything to the DCO yet and didn't want them changing their mind about her.

She forced herself to step back and put some much-needed space between her and Braden. "Thanks. It's good that at least one of us has some control left."

He nodded. "I'll see you in the morning."

Dreya got ready for bed quickly, refusing to let her mind wander in a sexual direction as she showered off, then hurried into her room. But then Braden hit the shower right after her, and she was forced to hold her breath to avoid inhaling his amazing scent. She didn't know how she could smell it under all the body wash he dumped on himself, but she could.

Knowing he was right there, barely ten feet away, wet and naked, made her want to caterwaul in frustration. The urge to walk into the bathroom and slip into the shower with him was nearly impossible to resist. But she did, because she needed to focus on doing well in training tomorrow and impressing the people who would decide if she was going to work for them.

She hated having to be all mature and adult about crap like this.

Dreya pulled on her Betty Boop sleepshirt, biting her lip to keep from moaning out loud as the cotton fabric rubbed against her tingling nipples. Then she climbed into bed and lay there under the covers, trying to think of something—anything—other than the kiss she and Braden had shared. Just the thought of that kiss had heat swirling between her legs.

What was it about Braden that got to her so much? Yeah, he was attractive and muscular and smelled amazing. But it was more than that. Part of it was the way he looked at her like he thought she was the most beautiful woman in the world, not just when he'd been helping her get naked, but back when he'd been interrogating her at the police station. Something told her it wasn't simply her body that he was attracted to either. It was all of her.

That was when it hit her. Braden had looked at her the same way right before they'd kissed…after he knew what she was. He knew she had fangs, and he still wanted to kiss her. That was incredible and arousing on a level she'd never experienced before.

The shower turned off, and Braden came out of the bathroom a few minutes later to turn off the lights. The scent rolling off him was almost enough to send her chasing after him. She was so excited, she wanted to jump him and sink her fangs into him. Dreya gripped the edge of the comforter, forcing herself to stay where she was.

In the next room, Braden climbed into bed. A moment later, she heard his heart rate slow and his breathing grow steady. He was already close to falling asleep, while she'd probably be lying there awake and frustrated for hours. How the heck could men change gears so quickly?

"Dreya?" he called, his voice barely above a whisper. "Can you hear me if I talk this softly?"

"Uh-huh," she said softly, then realized she was going to have to speak louder if she wanted him to hear her. "Yes, I can hear you."

"Good. Because I wanted to make sure you had one thing straight before you fell asleep tonight."

"What's that?"

"When I pulled away after kissing you and you said it was good that at least one of us still had some control. I want you to know that resisting the urge to drag you off to bed was the hardest thing I've ever done. Instead of saying I'd see you in the morning, what I really wanted to say was I hoped there was enough room in your bed for me. I just wanted you to know that, okay?"

Dreya smiled to herself and fluffed up her pillow. Why did it make her feel better knowing he'd come close to losing control, too? Maybe because if she had to lay here awake half the night, it was nice knowing he'd be lying awake just as long.

"Thanks," she said.

Then she tugged her blanket a little higher and closed her eyes, thinking delicious, if very erotic, thoughts.

"Do your best not to shoot me, huh?" Braden said with a smile.

Dreya thought that was anything but funny, especially since they were standing outside something known as a shoot house, about to start a session of CQC—Close

Quarter Combat—training using live ammo. In that regard, her partner wasn't joking. If she weren't careful, she could end up shooting him. Even if she didn't hit him, she still had to worry about taking out Clayne or Danica, who'd be walking around on the catwalks that overlooked each room of the shoot house she and Braden would be moving through.

Dreya was definitely of the opinion that this kind of room clearance training was way too advanced for her, especially since the first time she'd ever fired a real gun had been this morning, exactly eight hours ago.

Surprisingly, she'd enjoyed shooting a lot more than she would have expected, mostly because Braden had gone to great lengths to help her pick out the right handgun for her. The basic 9mm Glock 19 was the perfect size for her hand, didn't kick too much, and was easy to use.

It had also helped that Braden had stood right behind her through the first ten or fifteen clips of ammo, keeping her body in the right posture and steadying her arm. Having him so close, they were practically touching, had been seriously fun. Yes, she knew she should have been focused completely on the task at hand, but it turned out that shooting guns with Braden was kind of sexy.

But just because she'd been able to handle shooting holes in stationary targets set out at distances ranging from five to thirty yards didn't mean she was ready to get all SWAT cop and go kicking in a bunch of doors and shooting her way through a house full of simulated bad guys. Whatever happened to the concept of learning to walk before you tried to run? But like Braden had said last night, these people at the DCO were going to push her, and right now, that meant sending the two of them through this CQC course.

She stifled a groan. Thinking about last night was a bad idea, because it totally distracted her. Not that it took much to get her thinking about that kiss they'd shared before going to bed. It had been the last thing on her mind when she'd fallen asleep last night and the first thing she'd thought about the second she'd woken up this morning. Seriously, that had been one memorable kiss. Dreya only hoped that after her five-day recruitment period was up, she and Braden might get a chance to make a few more memories as amazing as the one from last night.

Beside her, Braden grabbed two sets of foam earplugs from the table and handed one to her.

"Don't overthink this, okay?" he said, his voice calm and steady. "We'll do this the same way we did on the walkthrough, moving slowly and carefully. I'll go first and cover the far left of the room, then sweep to the right corner. You immediately follow behind and cover the hinge side back corner first, then the knob side corner."

That was exactly the way he'd explained it on the walkthrough, and Dreya had barely understood it then. She took a deep breath and forced herself to relax, putting Braden's words into simpler instructions in her head. Basically, he would charge in first and worry about what was right in front of them, while she covered him by essentially dealing with "bad guys" who might be hiding behind the door, trying to shoot the first person through the door, namely him.

It had sounded scary tough on the walkthrough, and now that she was carrying a live weapon, it sounded even scarier. No, none of the pop-up "bad guys" in there would be shooting at them. But if she and Braden didn't communicate well, this could get dangerous.

He glanced at her as he slipped into the heavy tactical vest they would both be wearing for this exercise. "You'll be sweeping right across my back as you clear from one side to the other, so I'm trusting you, okay?"

She nodded as she tightened the straps on her own vest. The fact that he trusted her enough to let her carry a live weapon behind was important to her. She wouldn't let him down.

"Ready?" he asked.

"Ready," she said.

As she and Braden approached the shoot house in the fading light of day, he turned to give her a look. "No pressure or anything, but I think I just saw that guy you pointed out to me at breakfast—John Loughlin—walk up to the observation level. It looks like the big boss is going to be watching us."

She groaned. "Great. Someone else for me to accidently shoot."

Braden chuckled. "Don't worry. You'll do fine. You just stay on my ass and focus on covering me. I'll worry about getting us through the house."

Dreya nodded. Sounded like a fair deal to her. She definitely had no problem sticking close to his ass. It was sexy.

She pushed that thought out of her head and rolled her shoulders a few times, settling her tactical vest into place. Not only would the vest hopefully protect them from any stray round that might ricochet off of something hard, it also carried the sensors that would ring off if one of the targets "shot" them. She and Braden would lose points each time a sensor went off.

According to Braden, even a small house usually needed at least three or four well-trained cops working together to clear it safely. Doing it with two people, one of whom had never done anything like this, would have been considered suicidal in the real world. Here, it was just realistic training. She didn't expect them to do very well in this event, at least not the first few times through.

"You good?" Braden asked.

Dreya nodded, her heart starting to beat faster.

Giving her a nod in return, Braden stepped forward and kicked in the front door. He went in first, sweeping his handgun from left to right across the room. Dreya followed at his heels, checking the hinge side of the door to see if anyone was hiding there, then quickly sweeping across Braden's back to do the opposite corner of the room. If someone were there, they'd instinctively aim for her partner first, so while she moved carefully, keeping her finger away from the trigger anytime the weapon was pointed in Braden's direction, she also moved quickly.

As soon as they confirmed the first room was empty, Braden led the way to the next door. The moment he kicked it in, Dreya felt a funny tingle along the nape of her neck.

Braden was already moving before she could say anything, though. She darted after him, not worrying about which side of the room she was supposed to cover but instead going with the tingle and her instincts.

She turned to the left the moment she got in the room, lifting her weapon at the same time, her finger already squeezing the trigger as she saw the man-shaped target pop up in that corner of the room. She hit it in the center of the chest with two rounds before it had even gotten all the way up.

Pulse racing, she spun and checked the right back corner of the room, then took three quick steps forward to check a small closet on that wall, even though her instincts seemed to tell her there was nothing there.

She glanced over her shoulder at Braden to see him nodding at her in approval. She gave him a quick smile, but he was already heading for the next room.

They continued moving through the house like that, Braden using his experience, Dreya trusting the instincts she'd honed through years of being a thief and avoiding cops, surveillance cameras, and alarm sensors. It was amazing how similar what she was doing now was to breaking into a well-guarded high-rise apartment complex.

It wasn't long before her ears were ringing, even with the earplugs in, and there was a trail of brass cartridge cases, expended weapon clips, and bullet-riddled targets behind them. She didn't honestly have any way to judge, but something told her she and Braden were smoking this exercise.

Then the lights went out.

Braden immediately stopped in front of her. Dreya halted, too, her eyes automatically shifting to let in more light.

"No shifter vision," Clayne called out from above them. "We'll be able to see the glow of your eyes, so we'll know if you cheat, Dreya."

She looked up to meet his gold gaze. "Then how are we supposed to get through the rest of the house?"

"You'll have to figure out how to do it some other way."

That was patently unfair, but she turned off her shifter version of night-vision goggles.

"I can't see a damn thing in here, so I'm wide open to suggestions," Braden said softly.

Dreya thought a moment. Just because she couldn't use her night vision didn't mean she couldn't use the other talents available to her. Closing her eyes, she pulled up what she remembered of the house's floor plan from their earlier walkthrough. When she had it, she put her free hand on Braden's shoulder.

"The door is on our left." She gently nudged him that way. "Just go where I guide you."

Thankfully, Braden didn't question her but instead turned and headed in that direction. They had to move a lot slower, and getting through the doors was more of an adventure than it would have been if she could have seen where they were going, but they did it.

Figuring out where the "bad guys" were positioned was harder. Without her night vision, the only way she could tell if there were any targets in the room was when she heard the slight creak of their gears as they popped up. The moment she did, she'd call out a general clock direction of the sound, and then she and Braden would fire in that general direction.

Unfortunately, it was hard reacting to the sounds fast enough, and the buzzers on the vests she and Braden were wearing went off a few times, indicating that one or both of them had been hit. But they kept moving from room to room, getting better and more accurate with each one they moved through.

Dreya was getting in the groove when Braden kicked open another door, and the late afternoon sun came bursting in.

"Time," Clayne called from the catwalk above them. "Ten minutes, twenty-five seconds. You two were tagged three times, but you ended up with twenty-seven kills. Not frigging bad for a new team."

Braden turned and gave Dreya a high five. "Not frigging bad, my ass. That was damn impressive. When those lights went out, I thought we were done."

From the amount of pride surging through her, Dreya would have thought Braden had told her she'd won an Olympic gold medal. She started to thank him, but John interrupted her.

"Braden's right. That was impressive."

Dreya turned to see Danica, Clayne, and John coming down the steps from the catwalk, smiles on their faces.

"Considering this was the first time you've ever done anything like this together, you two were moving exceptionally fast," the director added. "How'd you'd get through the rest of the course in the dark so easily?"

Beside her, Dreya noticed Braden looked as curious as the rest of them.

She grinned. "Maybe I cheated and used my feline night-vision goggles."

Danica laughed. "Nice try, but like Clayne said, we would have seen the green glow of your eyes."

John regarded her thoughtfully. "I once heard about a wolf shifter whose nose is so good, she can navigate a dark shoot house like this by scent. Is that what you did?"

Dreya wished her nose was that good. "No, nothing

that amazing. I just memorized the building's floor plan when we did our walkthrough earlier."

"How'd you know we'd turn out the lights?" Clayne asked.

"I didn't." She shrugged. "I memorized it because it's what I do."

Braden had holstered his gun and now crossed his arms over his chest with a frown. "What do you mean, it's what you do?"

"I'm a thief," she reminded him, then quickly added, "or used to be one. I never knew what kind of safe I was going to run into or what kind of security system a place would have, never mind when I might have needed an alternate escape route. It's not like I could climb around with a laptop in my backpack, so I memorized everything."

That explanation didn't exactly clear up the surprise on the faces around her, especially Braden's.

"How long do you remember the stuff you commit to memory, like the floor plan of this shoot house?" he asked.

Dreya gave them another shrug. "Pretty much forever, I guess."

Braden looked even more stunned at that, as did Danica and Clayne. While John seemed equally amazed, he also looked intrigued, like he thought that might be another skill the DCO could have her use.

"That's even more impressive than your performance in the shoot house then," Clayne said. "We've got the computer analysis of what you guys did in there if you're interested?"

"Hell, yeah," Braden said.

Dreya almost laughed at the excitement on his face. He looked like a kid at Christmas.

"I wasn't just saying that, by the way," John said to her as Braden joined Clayne and Danica by the computer console inside the small room off the shoot house. "I really am impressed. Not just by what you were able to do today but how you've handled yourself since we brought you in. You've come a very long way from where you started."

She snorted. "I don't know about that. I've only been here four days. I haven't really accomplished much beyond running myself ragged."

Although if he measured her performance by how far she'd run since she'd gotten here, maybe she had done something. But she doubted that was what he meant.

John smiled. "Trust me, you've accomplished much more than you think." He tilted his head, regarding her thoughtfully. "What do you think of the DCO so far? Can you see yourself fitting in here?"

If someone had told her that she'd be contemplating going to work for a covert government organization, she would have told them they were crazy.

"Maybe," she admitted. "Though to be honest, I'm still not exactly sure what you expect me to do here."

John chuckled. "I wasn't real clear about it that first day, was I? Right now, the goal is simply to find a way for you to use your special skills to make a difference in the world. How exactly we do that is mostly up to you."

Dreya considered that. "Well, I'm good at two things—designing jewelry and stealing stuff. I'm not sure the DCO has a need for either of those skills."

It was kind of weird telling her prospective employer

something like that, but it wasn't like he didn't know she'd been a thief in her other life.

John's mouth twitched. "Maybe not jewelry designing, but someone who can steal things without getting caught? You'd be surprised how valuable that skill is."

She glanced at Braden. He was deep in conversation with Clayne and Danica, not paying attention to anything she and John were saying.

"I'm not so sure my partner would agree," she murmured. "Since he's a cop and all, I mean."

John followed her gaze. "How do you like working with Braden?"

She smiled. "Actually, I like it a lot more than I ever thought I would."

"Funny how these things work sometimes, isn't it?" John mused. "One day, a guy's trying to arrest you; the next, he's your partner."

Dreya laughed. She certainly hadn't seen it coming, that was for sure. But she couldn't deny that she and Braden made one heck of a team. Sometimes, like when they were going through the shoot house, it felt like the two of them had been working together for years instead of a few days.

She opened her mouth to ask John when she could officially start working for the DCO when his cell phone rang. He dug it out of the inside pocket of his suit jacket and checked the screen.

"I have to take this. Excuse me." He put the phone to his ear. "What do you have, Evan?"

Dreya wandered over to where Braden was standing with Clayne and Danica to give John some privacy. Despite having exceptional hearing, she didn't usually make a habit of listening in on other people's conversations, but she couldn't resist eavesdropping on the director's conversation with Evan, especially after she heard the guy say something about a *crisis*.

"And you're sure?" John demanded.

"We're sure," Evan said.

John cursed. "I'll be there in five minutes." He hung up, then glanced at her and the others. "Something has come up. I'll talk to you later. Good work today."

Giving them a nod, John jogged around the shoot house to where he'd parked his car.

"What was that all about?" Dreya wondered out loud.

Clayne shrugged. "Who knows? If it's something that involves you, you'll find out soon enough. If it doesn't involve you, then you'll never have a clue what it was about."

"Well, that stinks." She frowned. "Aren't you the least bit curious?"

The wolf shifter chuckled. "You ever hear about what curiosity did to the cat?"

Dreya sighed. She could have made some smart-aleck remark but didn't. She supposed if she were going to work here, she was going to have to get used to people keeping secrets.

Chapter 11

"It's not too late to change your mind and go to your room, you know," Trevor said.

He was following Brooklyn as she skulked along the wall of the dimly lit common room, being careful to stay out of sight of the nearest security station as well as any video cameras.

"I appreciate you trying to help me get into the isolation ward, I really do," he added. "But you're going to get yourself in trouble."

Brooklyn stopped abruptly and turned to look at him, her ponytail swinging over her shoulder. "Seriously? I saw the way those new doctors looked at me earlier. I'm already in trouble. Besides, you need someone to be your lookout while you snoop around."

Trevor shook his head. If Brooklyn ever came to work at the DCO, John would have to be careful, because she'd be running the place within a year.

As much as he didn't like the idea of Brooklyn helping him sneak into the isolation ward, he got the feeling he wasn't going to be able to talk her out of it. Considering her friend Ian was in there, he couldn't blame her. Regardless, they couldn't stand here in the middle of the common room, waiting for an orderly to come waltzing through. In theory, most patients in this wing of the facility were free to move around the common areas at night if they wanted, but he couldn't help noticing that none of them did. According to Brooklyn, that was because the orderlies tended to consider anyone they found outside their rooms troublemakers and treated them accordingly. Most patients quickly decided that getting up for a late-night walk simply wasn't worth the hassle. Not that he could figure out why anyone would wander around out here. With all the lights off but one tiny lamp and the cloying silence that filled the place, it was kind of creepy.

"Well, if we're going to do this, let's get on it before someone catches us." He motioned the teen girl forward. "Just promise me that if something happens, get to your room, and act like you never left."

"I told you, I will."

Then she took off along the wall, skirting the furniture and the camera coverage in a confident way that made him think she'd done this before. When she led him along a roundabout route to avoid the facility's cameras, he was sure she'd definitely done it before. No doubt about it, this girl would fit right in at the DCO.

A few minutes later, they passed a row of barred windows that overlooked the darkened gardens. Brooklyn slowed as they neared a T-intersection at the end of the hall. Trevor frowned when he realized where they were. Going right would take them toward the therapy wing. Left would take them to the isolation ward. No matter which direction they went, they were going to be seen either by the video camera at the end of the hallway or by the orderly at the security station.

Trevor opened his mouth to ask Brooklyn if she knew a way into the ward or if she was making it up, when she stopped short of the T-intersection at a wood door marked with a little brown placard that read *Janitorial Staff Only*.

Brooklyn peeked around the corner to check the hallway that led to the isolation ward. Cursing silently, he caught her arms and pulled her back. His nose and ears told him there wasn't anyone there, but he carefully poked his head around to check anyway. He was right. There was no one around, not even the orderly on guard. That was odd.

Brooklyn tapped him on the shoulder. When he turned around, she pointed at the door of the janitor's closet. "We need to get in here."

He frowned. "Why? What's in here?"

"The back of the room shares a wall with the wacky ward," she explained. "When you stand near the wall, you can hear people on the other side of it talking. You shouldn't be able to do that if it was concrete block like the rest of the walls in this place."

He looked around, taking in the concrete block construction and acoustic ceiling panels. Damn, this girl was sharp. "You think that there's a way into the isolation ward through the ceiling?"

"Maybe." She shrugged. "But like I said before, getting in here might be tough. This door used to have a cheap lock you could jimmy with a metal ruler, but they changed it a while ago. So unless you're better at picking locks than I am, I don't think we're getting in."

Trevor took one more sniff to confirm there wasn't anyone around, then grabbed the knob and gave it a savage twist. There was a metal-on-metal grinding sound, then a sharp pop as something inside the lock broke.

Brooklyn blinked in surprise, but then that familiar

look was on her face, the one that said she was wise beyond her years.

"It's still a cheap lock," he murmured.

"Sure," she said.

Trevor could practically feel her suspicious eyes boring into his head, and he opened the door and switched on the light. He ushered her into the room, then after another glance around, quickly followed, pulling the door closed behind them. Fortunately, it was heavy enough to stay in place.

He looked around as the overhead light flickered a few times before settling into that putrid institutional fluorescent glow. The place was bigger than he thought it would be. In addition to the typical racks of maintenance and cleaning stuff, there were also a refrigerator and a sofa. The custodians must use the place as a break room as well as a supply closet.

"You used to break in here?" He glanced over his shoulder at Brooklyn as he headed toward the back wall. "Why?"

"Ian and I used to slip in here all the time at night so that we could—"

Trevor turned and cut her off. "TMI. Don't want to know."

He didn't have to wait to get the ceiling panels pushed aside to know that Brooklyn had been right. He could already hear people talking on the other side of the wall. He could also pick up a mishmash of hybrid and shifter scents wafting from the ceiling. Unfortunately, none of them were clear enough to tell him exactly what was going on in the isolation ward.

He was looking for a chair he could climb so he could

reach the ceiling tiles when an ear-splitting scream ripped through the air. The tortured sound climbed higher and higher until he swore the vocal cords of whoever was making the sound would surely tear apart. But instead, the scream transitioned into a pain-filled growl.

The sound was so primal and raw that Trevor felt his claws and fangs extend, regardless of the fact that Brooklyn was standing right there beside him.

"What the hell was that?" she asked fearfully from behind him.

He didn't answer. He was too busy clenching his hands into fists and fighting down the need to shift, something he hadn't needed to do in frigging years, not since he was fourteen. But the urge to let out the animal inside was difficult to get a handle on.

He was just getting a grip on his coyote half when a completely different sound reached his ears—the creaking and rending of leather and the snapping of metal. At the same time, the growl changed tone, becoming angrier and more savage.

Terrified voices rose on the other side of the wall before turning into high-pitched screams as panic reigned in the isolation ward.

There was a slash of claws, followed by cries of pain, then running feet. It wasn't hard to figure out where the footsteps were heading.

Trevor spun around and gave Brooklyn a stern look. "Stay right here. Don't frigging move!"

He'd barely made it into the corridor when he heard the crash of the heavy metal doors of the isolation ward smashing open. The smell hit Trevor at the same time as a teenage boy rushed around the corner in full-flight mode and slid to a stop a few feet from him. The kid couldn't have been more than sixteen or seventeen years old. He was thin with dark hair sticking up all over the place, pale skin, and angular features.

It wasn't the short fangs protruding from the boy's snarling mouth or the blood-smeared claws that kept partially retracting and advancing every few seconds that gave the creature away as a hybrid. In fact, his claws and fangs looked more like a shifter's. It was the scent. Hybrids smelled…well…wrong was the only was Trevor could think to describe it.

He couldn't tell exactly what shifter animal was mixed in with the kid's DNA as part of the hybrid process that had changed him, but if he had to guess, he'd say some kind of canine blend. The smell and facial shift weren't right for a coyote, but maybe something smaller. A fox?

Oddly enough, the kid didn't have the red eyes hybrids usually had. He sure as hell still had the typical hybrid rage thing going on, though. And he didn't seem to like the fact that Trevor was standing in the way he wanted to go.

The hybrid took a threatening step toward him, his mouth opening wider, his hands coming up with fingers spread and claws extended, ready to swipe.

Shit.

Trevor didn't want to get into a scrap with the kid, not when there was a facility full of Taser-toting orderlies sure to descend on them any moment. But it didn't look like the hybrid was going to give him any choice.

"Ian?" Brooklyn asked softly from behind Trevor.

Trevor groaned silently. Dammit. He should have

realized who the kid was. He started to warn the girl and tell her this wasn't the Ian she'd known before, but it was too late for that. She stepped around him and reached out a hand toward Ian.

All at once, the fangs disappeared, and the claws retracted until only the tips remained visible. The rage that had filled his features seconds earlier faded.

Even so, when Brooklyn took another step forward, Trevor had to fight the urge to reach out and pull her away. He doubted Ian would take it well. Seeing some guy grab his friend—especially since the two teens were clearly more than that—would freak him out.

Trevor thought Brooklyn might bring Ian completely out of his hybrid state, when the pounding of footsteps echoed in the hallway. Just like that, the rage-filled hybrid was back.

Trevor reached out and jerked Brooklyn back just as Ian's claws and fangs extended again. With a growl, the kid took off running down the hallway in the opposite direction from the approaching footsteps.

Trevor grabbed Brooklyn's hand and followed after the hybrid. Brooklyn didn't need any extra urging to run after her friend.

Trevor had horrible visions of the hybrid teen running loose through the common area and around the three floors of patient rooms. If there was one thing the patients here at Stillwater didn't need to see, it was an enraged hybrid running through the halls. They'd never be right again.

But when Ian reached the end of the corridor and didn't slow down, Trevor realized that the hybrid wasn't planning to terrorize the halls at all. He was planning to escape.

The kid—who couldn't be more than a hundred and

sixty-five pounds soaking wet—threw himself at the first window he saw, smashing through the glass and the steel security bars like they were dry sticks. Trevor cringed at the force of the impact. Hybrid or not, that had to hurt like hell.

Trevor got to the window first, but Brooklyn was a close second. Two stories below, Ian raced through the dark for the wall. He hurdled it like it wasn't even there, then disappeared into the woods.

Trevor and Brooklyn were still standing there when Brand, Mahsood, and eight big orderlies came running up. He'd expected them to be carrying Tasers, so he was shocked to see three of the beefy men carrying handguns. Where the hell had they gotten those?

"What are you two doing out of bed?" Brand demanded.

The psychiatrist's heart was pounding like a drum, but that could have been the excitement of the moment and his mad dash down the hallway. It was difficult to tell. There was no mistaking the spatter of blood along one side of the doctor's lab coat. Or the fact that it wasn't Brand's. Which meant the man had been in the isolation ward when Ian had escaped his bonds and laid into some of his torturers.

So much for the good Dr. Brand being an innocent bystander.

"I couldn't sleep," Trevor said. "I'm not used to the place yet, I suppose. Brooklyn and I were walking around the common area when we heard a god-awful screaming and crashing sound. We came to investigate and found the window like this."

Beside Brand, Mahsood's dark eyes narrowed suspiciously. "You didn't see who broke it?"

"No," Trevor said. "Whoever crashed through the window was gone before we got here."

Brand stared at him for a long time before turning his gaze on Brooklyn. "What about you? Did you see anything?"

Trevor glanced at Brooklyn, hoping she didn't lose it and start ranting about her boyfriend smashing through a window while sporting fangs and claws. She looked worried as hell about Ian, but she was keeping it together.

"I didn't see anything, Dr. Brand." She eyed the orderlies. "Did someone escape from the wacky ward? Is that why you have guns?"

Brand scowled. "No one escaped. And the Stillwater facility does not have a *wacky ward*, Brooklyn. You and Miles need to go to your rooms immediately. And I don't want either of you telling the other patients about this. We don't want to alarm them. Understood?"

Brooklyn nodded. Trevor did the same, then put his hand on her back, urging her forward. As they made their way down the hallway, Brand began giving orders for the orderlies to get their butts outside and start searching the grounds.

"What did they do to Ian?" Brooklyn asked softly, glancing nervously at Trevor. "It's like they turned him into an animal."

"I'll explain everything later," Trevor told her.

"Do you think Ian will be okay out there?"

"I hope so."

Luckily, Ivy and Landon were camped out in the woods in case he needed backup. He only prayed they found Ian before Brand and Mahsood did.

As he and Brooklyn rounded the corner, Trevor glanced over his shoulder to see Mahsood watching them. Something told him the man hadn't believed a word he and Brooklyn said. That was likely going to be a problem.

~

"I almost have it." Dreya's voice came through softly over his headset. "Just another few minutes."

"You don't have another few minutes," Braden told her, fighting to keep his voice even as he watched the monitors set up in the back of the van. "The security guard doing room-by-room checks is already on your floor. You need to shut down that computer and get out of that office."

"I can't," she said. "Not until I find the file we need."

Dreya's voice was so calm, it made him want to growl like Clayne so often did. You'd think the woman was surfing the Web while sitting at a table in one of her favorite Starbucks locations in Foggy Bottom instead of hacking into the computer of a senior partner at a law firm in Miami that only had one client—the Zeta drug cartel.

This had to be the most insane undercover job he'd ever been part of as a cop. It was also likely the most illegal thing he'd ever done as a cop. They had no warrant, no backup, and no real plan. Just him and Dreya breaking into the well-guarded office of the Martz Law Firm, looking for a list of U.S. federal attorneys targeted for assassination. It was an impossible task that would get one or both of them shot or arrested if they didn't pull it off just right.

Somewhere, he could hear Tommy laughing his ass off at the irony of what Braden had become. A fly-by-the-seat-of-your-pants, make-it-up-as-you-go cop who ignored issues of questionable legalities and had a thief for a partner.

How the heck had he gotten himself here?

Here being inside a rental van full of expensive surveillance gear, parked on the street a mere few blocks down the street from an extremely nice high-rise office building with unobstructed views of Biscayne Bay and the Port of Miami. Thank God it was four o'clock in the morning, or this place would have been crawling with people. As it was, he figured they only had another hour at most before the suit-and-tie crowd started showing up for work. Hopefully, they'd be long gone before then.

If he could get Dreya to hurry up and get her sexy ass out of there.

He swallowed the urge to tell her to abort the mission, focusing instead on the monitor that was tied into the building's security system—the one that showed the security guard moving around the thirtieth floor of the building, getting closer to Dreya with every passing second. She needed to hurry the hell up.

Braden looked from one monitor to the next. He had a bad feeling about this mission from the moment John had pulled him and Dreya into one of the conference rooms when they'd gotten back from the shoot house yesterday afternoon. Braden had been surprised either of them had been included in what was clearly an official briefing with a room full of DCO agents as well as both director and deputy director of the agency. He and Dreya weren't even on the payroll.

"We have a major situation on our hands, and I'm clearing the benches for this one," John had said without preamble. "A few days ago, our source in the Zeta drug cartel informed us that one of their rogue lieutenants was planning to make a move against one or more federal attorneys as a way to disrupt the ongoing trials involving his particular cartel members. We assumed they were going to target attorneys in Houston or Dallas, since that's where their biggest players are being prosecuted, but an hour ago, we discovered we were wrong. Our source came through with significantly more information, specifically, the identity of approximately twenty cartel assassins who entered the United States this morning. They intend to take out a dozen targets, maybe more. The hits are going down sometime early tomorrow morning, and they're synchronized to happen all across the country within minutes of each other."

"If that isn't bad enough," Coleman added, "we don't know where the cartel assassins are currently located or exactly which federal attorneys are being targeted."

"Each of your teams is being given folders with everything we have on the killers," John continued as a dark-haired guy with glasses handed out manila folders. He picked up the remote for the projector and clicked a button. Photos of men and women filled the screen at the front of the room. "These are the federal attorneys our analysts tell us are the most likely targets. You'll find the names, addresses, and background information on the ones in the city where we're sending you and your team."

"Unfortunately, we can't tell the Justice Department about any of this, because we don't know how many people the cartel has on the inside," Coleman said. "If the assassins get word that we're on to them, they could disappear into the wind, move up their timetables, even go after alternate targets. We have to wait and take them down all at once before they know what hit them. It's the only way to get them all."

The guy in the glasses passed Braden and Dreya, handing a folder to Danica.

"Wait a minute," Danica said as she scanned the papers in it. "John, there are seven names on the list you gave Clayne and me, and they're scattered all over San Diego. There's no way we'll be able to cover all of them at once."

"We need a better idea of who the real targets are, or we're earning a lot of frequent flyer miles for nothing," Clayne put in.

John's mouth curved into a smile as he looked at Braden and Dreya. "That's where our newest team comes in. Braden and Dreya get the most important city—Miami. That's where the cartel's stateside law firm is located. We're hoping they'll have a list of the real targets."

"Why would a law firm have a list like that?" Braden asked.

He couldn't believe John was serious. He and Dreya had been at the DCO for four days, not to mention partners for all of twenty-four hours.

John lifted a brow. "Who do you think decided which federal attorneys would make the best targets? They know which ones to kill to cripple every major federal case against the cartel. According to our source, the Martz Law Firm of Miami didn't merely come up with the list but proposed the entire idea. Apparently, they're coordinating the entire operation."

"What do you want us to do?" Dreya asked.

"We need you and Braden to break into their offices and find the list of targets, then get the names to us in time to stop the assassinations."

Sitting there in the van, Braden snorted at the memory. John had made it sound so simple.

He glanced at his watch, then at the monitors. Dreya had already been in there thirty minutes. If she didn't find that list soon, she wouldn't be the only one in trouble. There were going to be a whole lot of federal attorneys in deep shit, too.

If he and Dreya were going to be a team full-time, they were going to have to go out in the field at some point, but this was too soon. Dreya was too new at this whole superspy crap. And he was too damn far away from the building if she needed backup.

"Almost got it," Dreya whispered in his earpiece.

Braden shot another look at the guard's progress, biting his tongue to keep from pointing out that Dreya had said that same thing five minutes ago. He took a deep breath. She'd been a thief for most of her adult life. She knew what she was doing. She simply needed more time.

At least he had eyes on her for most of it. Using the detailed set of instructions that came with the gear, he'd hacked into the building's security system when they had first arrived. Dreya had slipped over to the upscale high-rise tower through the adjacent multilevel parking garage and climbed up three stories, clawing her way along the seams between the panes of glass until she reached a terrace that gave her access to the tenth floor. Then Braden had momentarily cut into the feed of each of the building's security cameras, one after the other, running short loops of empty background space for the guard in the control room to see while Dreya had taken the stairwell up to the thirtieth floor where Martz had their offices.

Unfortunately, there weren't any cameras in the corner office of the partner who was supposedly running this whole assassination show, so he couldn't see her now. But she kept up a constant dialogue to let him know what was going on. He had to admit that while she might be new at this covert ops stuff, she was damn good at it.

Of course, his objectivity might be a little compromised when it came to Dreya. Thanks to that kiss the other night, he was starting to feel things for the feline shifter he shouldn't feel for a partner. He hadn't planned on kissing her, but they'd been standing so close to each other that he couldn't stop himself.

Dreya had tasted so sweet and felt so right in his arms. He still wasn't sure how they hadn't ended up in bed. When she'd started undressing him, it had taken everything in him to pull away from her. He'd dated a lot of women, some of them seriously, but he couldn't ever remember feeling like this about any other woman. It was like he was on fire every time they got close to each other.

Even more amazing, Dreya seemed to feel the same way. That was why he'd admitted to her later how hard it had been for him to stop. He didn't want her to think that she was the only one who felt this thing between them. He wanted her, too. He was willing to wait until the right time.

He knew it was stupid to get involved with a person he worked with. He'd seen fellow cops in the MPD try to make it work as lovers, and more often than not, the results had been disastrous.

But there was something about Dreya that made it impossible to resist her. Hell, maybe it was some kind of shifter DNA thing. After the stuff he'd learned over the past few days, he was ready to admit he didn't know nearly as much about the way the world worked as he'd once thought.

Besides, he had no idea how long this DCO partnership thing was going to last. One more day, another week, a month? He wasn't prepared to mess up this thing he had going with Dreya when he could be back in the MPD burglary section next week.

And if he ended up being partnered with Dreya for longer than he expected? If John decided to keep him around for a while?

Then he'd find a way to make it work with Dreya. Hell, Danica and Clayne were partners, and they were married. If that odd couple could make it work, he and Dreya sure as hell could.

Braden was still pondering that when he caught a sudden movement on the main monitor.

Shit.

"Dreya," he said into the mic. "There are two more guards on your floor now. They're moving faster than they should, too. I think you must have tripped an alarm or something."

She snorted. "I've never tripped an alarm in my life.

By the way, I think I've found the right file. Just give me some time."

Braden ran a hand through his hair. Dammit! Dreya was as stubborn as Tommy had ever been, maybe worse. She was still in the lawyer's office, and the guards—three of them now—were getting closer.

He had to buy Dreya that time she asked for.

He looked around the van, his eyes locking on the row of switches that let him cut into selective camera feeds in the building.

"Well, fuck."

Reaching over, he slapped all the switches to the intercept position. Without having run a loop first, the effect was instantaneous and obvious. One by one, every monitor in the van faded to black. Inside the security control room, the effects would be even more pronounced as every camera in the building simultaneously went down.

Braden jumped out of the van and ran up the sidewalk along Biscayne Boulevard toward the main entrance of the building Dreya was in.

"I have the file," she whispered in his earpiece. Her voice was so soft, Braden could barely hear her over the pounding of his feet on the pavement. "But now I can't get out of here, because the guards are right outside the door."

Shit.

He knew this would happen. His heart beat faster. Not from the sprint, but from fear.

"Stay where you are," he told her. "I'm on the way with a distraction."

"What are you going to do?" Dreya asked.

Braden didn't answer. Instead, he skidded to a stop in front of the office building and banged on the big glass door with his fist. The uniformed security guard standing behind the marble-topped counter looked up with a start, the phone he had to his ear all but forgotten. Frowning, the guard waved him away.

Braden smacked his MPD badge against the glass and pointed at the lock. He should have used the DHS badge John had given him and Dreya to allow them to carry their guns on the flight as well as have jurisdiction in Miami, but reaching for his police one was just second nature. Besides, he figured there was a good chance he was going to lose that badge after this insanity. Might as well get some use out of it.

The guard said something to whoever was on the other end of the line, then hung up the phone and strode over to the door. The moment the man unlocked it and pulled it open, Braden punched him—hard. The blow snapped the guy's head back, banging it against the metal door frame. Eyes glazing over, he started sliding to the floor. Braden caught him before he could hit and dragged him inside the lobby, all the way across the floor and behind the big marble-topped counter.

He didn't hesitate, jogging across the lobby, past the gray and white marble walls and all the high-end shops to the elevators. He stepped in one that was already open and waiting. He reached out to push the button for the thirtieth floor, but then hesitated for a split second before finally thumbing the one of the twenty-ninth.

"Okay, I'm in the building," he said softly into his mic. "Are you still in the office?"

"I'm in the executive washroom that connects to

it," she whispered. "I think you were right. I must have tripped something when I came in here. Or maybe when I powered up the computer. I shut everything down, but now all three guards are looking around the office. They're going to look in here next. What should I do?"

Braden glanced at the display showing what floor the elevator was on. "Is there anywhere to hide in the washroom?"

"No."

"Hang tight. I'm almost there"

When the elevator doors opened on the twenty-ninth floor, he darted his head out for a quick peek, then jogged down the empty hall to the fire alarm on the wall.

"Here comes that distraction," he said as he yanked on the handle.

The clang of the alarm pierced the silence of the empty building, echoing in his ears as he hauled ass to the stairwell and raced up the steps. He'd just made it to the landing on the thirtieth when the door flew open.

Braden darted behind it, using it as cover as he squeezed into the corner of the stairwell. Two security guards ran down the steps. It would have been nice if all three guards had gone downstairs, but the odds were still better against one than three.

When they disappeared from sight, he came out from behind the door and hurried down the hallway to the corner office where Dreya was trapped.

"Dreya?" he said into his mic, hoping she could hear him over the fire alarm.

No answer.

Dammit!

Braden ran faster. He got to the corner office in time

to see the security guard jerk open the door to the washroom and point his gun in that direction.

"Stay right where you are, and don't move!" the man ordered Dreya. "You're under arrest."

"I was only looking for a clean restroom," Dreya said. "Is that a crime in Miami?"

Braden would have laughed if he wasn't so terrified for her. She was definitely quick on her feet.

He didn't know whether the security guard heard him or simply sensed someone behind him, because he spun around and aimed his gun in Braden's direction.

Braden knocked the man's arm aside before he could line up a shot, then punched him in the jaw. He quickly followed that haymaker up with another one, then he grabbed hold of the lapels on the man's suit jacket and shoved him backward, slamming him hard into the big mirror over the sink. The guard's head bounced off the glass, breaking it and knocking him out cold. Braden let the guy collapse to the floor, then took the weapon from his limp hand and dropped it in the toilet.

He turned to find Dreya standing there with a shocked look on her face.

"What?" he asked.

"You came to get me," she said.

"I'm getting the feeling that's going to be my role in this partnership," he said, grabbing her hand and heading for the door. "You steal things, and I come get your sexy ass out of trouble."

She caught up to him as he led her to the stairwell and headed down the steps. He hoped they didn't run into any more guards on the way out of there. They might work for a drug cartel, but he'd still rather not shoot them.

"Speaking of getting your ass out of trouble, we need to come to an agreement of some kind," he said as they hurried downstairs. "If I tell you the situation is bad and that you need to bail, you need to listen to me, okay?"

Dreya didn't answer.

Braden ground his jaw. If they were going to be partners, they needed to agree on how they were going to do things.

He glanced at her to see her grinning.

"What?" he asked.

"You think I have a sexy ass?"

Braden stifled a groan. Being her partner was going to kill him—or drive him nuts. Tommy was probably laughing so hard, Braden was surprised he couldn't hear the sound coming all the way down from heaven.

It would have been a lot easier to track the hybrid who escaped from Stillwater if there weren't so many other people running around the woods at the same time, Ivy thought as she and Landon slowed down to avoid running over the clueless hospital orderly stumbling along the nearly pitch-black trail ahead of them.

She and Landon had been hiding in the woods outside the psychiatric facility in case Trevor needed help and was able to get a signal out to them, when the insane hybrid scream had torn through the still night. A few minutes later, they'd heard a crash and the sound of glass breaking. Next thing they knew, a hybrid had come hurtling through the trees.

She and Landon had hesitated, torn between checking on Trevor and going after the hybrid. In the end, the decision had been simple. Trevor was a trained operative who could take care of himself. The people who lived in the rural area near Stillwater, on the other hand, weren't trained to deal with a hybrid. After seeing firsthand what innocent people who'd been turned into hybrids had to deal with, Ivy hoped they'd be able to capture the kid, but one way or the other, they needed to get him out of these woods before he killed someone.

But within ten minutes of tearing off after the hybrid, she and Landon both realized the task wasn't going to be as easy as they thought.

For one thing, a handful of orderlies had showed up carrying handguns, making a buttload of noise and poking under the brush like they were looking for a lost puppy. They might be big, but they seemed better suited to intimidating helpless patients in a mental facility than chasing rogue hybrids. There was a good chance that one of them would end up shooting a coworker long before they actually found the hybrid.

The armed orderlies weren't nearly as difficult to deal with as the hybrid was, though. The creature who'd escaped from Stillwater didn't behave like any other hybrid she and Landon had run into in the past. If this had been one of the creatures they'd dealt with in Washington State, Costa Rica, or Tajikistan, he would have already turned around and attacked someone by now. But this particular hybrid seemed to have no interest in going after any of the people who were tracking him.

On the flip side, he didn't seem interested in leaving the area either. Instead, he kept moving in large circles around the Stillwater facility, avoiding the orderlies—and them—with relative ease. Ivy even got the feeling that the thing knew what she and Landon were going to do long before they did.

"This hybrid is smarter and way more in control than any we've dealt with before," Ivy whispered to Landon as they crouched behind some bushes to wait for the disoriented orderly to wander off. "The kid's running us around in circles like it's a game to him."

"Tell me about it. Why hasn't he escaped already?" Landon wondered. "He could have been miles from here if he'd run in a straight line. It's like he's afraid to get too far from the psychiatric center."

"Maybe it's something we can ask, when we finally catch up to him."

When the orderly finally made his way down the trail, they took off through the woods again, Ivy focusing on tracking the hybrid's scent while Landon worried about the hospital orderlies. She was so intent on her part of the mission that she almost completely missed it when a half dozen new scents hit her nose.

Ivy reached out and stopped Landon with a gesture. He immediately halted.

She stared into the clearing about sixty feet away from where they were, looking for movement. A few moments later, a group of men entered the area. They were all heavily armed and moved with sure, confident steps, but Ivy was only interested one of them—Douglas Frasier. What the hell was he doing here?

Frasier and the others skirted the clearing, staying close to the tree line as they moved in the same general direction Ivy and Landon had taken ten minutes earlier. She blinked in amazement as one of the men crouched to look at something in the dirt. Crap, he was tracking the hybrid by footprints—in the dark.

Beside her, Landon tensed. He must have figured out it was Frasier, too. Not by picking up his scent but from seeing the way his right arm hung slightly loose as he moved.

She held her breath as Frasier and his men disappeared into the woods after the hybrid.

"What the hell is Frasier doing here?" Landon asked softly. "When Thorn excluded him from the meeting he had with us about Mahsood, I didn't think Frasier was even aware of what was going on up here. Now he's out here, personally hunting hybrids?"

"I don't understand it either," Ivy said. "Do you think he can track down the hybrid?"

Landon shook his head. "Not a chance. That hybrid is going to be out there running laps around those guys. That doesn't mean we don't need to worry about them. Frasier is here for a reason, and until we know what that reason is, we're going to have to spend half the time keeping our eyes on him."

Ivy silently agreed. Unfortunately, that distraction could be dangerous with an unpredictable hybrid on the loose.

Chapter 12

Braden pulled the van away from the curb as the cop cars and fire engines swarmed the building. Dreya let out a breath and flopped back in the passenger seat.

"That was close," she said.

Braden glanced in the rearview mirror, but he didn't say anything.

She dug her cell phone out of her pocket. "I'm going to call John and make sure he got the file."

If he didn't, there wasn't much she or Braden could do. It wasn't like they could go back to the Martz Law Firm and break in again.

Before she could pull up her contacts, her phone rang. When she saw John's name, she thumbed the button and put him on speaker.

"Did you get the file?" she asked.

"We got it. That was good work," John said. "Is Braden with you?"

"I'm here," Braden said.

"Good. Did either of you look at the list you sent me?" John asked.

"No." Dreya pushed some hair that had come loose back into her braid. "We ran into a little trouble, so the moment I knew I had the right file, I copied everything and sent it to you, then we got the hell out of there. It's the right one, isn't it?"

Finding the file had taken her a lot longer than she'd

thought it would. It was buried in with a handful of others, and she had to do some digging. It would have been nice if the cartel lawyers had labeled it "Hit List," but no such luck.

"It's the right one," John said. "I've got teams moving on the cartel assassins as we speak. But it turns out that one of the targets is in Miami. We don't have any other agents there, just the two of you. I need you to get to that attorney's house as fast as you can and stop that killer."

Dreya's heart started to pound. Breaking into a building, hacking into a computer, and stealing a list of names was one thing. She had been stealing for most of her adult life. Going up against a cold-blooded assassin was something else entirely. She wasn't trained enough to try that. She wasn't sure if she'd ever be that well trained.

She looked at Braden to see him frowning.

"There's no way you can call the local police or the feds and give them an anonymous tip or something?" Braden asked.

"If we call the feds, there's a good chance the killer will know about it five minutes later," John said. "And if we call the local police, the dispatcher will likely send a couple of uniform cops to check out the situation first. You want to be the one to get two cops killed by putting them up against a trained assassin?" He sighed. "You know I wouldn't ask you to do this if there was any other way, but we have thirty minutes at most to save that attorney. Probably her husband and two children, too. There's no time to call anyone else."

Braden must have seen the look of panic on Dreya's

face, because he took one hand off the wheel and reached out to give hers a squeeze. "I know you're scared, but we can do this, Dreya."

She hesitated, then took a deep breath and nodded. She *could* do this, because Braden would be with her. It was the only reason she would even consider it.

"Send us the address and everything you can on the target and the killer," Braden told John.

"The attorney's name is Barbara Herrera. She lives in Cutler Bay right off Highway 1," John said. "I'm sending everything to Dreya's phone now. But be careful. This guy you're going after is dangerous."

Braden spun the van around and was heading south before John even hung up.

"The assassin is six foot two with long, dark hair, and he's from Argentina," Dreya said as she tried to hold the phone stable enough to read. "His name is Lucas Alvarez, but he goes by the nickname Cabo."

She skimmed the rest of his bio. "Oh, here's a heartwarming tidbit. While it says that Cabo is proficient in almost all forms of firearms, he prefers to use a knife when he can. Great."

Braden turned the van onto Highway 826. It was still an hour until the sun came up, but the road was already starting to get crowded. Braden weaved the big van through the maze of vehicles with the skill of someone who spent years driving in DC traffic.

"That's good to know," he said. "It's something that could come into play if I have to get close to this guy."

Dreya frowned. "You mean if *we* have to get close to this guy, right?"

Braden shook his head. "Dreya, this guy is too

dangerous. When we get to Herrera's house, I want you to stay in the van."

"No way." Dreya bit back a growl. "There's no way I'm going to sit in the van and play games on my cell phone while you go fight a cold-blooded killer by yourself."

His jaw flexed. "I'm a cop, Dreya. I'm trained for this kind of stuff."

"And I'm your partner," she said. "I'm not letting you go in there alone, not when I have senses and talents that can help you."

"Dreya..." He swallowed hard. "I can't stand the thought of you getting hurt."

If she weren't so busy trying to convince him to let her do her job, she would have basked in the glow of those words. "Yeah, well, I can't stand the thought of you getting hurt either. So we both do this, or neither one of us will." She glanced at the map on her phone. "Turn right at the next street."

Braden gripped the wheel tighter, and Dreya braced herself for more of his macho crap. But instead, he surprised her by nodding. "Okay, but at least promise me that you won't do anything crazy."

She snorted. "Right. Like going after an assassin isn't crazy enough?"

Fifteen minutes later, Braden stopped the van near the curb on the quiet subdivision street three houses down from the Herrera residence. The house was a two-story hacienda style with a stucco exterior and tile roof. The inside was still dark, but it was a workday, so there was a good chance that everyone on the street—including Barbara Herrera—would be stirring soon. If the assassin wanted his job to go easy, he'd do it now. If he hadn't done it already.

"You think we got here before Cabo?" Dreya asked.

She couldn't bear the thought that Barbara, her husband, and their kids were already dead because she and Braden hadn't been fast enough.

"I hope so. But I guess there's only one way to know for sure." He turned off the engine and pocketed the keys. "It's unlikely he would have gone in through the front. So we'll go around the back and see what your kitty senses tell you. If Cabo hasn't shown yet, we'll wait for him there."

Luckily, the houses in the subdivision were far enough apart that she and Braden didn't have to walk right by anyone's window. When they got to the Herrera house, they found the gate to the backyard fence wide open.

Dreya sniffed the air. She didn't know what Cabo smelled like, so she wouldn't be able to pick up his scent, but she did pick up a smell on the early morning breeze that didn't fit with the rest of the backyard smells—a strong men's cologne. It could have belonged to Mr. Herrera, she supposed, but whoever wore it had been out here recently, which made her think it was more likely Cabo.

"He's here," she said softly. "His scent is fresh. He got here a minute or so before we did."

"Shit," Braden swore.

Pulling his gun, he headed for the back door. Dreya did the same. Despite the target practice and training they'd done yesterday, it still felt strange to carry a weapon.

They were still a few feet away from the ornate stone and wood pergola when Dreya noticed the French doors were open. She heard a sound from inside the house that could have been a whimper, followed by soft, guttural, heavily accented words.

Dreya tightened her grip on the gun, her mind replaying every single piece of instruction that Braden, Danica, and Clayne had given her. No safety, keep her finger off the trigger until she was ready to shoot, take slow, steady breaths, use a firm but gentle grip, aim for the center of the target, don't jerk. The list of things she needed to do seemed endless, and suddenly, she wished the DCO would have spent a lot more time teaching her to shoot than having her run around obstacle courses.

But none of that mattered now. Braden was moving through the French doors already, and she was going with him.

Her eyes immediately shifted as she entered the dark living room. She didn't bother to try to stop it. She didn't care if anyone saw the strange green glow of her reflective pupils. She needed to be able to see clearly.

What she saw almost made her heart stop. On the far side of the living room in the open-concept kitchen, a curly-haired middle-aged woman in a robe and slippers was standing beside the refrigerator, a carton of milk in her hands. A tall, dark-haired man stood behind her. He had one arm wrapped around her middle in an embrace that almost seemed romantic—if it hadn't been for the woman's completely rigid stance and the gun Cabo was pointing at her head.

"Drop the gun, Cabo!" Braden ordered, moving slightly to the left to get a better angle on the killer.

Pulse beating fast, Dreya mimicked his movements, sliding to the right.

The cartel assassin spun around to face them, dragging Barbara Herrera with him, using her as a shield.

Dreya pointed her weapon at the man, but she kept her finger away from the trigger. Even though Cabo was a good six inches taller than the attorney, he held the woman tightly against him, which made the target he presented too small for Dreya to consider taking a shot. She simply wasn't that comfortable with a weapon yet.

The killer looked at Braden, then Dreya, his eyes widening a little in surprise when he met her gaze. No doubt the glow of her eyes freaked him out. Unfortunately, it wasn't enough to get him to let Barbara Herrera go. Instead, his expression hardened, and he pressed the barrel of the gun's silencer harder against the side of the woman's head, making her groan.

"I don't think so," Cabo said. "If you two don't move away right now, I'll shoot her while you watch."

Dreya's stomach clenched at the threat. She hadn't realized you could smell fear, but the terror coming off the woman filled the air.

"You shoot her, and we both shoot you. I'm guessing you're not in this line of work to die," Braden told Cabo. "Right now, you're looking at breaking and entering, assault with intent, maybe a few misdemeanor gun charges. With a good cartel lawyer, like the ones at the Martz Law Firm, you'll be out in three to five years. But if you pull that trigger, it's all over."

Cabo stared at Braden for a moment, like he might be considering Braden's words. Barbara stayed perfectly still, her gaze nervously flicking back and forth between Dreya and Braden.

Dreya thought talking Cabo down might actually work, but then a little girl with a tangle of dark hair and a stuffed pony in her hands walked into the kitchen and stopped halfway in between Dreya and Barbara.

"Mommy, Starlight wants a cookie," the girl said in a sleepy voice.

Pure panic washed over the woman's face as tears welled up in her eyes. "It's too early for Starlight to eat cookies," she said, half sobbing. "Go back to bed, baby."

But it was too late for that. Cabo realized that he'd been given a gift that drastically changed the standoff between him and them. In a heartbeat, he pulled the gun barrel from Barbara's head and swung it toward the little girl.

Dreya lunged for the child, her shifter reflexes and strength kicking in. She tried to be gentle as she scooped the little girl up in her arms and hit the floor rolling, but she was moving fast, and there was only so much she could do. The scream of shock the girl let out was louder than the *pop, pop, pop* of the silenced weapon being fired at them.

Bullets hit the floor, tearing into the wood and ricocheting under Dreya as she tumbled into the living room with the girl wrapped in her protective embrace.

Left with no other choice, Braden fired.

A split second later, more pops from the silencer filled the air.

Dreya's heart lurched.

Her shoulder slammed into a wall, bringing her to an abrupt stop. Telling the little girl to stay put, she sprang to her feet and charged into the kitchen, not knowing what she was going to find. Had Cabo shot the attorney—or Braden?

Barbara Herrera was lying unmoving on the floor of the kitchen while Braden and Cabo were fighting hand to hand and trying to kill each other a few feet away from the woman. Dreya smelled blood, but it wasn't Braden's, thank God. However, whether it was the attorney's or Cabo's, she didn't know.

Braden and Cabo were moving and twisting so fast as they punched, jabbed, and kicked each other to keep their opponent's gun pointed in a safe direction that there was no way Dreya could take a shot at the Argentinian hit man. She wasn't going to stand there and watch either. Taking a deep breath, she closed the distance between her and the two combatants, claws extended.

Cabo must have seen her coming, because he twisted around to put Braden between him and Dreya. She didn't slow but simply dropped to the tiled floor of the kitchen, sliding on her hip the last few feet like a baseball player at home plate. As she passed Cabo, she lashed out with her left hand, letting her claws rip through the blue jeans he wore all the way to the muscles of his left thigh. Her claws dug so deep, she was sure they hit bone.

She'd never done anything so violent before—had never wanted to—but she would do anything to keep Braden safe.

Paying no attention to the shout of pain Cabo let out, Dreya twisted and jumped to her feet, ready to strike again. But Braden had already ripped the weapon out of the man's hand and thrown him to the floor.

Even then, Cabo refused to give up, his hand whipping

behind his back and coming up with a wicked-looking knife. Braden was ready for the wild swing that came at his legs, leaping away from the blade and aiming his gun at the man's head.

"I'm going to tell you one more time," Braden said. "Drop it, or I shoot you. And you don't have a woman to hide behind this time."

Cabo glared at Braden, then swung his ire on Dreya before he cursed and tossed the knife away. It slid across the floor to come to a stop by Braden's booted feet.

Braden reached behind his back and came out with a pair of handcuffs. He held them out to Dreya. She couldn't believe he'd thought to bring them. Once a cop, always a cop, she supposed.

While Braden kept the man covered, Dreya flipped him over and yanked his arms behind his back. Cabo howled in pain. That's when she realized the man was bleeding from a wound in his shoulder. Ignoring his protests, she pressed one knee into his spine and cuffed him. She'd never been trained in their use, but after having them slapped on her several days ago, she understood the basic concept.

"Is that a bad man, Mommy?" a tiny voice suddenly said from behind her.

Dreya turned to see the little girl standing beside Barbara Herrera. There was a dark bruise already forming along one of the woman's cheeks, but other than that, she seemed okay. She reached out and pulled her daughter in for a hug, but before she could answer the little girl's question, the lights flicked on, and a thin, middle-aged man in pajamas hurried into the kitchen with a small revolver in his hands. His eyes widened at Cabo, lying facedown on the floor, cuffed and still, before he pointed the gun at her and Braden, nervously alternating between them.

"It's okay, Mateo," Barbara told her husband as she slowly got to her feet. "They're feds." She eyed Dreya and Braden warily. "You two are feds, right?"

Dreya looked at Braden, not sure how to answer the woman. Technically, she hadn't been hired by the DCO yet, and she couldn't very well say she was a thief—or a jewelry designer.

Braden's mouth curved. "It's complicated, but yeah, you can call us feds."

Chapter 13

"When you said you spent most of your time at work, I expected your place to be kind of Spartan." Dreya looked around his small one-bedroom apartment in Arlington as she sat at the kitchen table. It was surprisingly clean and neat, with a comfy-looking sectional couch in the living room, framed pictures on the wall, and even a few plants. "This is nice."

Braden chuckled as he took the Chinese takeout they'd gotten out of the microwave and brought it over to the table. "I went out with an interior designer a while back. She made it her mission to give my place a makeover. She was of the opinion that I had zero decorating skills. She dumped me after she realized the reason I never bothered to decorate my apartment is because I'm never here."

Silly woman. Well, her loss was Dreya's gain. She inhaled appreciatively as Braden opened up the takeout containers from P.F. Chang's. "Mmm, that smells so good. I'm starving."

Mouth twitching, he dumped a whole carton of brown rice on her plate, then did the same with his own. "You know, you wouldn't be nearly as hungry if you ate what they gave us on the plane."

She dipped her fork in the different containers, trying to decide which one she wanted. When he'd suggested stopping by the Chinese restaurant on the way home from the airport, she'd been too tired to think about food, but now that she got a whiff of it, she hoped they had bought enough.

"That wasn't a meal," she told him. "It was a can of soda and a pack of pretzels. I'm not picky about my food, but no one considers a pack of pretzels to be a meal."

"There is that," he agreed. "So, what's it going to be? Mongolian beef or spicy chicken?"

"Can we share?" she asked. "They both smell so good that I can't decide."

He shrugged. "Works for me."

While she spooned some of each onto their plates, Braden grabbed the soy sauce from the fridge, then joined her at the table.

They'd landed at Reagan two hours ago. Braden had been going to drop Dreya at her apartment in Foggy Bottom, but the president was speaking at George Washington University that evening, so the Secret Service and Metro Police had all the roads in and out of her street blocked off. Since they wouldn't reopen for hours, they'd decided to grab takeout and go over to his place while they waited. That was fine with Dreya. Truth was, she'd been curious as heck to see his place. She had expected a typical bachelor pad, but like everything else about the man, his apartment had surprised her. Bottom line, Braden was a man who defied simple and cliché stereotypes.

As they ate, they talked about the mission in Miami, discussing everything that had happened from the moment they'd broken into the Martz Law Firm to when the local FBI and Justice Department had finally stopped asking them questions they couldn't answer and let them leave. Luckily, their Homeland badges spoke volumes.

"I haven't been that worried about a partner in a long time," Braden admitted quietly.

Dreya knew he was talking about Tommy. She sipped her iced tea, setting the glass on the table before answering. "I've never worked with a partner, so I never had one to worry about, but I was terrified when I saw you fighting Cabo. I've never felt an urge to hurt someone before, but I wanted to rip him apart with my claws."

Braden's mouth edged up. "I know how you feel. I wanted to kick the crap out of the security guard who had a gun on you at the law firm."

Dreya felt an unfamiliar yet extremely pleasant sensation warm her middle and spread up into her chest. She refused to admit it out loud, but she swore she'd never had a man say anything so romantic to her in her life.

Across from her, Braden polished off what was left on his plate. "I'm not sure if you realized it, but we spent day five of your DCO recruitment deal in Miami, fighting crooked lawyers, security guards, and a cartel hit man. Tomorrow morning when we go to work, you're officially done with your obligation to them. If you decide to stay, it'll be because you want to, not because you have to."

Crap. She hadn't even thought about it, but Braden was right. She was free to do anything she wanted. And she wanted to stay at the DCO…with Braden. She smiled, unable to help herself.

"I take it by that grin on your face that you're going to take the job, huh?"

She nodded. "I can't believe I'm saying this, but yeah."

"I'm glad." Braden regarded her thoughtfully for a moment. "Since that means we'll have to get up early tomorrow, I guess I should probably take you home. Let me check to see if the roads are open yet."

Dreya wouldn't have minded giving up a little sleep if it meant hanging out with Braden some more, but he was right. Besides, she could use a shower.

Across from her, Braden was frowning at something on his phone. "The president's speech was delayed. He's going to be at GWU for another couple of hours."

She sighed. "That means I won't get home until almost midnight." And while she'd joked about not needing much sleep, the adrenaline rush she'd felt in Miami had long since worn off, and she was tired.

On the other side of the table, Braden had that thoughtful look on his face again. "You want to crash here for the night instead?"

Dreya paused, her glass of iced tea halfway to her lips. It wasn't exactly the way she imagined getting an invitation to spend the night with Braden, but it was a start. Besides, it would be easier than fighting late-night traffic.

"Sure," she said. "If you don't mind."

Braden's mouth curved. "I don't mind at all."

"Any chance you have a T-shirt or something I can wear?"

They hadn't taken any luggage with them to Miami, so if not, she'd be sleeping in the clothes she'd been wearing since they left DC yesterday. Either that or go naked, which probably wouldn't be a good idea, since she'd be sleeping on the couch.

"There are some in the bedroom. Feel free to grab anything you want." He pushed back his chair. "There are clean towels in the linen closet if you want to take a shower."

There were some nicely framed photos of historical DC sites in his bedroom, as well as a few on the dresser of Braden and a man who looked like he could be an older brother with a smiling couple who had to be their parents. And in the center of the room against the far wall was a gigantic king bed with a comforter that looked as soft and fluffy as a cloud.

She strolled into the walk-in closet, smiling at how organized everything was. He had suits and dress pants in one section, MPD blues in another, and casual clothes in a third. She couldn't help noticing there was a lot of room in here for other clothes. Hers would fit just fine, for example.

That brought her up short. Now that was a completely crazy, improper, way-too-soon-to-be-thinking kind of thought. She had no clue where it had come from. But it made her smile.

While she was tempted to pick one of his dress shirts to wear, she walked into the bedroom to check out the two dressers he had against the far wall, figuring he'd have some T-shirts in there. She was right. His scent was even stronger on the clothes in the drawers, making her think he wore them a lot. When she found one she liked—a gray shirt with the words *Property of the Metro PD* across the front—she laughed. A thief wearing a shirt like this should be in a dictionary somewhere under the definition of irony.

She held the material close to her face, breathing in his scent. While it had been laundered, a hundred washings would never get his scent out enough that she couldn't smell it. She breathed deep again, letting the smell wash over her like a gentle wave. Damn, he smelled good.

T-shirt in hand, she headed to the bathroom, smiling as she heard the quiet rattle of Braden putting dishes in the dishwasher. She closed the door, then slipped out of her clothes and into the warm spray of the shower. Even with the water running, she could smell Braden's T-shirt filling the small room, hear him moving around in the kitchen, and pick up the steady beat of his heart. Suddenly, she wasn't nearly as tired as she had been only a little while ago.

Sighing, she finished showering, then dried off and slipped into Braden's T-shirt. It hung to midthigh and felt as soft as she imagined it would. After drying her hair, she walked out of the bathroom, expecting to find Braden already in his bedroom and the door closed. Instead, he was in the living room, spreading a blanket out on the couch.

She padded over to him. "You didn't have to do that."

He looked up from the blanket, heat flaring in his eyes at the sight of her. If the scent of arousal rolling off of him was any indication, he liked the way his shirt looked on her as much as she did.

He straightened. "I figured that since I'm the one sleeping on it, I should make it up."

She blinked. She hadn't expected him to give up his bed. "You're sleeping on the couch?"

His mouth quirked. "That was the plan. Unless you have a better idea."

Dreya hadn't come out here intending to seduce him. But they had already come damn close to sleeping together two nights ago. The only reason they hadn't was that they were afraid of messing up her shot of working at the DCO. Well, that excuse was off the table now, and after today, it was obvious they were a perfect match for each other in every way that mattered. Why shouldn't they finally act on the feelings they'd been putting on hold for days?

She smiled and jerked her head in the direction of the bedroom. "I couldn't help but notice that you have a big bed in there. What kind of partner would I be if I let you sleep on an uncomfortable couch while I hogged the bed?"

The fire in his eyes blazed into new life. "Oh, I don't know. I've fallen asleep on this couch a few times watching TV. It's pretty comfortable."

Now he was just messing with her. Two could play that game.

Dreya sighed and turned to head toward the bedroom. "If you'd rather sleep on the couch instead of in a bed with me, that's okay."

She hadn't taken more than two steps when Braden caught her hand and spun her around. Groaning, he pulled her into his arms and kissed her with a passion so hot, it almost scorched her skin. His tongue plunged into her mouth, making her moan as he teased her with a little taste and then withdrew to nibble on her lips, tugging and nipping gently with his teeth.

She wrapped her arms around his neck, kissing him even more fiercely and tangling her tongue with his. Mmm, he tasted delicious.

She didn't think about what going up on tiptoe and wrapping her arms around his neck would do to the T-shirt she was wearing until he cupped her bare ass cheeks and tugged her against him hard enough that she could feel his cock pressing against her through his jeans.

She wiggled against him, just to let him know she approved. Holding on to his neck even tighter, she lifted one leg up to hook it around his waist. Then she lifted the other and wrapped it around him, too, locking her ankles together behind him.

Braden didn't seem to mind. Instead, he got a better grip on her ass and headed for the bedroom.

She dragged her mouth away to smile at him. "I guess that means you'll be sleeping in the bed with me tonight?"

He stopped long enough to shove her up against the wall beside the bedroom door, his hands still supporting her ass as he rocked himself against her and nuzzled her neck. She practically purred as his jean-clad cock pressed against her pussy.

"Yes," he rasped against her throat, making her shiver. "I'll be joining you in the bed tonight, although I don't think we'll be getting much sleep."

She laughed. "You won't hear me complaining."

Kissing her again, he pulled her away from the wall and carried her into the bedroom, then tossed her lightly on the bed. She giggled as she bounced on the comforter. It was as soft as she thought it'd be.

Braden's eyes smoldered as she reached down and whipped the T-shirt over her head, tossing it toward the dresser across the room. It might have made it there—she didn't bother to look. She was much more interested in watching as Braden's eyes raked over her naked body. Men had looked at her before but never devoured her like this. It was amazing the way a simple look could make her feel wanted—powerful.

Gaze still on her, Braden yanked off his clothes. As

much as she wanted him just as naked as she was, Dreya almost found herself urging him to slow down and let her enjoy it. But then she realized she wasn't patient enough for that. She'd enjoy his body at her leisure later. Right now, she wanted him naked and in her arms.

That didn't mean she couldn't appreciate the pure artistry of his body as his clothes came off. She couldn't believe how beautiful he was, all the way from his broad shoulders to his muscular pecs and arms, to the deep cuts of his abs and the powerful legs of a man who ran a lot.

Then there was his cock, yet another thing of beauty. It was thick and hard, pulsing with his excitement. She squirmed a little at the thought of what it was going to feel like to have him inside her. The mere thought of it made her fingertips tingle and her fangs throb with the need to let go and extend. She clamped down on that desire. The words erection, claws, and fangs didn't deserve to be mentioned in the same sentence together, much less be allowed in the same bed.

Dreya's heart suddenly constricted when she saw what else was exposed as Braden's clothes hit the floor—the evidence of his violent job. There was one well-healed scar on the front of his right shoulder, maybe an inch below his collarbone. Another graced the outside of his left thigh, the lines spreading out from it implying extensive surgery to repair all the damage that a bullet had likely done to him. There were other, smaller scars here and there on that amazing body of his, too, including thin lines that a knife might make as well as the more jagged ones that seemed more suited to a broken bottle.

But rather than mar the beauty of the man, the scars only seemed to enhance it, highlighting the fact that his body hadn't been created in a gym or through the use of a personal trainer. It had been honed to perfection by a hard life, one that had left its mark on him in so many different ways.

After Braden cast the last piece of clothing aside, he moved over to the nightstand beside the bed to pull open a drawer and rustle around inside. She opened her mouth to ask what he was looking for when he came out with a strip of condom packets.

There was a momentary spike of something she knew was jealousy as she realized that a man only kept condoms in his bedside nightstand if he needed them on occasion. She told herself that was a stupid thing to feel, that she had no say in the life he'd lived before he met her. Still, it bothered her anyway.

But then she saw him holding the packets up to the light, turning them this way and that, and she finally figured out he was looking for the expiration date. He must have been worried about it, because a look of relief flashed across his face when he found it. Apparently, Braden didn't use his condoms very often, a realization that made her feel warm all over. Again, it was a totally stupid thing to feel, but it made her ridiculously happy.

He turned to her, pure lust making his eyes heavy, and the urge to simply lay back on the bed, spread her legs wide, and invite him in was suddenly tempered by the knowledge that they had all night...and there were so many different things she wanted to try with him.

In a flash, she sat up and flipped over, slowly crawling

away from him on the big soft bed, deliberately letting her hips sway back and forth.

“By the way,” she said, looking playfully over her shoulder at him. “You never did answer my question in Miami…about whether you think I have a sexy ass.”

Dreya knew she didn’t have a mountain of curves. She was an athletic feline shifter, more gymnast and less harem dancer. But the look that came over Braden’s face right then as he gazed at her bottom made her feel like the curviest woman who’d ever walked the earth.

“Hell, yes.” He reached out and got a hand on each of her hips, dragging her closer to him. “You have the sexiest ass on the planet.”

Dreya laughed, letting him tug her to the edge of the bed. *Sexiest ass on the planet?* Yeah, she could live with that. Especially since Braden leaned forward and started kissing and nibbling every square inch of her bottom, finding sensitive little areas she never even knew she had. Like that one above the cleft of her ass, right at the base of her spine. Oh boy, did his mouth feel good there or what?

As he teased her with his mouth, Braden’s hands roamed all over, running up her thighs, massaging her cheeks, even spanking now and then before moving slowly along her sides and slipping around to tease her clit. Dreya had never had a man pay so much attention to her body. Moaning, she dropped her face and arms to the downy comforter, deciding she could get used to it.

She didn’t realize how excited she was until she looked up and realized that her claws were partially extended and that she was kneading Braden’s comforter like she was a happy kitty cat getting her belly rubbed. For one wild second, she worried that seeing her claws might freak him out. But one glance over her shoulder confirmed that yes, he could see them, and no, he didn't care. He was totally focused on her body and making her feel good.

Knowing her shifter side didn't bother him was unbelievably amazing. It was like someone had finally given her permission to be herself.

She rested her face on the blanket again, smiling as she gave in to the experience and enjoying the fact that this man had her wrapped around his little finger.

Braden seemed to know it, too. He teased and caressed her until she thought she was going to scream. She was so close to coming that she yowled in disappointment when he stopped what he was doing and took his hands away. But the sound froze in her throat as she felt him firmly grip one of her hips and nudge her a little higher on her knees.

Dreya melted as he pushed his thickness inside her, a deep, pleasure-laced growl escaping from her lips. She was so wet and ready for him that he had no problem sliding in deep, and the sensation of being completely filled was almost a transcendent experience. He felt so perfect, it was like he'd been made for her.

When he began to thrust, the movement was almost agonizingly slow, with him pulling almost all the way out until he was barely inside, then plunging in slowly. Her body tingled all over from that single thrust, and she felt her fangs slip out.

With any other man, she would have immediately tried to control her shift, but with Braden, she just relaxed and let go, allowing her feline side to enjoy the experience, too.

The second thrust was faster, and the third faster still. Then, when he must have felt she was ready, he began to pick up speed...and she just about lost her mind.

The slap of his hips and thighs smacking against her ass, the feel of his strong hands clutching her hips, not to mention the sexy, primal grunt he made each time he pumped into her, turned her on as much as the physical pleasure his cock provided.

She tried not to shred his comforter with her claws, but what he was doing felt so damn good, it was hard to control anything her body did, especially her shifted side. The animal seemed to have a mind of its own as pleasure spiraled through her, making her purr and yowl like the feline she was.

Her body shook as Braden pounded into her harder. Then she was exploding, her back bowing as her head came up to cut loose with a loud scream of pure pleasure.

Dreya was just coming down from her high, her body spasming around him so tightly, she couldn't imagine how he was still able to move inside her, when he flipped her over, spread her legs wide, and slipped right back inside.

The move was so smooth and powerful that it took her breath away almost as much as the expression on Braden's handsome face. Her fangs were out, and her eyes were probably glowing so bright, they looked like green neon, and yet, all she saw on his face was total lust—and total acceptance. He had flipped her over like this on purpose, so he could look her straight in the eyes as he came.

She wrapped her legs around his waist, pulling him in tightly as he thrust. He plunged so deep, it was almost shocking, but she never looked away, never broke eye contact with him. With every thrust, she lifted her hips to meet his.

When he climaxed, she came again with him, not as hard as before, but still more powerfully than any other orgasm she'd ever had. This time, though, she focused on him and his pleasure and the emotions reflected on his face.

Their joining was the most intense thing she'd ever experienced, and when both their orgasms were done, when every trace of possible pleasure had been wrung out of them, she pulled him down and kissed him. It was tricky with her fangs out, but they managed.

After her fangs and claws retracted, Braden lifted his head and gazed at her. His shaft still pulsed inside her ever so slightly, and his breathing was ragged.

"Is it like that every time for you?" he asked huskily. "Your claws and fangs coming out, I mean?"

Dreya smiled and shook her head. "It's never been like that for me. No one has ever made my body shift like that. Not like you do."

Braden regarded her for a long moment, then a slow smile spread across his face. "Well then, what do you say we see how many times we can get those claws and fangs to come out tonight?"

Braden was walking out of the bathroom the next morning, a towel wrapped around his waist and his hair damp from the shower, when the door to his apartment opened, and Mick walked in with a stack of mail in his hand.

Mick stopped cold a few feet inside the door. “You’re home.”

“Yeah,” Braden said. “Last night.”

His friend closed the door. “You should have called me. I wouldn’t have bothered stopping by to pick up your mail if I’d known you were going to be off for the weekend.”

Braden opened his mouth to point out that technically, he wasn’t off today, when Mick’s eyes suddenly widened. Braden turned to see Dreya saunter out of the bedroom, wearing nothing but the T-shirt she’d had on last night.

“Morning, Mick.”

Giving them a smile, she walked past him and a flabbergasted Mick into the kitchen. Taking one of the MPD mugs out of the cabinet, she poured coffee into it, then added a packet of sweetener and some milk.

Mick stared at her as she padded down the short hallway and into the bedroom, his gaze on Dreya’s perfectly toned legs. Only when she had closed the door behind her did he turn and look at Braden.

“Um…that was Dreya Clark, right?”

Braden nodded. “Yeah.”

Mick seemed to consider that. “And she just came out of your bedroom half-naked, wearing one of your T-shirts, right?”

Braden’s mouth twitched. “Yeah.”

“And she’s, like, your partner in Homeland these days, right?”

“Yes, she’s my partner at the place where we’re

working," Braden said. "So, if you have something on your mind, why don't you say it, Mick? If not, you only have about seventeen questions left in this game of twenty."

Mick crossed the living room until he was standing a foot away from Braden. Then he leaned in even closer. "Are you two sleeping together?"

"You don't have to whisper, Mick. Dreya has exceptional hearing. Plus, she's smart enough to know what we're talking about out here."

Mick threw a glance at the bedroom door. "Well… are you?"

"Would it bother you if we were?" Braden asked.

Mick frowned. "It doesn't bother me, but you don't think Homeland is going to have a problem with it?"

Braden had been thinking about that all morning. He was sure an organization like the DCO likely had a fraternization policy in place. Every large, bureaucratic organization did. But he also knew the DCO seemed to do anything it wanted to do, whenever it wanted. Danica and Clayne were married, and they still worked together.

He shrugged. "It's complicated, but Homeland doesn't have much of a say in it. The people who would don't seemed overly concerned with things like administrative rules and crap like that. They just care about getting the job done."

Mick snorted. "Refreshing, I guess. You sure you're working for the United States?"

"Yeah. They're different. I'll give you that, but they're a U.S. agency."

"So, I guess that if I asked Dreya out on a date, she'd probably say no?" Mick asked.

Braden chuckled. "Probably."

Not that it would stop Mick. The man was a little delusional like that. He'd probably think Dreya would consider him a step up from Braden.

Mick walked over to the kitchen counter and tossed the mail he'd brought with him onto the stack. "There're a few bills in the pile you need to take care of." At the door, he turned and looked over his shoulder at Braden. "And by the way, stop by and see your parents. Your mom has been worried sick."

His friend was already half out the door when Braden stopped him. "Hey, Mick."

The man turned and looked at him again. "Yeah?"

"Thanks."

Mick grinned. "No problem. Just call if it turns out you need a hand."

"I appreciate it, but it's not really the kind of job I can ask for your help with."

Mick's smile broadened. "I wasn't talking about the job. I meant with Dreya. Let me know if she turns out to be too much for you, and I'll take her off your hands."

Braden was still laughing when Dreya came out of his bedroom. Wrapping her arms around his neck, she went up on tiptoe and kissed him. He dipped his tongue into her mouth, his hands naturally finding their way to her ass. Man, he loved her in that shirt. If he had his way, she'd never wear anything but this when she was at his place.

"I didn't cause any trouble, did I?" she asked. "Letting Mick see me, I mean."

Braden shook his head. "Nah. If there's anyone I want to know about us, it's Mick. He's cool with it. Disappointed he can't have you himself, but cool with it."

She laughed and kissed him again, and he felt his cock fighting to find a way past the bath towel keeping him away from Dreya.

He groaned and took a step back. "We'd better get ready, or we won't make it to the DCO on time."

She sighed but turned and walked into the bedroom, the sway of her hips reminding him of what he was missing out on. "If you're good, I'll make it up to you later."

He chuckled as her beautiful ass disappeared from sight. With a promise like that, he could be very good.

Chapter 14

"YOU'RE QUIET," DREYA REMARKED AS THEY DROVE toward his parents' place in New Carrollton. "I thought you'd be stoked to have the rest of the day off."

He gave her a sidelong glance. They'd stopped by her place after going to the DCO complex, and she'd changed into a sleeveless dress that showed off her gorgeous legs.

Braden smiled. "Sorry. I'm thrilled to spend the day with you. I'm just exhausted. It's your fault. You kept me up too late last night."

"You sure that's it?" She eyed him dubiously. "Because, if I didn't know any better, I would say you're a worried about me having lunch with your parents, especially since your father is a retired cop."

He wasn't concerned about that in the least, but since he didn't want to get into what was actually bothering him, he went along with it.

He shrugged as he signaled to change lanes. "Maybe a little bit. It's just that my dad doesn't have a very good filter on his mouth. I'm worried he's going to say something that pisses you off or offends you."

Dreya laughed. "Don't worry about that. I've spent my life around some pretty rough characters. You should be more concerned that I'll end up saying something that offends your father."

He couldn't help smiling. "That would be funny to see."

"There you go. Nothing to worry about then," she promised. "I'll handle your dad fine. Just don't be shocked when I mention that you've used your cuffs on me already."

Braden chuckled. He could only imagine how his parents would deal with that. His mom would laugh her butt off, but his very uptight dad would almost certainly have a cow.

While Dreya carried on a mostly one-sided conversation about messing with his dad, Braden thought about what had happened at the DCO complex that morning.

Since it was Saturday, the complex had been relatively quiet compared to what they were used to. There wasn't a lot of gunfire to be heard in the distance, the parking lots were almost empty, and the main admin building was nearly deserted.

Braden had expected Clayne and Danica to meet them there, but instead, John met with him and Dreya in his big office in the main building. The director had told them again how impressed he was with the way they'd handled the situation in Miami and that he was ready to offer Dreya a job at the DCO if she was interested.

Braden could have told John she was. It was all she'd talked about on the drive from his apartment.

But instead of asking John where to sign right away, she said, "Only if Braden is my partner."

John glanced at him. "That's up to Braden. I don't know if he mentioned it, but he's already on long-term loan from the Metro Police Department. He can work here with you as long as the two of you want."

When Dreya looked expectantly at him, he nodded. After she'd fallen asleep last night, he'd held her, thinking about that very thing. Deciding to work at the DCO with her hadn't been difficult. They made a good team, and in all honesty, he couldn't stomach the idea of her working with anyone else, especially a guy.

He'd fallen for her all right—hard.

While John had taken Dreya to HR to sign some paperwork, Braden had wandered over to the cafeteria to grab some coffee and ended up running into Coleman. He and the deputy director seemed to have an uncanny habit of meeting like that.

Coleman had immediately congratulated him for the amazing job he and Dreya had done in Florida.

"Where is Dreya, by the way?" Coleman asked.

Braden jerked his head at the admin building. "She's with John, filling out HR forms so she can officially start working here."

Coleman nodded. "That's good. You two can do good things here."

Something about the way he said the words made Braden's hackles rise. "Meaning?"

The words came out a little sharper than he'd meant them to, but he couldn't help it. If he was protective when it came to Dreya, so be it.

"Nothing," Coleman said, then sighed. "I'm a bit worried, that's all. You know Dreya better than I ever will, so maybe I'm off base here. To put it bluntly, you two went through the most exhilarating, euphoria-inducing mission that a new team at the DCO has ever gone through. And both of you did an outstanding job. But the problem is that Dreya is in there right now, signing up for a job in which she thinks she's going to be doing stuff like that every day, or at least frequently.

But the truth is, you two may never do anything that dramatic again the rest of the time you're here."

Braden folded his arms across his chest. "I don't see how that's a problem."

Coleman regarded him thoughtfully. "Why do you think Dreya climbs high-rises and steals things? Do you think it's because she needs the money?"

"No," Braden admitted. "She makes enough from the legitimate jewelry business she runs. Plus, I'm pretty sure she didn't fence most of the stuff she stole. It's one of the biggest reasons I was never able to pin anything on her."

"That's what I thought," Coleman said. "Simply put, I think Dreya is an adrenaline junkie. And the other night's mission gave her the biggest shot of adrenaline she's ever had. If it turns out that the two of you don't go on another crazy mission for a long time to come, what do you think Dreya is going to do to get her next rush?"

Braden didn't answer.

"I don't know," Coleman said. "Maybe I'm simply worrying over nothing, but keep an eye on her, huh? Let me know if you see anything that makes you think she's going back to her old ways. If you even suspect she is, call me. We have some excellent people she can talk to at the DCO."

Braden frowned. "Psychologists, you mean?"

Coleman smiled. "Think of it as an intervention."

Braden had still been standing there, thinking about the deputy director's words, when Dreya came out of the admin building. She was so excited about how much she was going to make, not to mention what kind of housing allowance they were giving her and the free motorcycle insurance, that he couldn't help smiling, despite how preoccupied he was.

He was genuinely happy for her, but at the same time, Coleman's words kept playing over and over again in his head. Braden hated the idea of snooping on Dreya, but what if the deputy director was right? What if Dreya was one stumble away from doing something incredibly stupid and screwing everything up? Given her background, Braden had to at least consider that as a possibility, didn't he?

"What kind of law enforcement background do you have, Dreya?" Braden's dad asked, glancing at her as he flipped the burgers on the grill.

Braden was pretty sure that was the most heavy-handed attempt to fish for information he'd ever witnessed. There was a reason his dad had never wanted to be a detective—his questioning technique sucked. Braden was surprised it had taken almost a whole hour for his dad to bring the subject up.

When Braden had called to reassure his mom that he hadn't fallen off the face of the earth but was instead working with Homeland on a joint mission, she had cajoled him into coming over for an impromptu cookout. Sitting with Dreya at the umbrella table on his parents' deck in the backyard now, he wasn't sure that had been such a good idea. Even his parents' orange tabby cat, Merlin, who was currently curled up on Dreya's lap, seemed to doubt the decision.

"Joseph, you stop badgering her right this minute," his mom scolded as she set a plate full of condiments on the table to join all the other food she'd already brought out, including sliced tomatoes, lettuce, cheese, three kinds of chips, and two kinds of dips. His mom did nothing halfway. "Our son already said he can't talk details about the type of work he and Dreya are doing for Homeland, so stick a sock in it."

Tall with salt-and-pepper hair and a matching mustache, his dad tried to put on an injured expression and failed miserably. That didn't stop him from trying to defend himself. "Janice, doesn't a father have a right to know what kind of partner his son is working with? I mean, it's bad enough that he won't tell us what the feds need a burglary detective for. Now you're saying I can't even ask if the woman is qualified to keep my son from getting his ass shot off?"

She put her hands on her hips and glared at him. "Joseph Hayes!"

His father ducked his head, looking chagrined. "Excuse my French. I'll put a quarter in the jar later."

Braden shook his head. His mother had been making his father put a quarter in a jar in the kitchen every time he cursed since Braden could remember. Unfortunately, the penalty had never really worked well, and now there were so many jars lined up on a shelf in the basement that they could probably pay for their first grandkid's college tuition in full—if he or his brother, Nate, every got around to having any.

His mom continued to stare daggers at his dad until he relented and shrugged. "I'm sorry, Dreya." Spatula in hand, he sat at the table, giving her an apologetic look. "But I'm just an old street cop through and through. This talk of feds, Homeland Security, and long-term reassignments scares the…" He stopped and regrouped, his gaze going to his wife, then to Dreya. "It scares me. I want to make sure my son is going to have backup he can trust when the time comes."

Braden was about to tell his dad to stuff the scared old man act. Nobody was buying it. But unfortunately, it seemed that Dreya did.

"I completely understand," she said, gently running her fingers over Merlin's fur. "I don't have what you would call a traditional law enforcement background."

Braden cursed silently. He'd put enough quarters in the jar over the years, thank you very much.

His father's head whipped around like the turret on a battle tank as he fixed her with a sharp look. "And what exactly does that mean? Are you a cop or not?"

"You don't have to answer that, Dreya," Braden said.

He was ready to take her hand and walk right the hell out of there. He loved his dad, but in this case, the man was out of line.

But Dreya shook her head. "Actually, I think I do, Braden. Your parents have a right to know who's covering their son's back."

Even his mom looked worried at that. She pushed her dark hair over her shoulder and sat beside her husband, her dark eyes intent on Dreya. "You're not a cop or a fed?"

Dreya smiled. "I was officially hired as a fed at eleven o'clock this morning. Before that, I was a professional second-story thief and have been for the better part of ten years. In all the time I worked, nobody has ever come close to arresting me, until Braden. Homeland wanted someone with my talents and decided that if he was good enough to catch me, we should be good working together. They were right. We make a very good team."

His father's jaw dropped while his mom lifted a hand to her mouth in surprise. Oh hell, now the crap had hit the fan.

"The feds partnered my son up with a thief!" his father demanded when he'd finally found the ability to speak again. "What kind of backup are you going to be if someone pulls a gun on Braden? What are you going to do, pick the guy's damn pocket?"

Braden cringed. His father was yelling so loudly, he'd be surprised if the entire neighborhood didn't hear. That was all he needed.

"No, she's not going to pick his pocket, Dad, because she'll be too busy kicking his ass," he said. "If you need proof, there's an Argentinian cartel assassin in Florida heading to a federal prison right now with a limp he'll have for the rest of his life thanks to Dreya. As far as I'm concerned, she's already proven herself a solid partner in the only way that matters, and she did it while covering my ass."

He wasn't sure if his mother had heard enough to satisfy her or she was just concerned about the burgers, because she took the spatula out of her husband's hand and went over to the grill to pull them off the heat.

His father looked at him sharply, then at Dreya. The man read state and federal police blotters over breakfast every morning, so Braden knew he'd leaked more than enough information for his dad to figure out exactly which cartel assassin he was talking about.

"I see." His dad sat back in his chair and regarded

them thoughtfully. "So you two go around stealing stuff for the federal government, is that it?"

"Joseph, stop fishing," his mom said. "You've gotten everything you need to hear."

"Oh, for crying out loud, Janice. I'm just asking a simple question."

His mother stabbed him with a stern look.

"Fine," his father grumbled. "Make sure my burger is well done. You know I hate when the inside is raw."

"And?" his mom said softly.

His dad smiled at Dreya. "Welcome to the family, Dreya."

"And?" his mom prompted again, pausing to look at her husband for a moment as she took the last burger off the grill.

He sighed. "And I'll put another quarter in the jar."

"Thank you, dear." His mother picked up the tray of burgers and brought them over to the table with a smile. "Who's ready to eat?"

Dreya lay beside Braden in his big bed Sunday night, her head on his shoulder, her human nails tracing the light scratches that her shifter claws had made during their most recent round of lovemaking. Almost as if her fingers had a mind of their own, they slowly moved onto the real scars, caressing the straight slice on the right side of his rib cage before moving to the almost star-shaped pattern on his right shoulder. She didn't know much about these kinds of things, but something told her the scar had been made by a bullet. It pained her to think of someone shooting him, and she felt her claws start to extend as the urge to hurt someone reared up out of nowhere.

"How did this happen?" she asked softly, running her fingertips over the scar on his shoulder again.

"It happened in the same shoot-out where Tommy got killed. It was a long time ago," he said just as softly. Beneath her ear, his heart thumped with a steady rhythm. "When I was younger—and dumber. You don't have to worry about something like that happening again."

She smiled, adoring the fact that his first instinct was to say something to make her not worry. It was such a guy thing to do.

"I know," she told him. "But it happened to you, and therefore, it's important to me. I want to learn everything I can about you so I can be a good partner."

He chuckled, the sound a deep rumble in her ear. "You're already a good partner."

She waited for him to continue, but he didn't. Instead, he simply glided his fingers up and down her bare arm. That was okay. If it was something he couldn't share right now, she wouldn't pry. They might be partners—in more ways than one—but they were still new at this whole thing.

Beneath her ear, his heart sped up a little. "I was a brand-new detective level II and naive as shit. I thought I was going to save the world—or DC at least. I didn't know it for sure, though, until I got partnered up with the best detective in the burglary section. Hell, he was probably the best detective in the whole MPD."

Braden paused as if collecting his thoughts, and Dreya didn't push.

"Tommy was amazing, the most instinctive cop I've

ever worked with. He just knew when people were lying to him. It was like he had this sixth sense about it. I swear he could smell people breaking the law." Braden's mouth edged up. "He took down so many bad guys—a lot of times on his own—that he was pretty much a legend in the department. He had so many commendations and had been wounded in the line of duty so many times, it was like he was the real-life police officer, and all the rest of us were kids playing a game of cops and robbers."

Another pause, followed by another slight increase in heartbeat.

"But Tommy hated playing by the rules. He couldn't stand what he called do-nothing cops—guys who used the rules to justify not getting their jobs done. And I have to admit, for a brand-new detective like me, it was one hell of a rush getting to work with a partner like that."

Braden took a deep breath, letting it out slowly. "There was a burglary ring working the city then, nasty guys who didn't have a problem hitting the homes when the owners were still in them. They'd already made off with over a half million in cash, jewelry, and small art pieces—all stuff that was easy to move—but the bigger problem was the violence. They seemed to be developing a taste for it."

Dreya grimaced. She'd met thieves like that. The ones who started in a dark place and only got worse, the more they let themselves go. She'd never worked with any of them, even though many had tried to strong-arm her into pulling jobs with them. But she didn't get strong-armed easily.

"Tommy's informant—the piece of crap I told you about—claimed to know who was on the crew and where they were hiding the crap they'd bagged. Tommy decided we were going to take them down on our own."

She cringed. That didn't sound like a very good idea to her, and she wasn't even a cop. "How many of them were there?"

"There were supposed to be three, but it turned out there were five." Braden folded his free arm beneath his head. "It went bad almost the moment Tommy and I walked in. The two guys we didn't know were there walked out of a back room and just started shooting."

His heartbeat spiked, his chest rising and falling faster. "It all happened in a blur. One second, we were taking down the bad guys, and the next, Tommy was lying in my arms, bleeding out from five hits to the chest. Doctors told me later the mean son of a bitch should have died instantly, but instead, he hung on long enough to finish the fight, then tell me not to be scared with his dying breath."

Tears filled Dreya's eyes. She'd never even met Tommy, and yet, she wanted to cry for the man simply because he'd been someone important to Braden.

"What did he mean by that, not to be scared?" she asked quietly.

Braden snorted. "Hell if I know. As much as I've thought about those words over the years, you think I would have figured it out, but I never did."

"What happened after that?" she asked, something telling her that Tommy's death had only been the beginning of this story.

"First, there were the investigations, then the

commendations." Braden's voice was laced with bitterness. "It's what the department does when their people get shot and killed. Worthless as shit to me, of course. I threw mine away and had a friend in admin get it pulled out of my permanent record. I couldn't stand the idea of receiving a commendation for letting my partner get killed."

Dreya wanted to tell him that he was wrong, that he had nothing to do with Tommy's death, but she didn't bother. Braden had spent eight years convincing himself it was true. There was nothing she could say in a few words that would change anything.

"After that day, I became the most by the book cop in the department," he continued. "I was convinced that if we'd done things the right way, Tommy would still be around. Sure, every once in a while, I'd stretch or bend a rule a little. I used to laugh and say that it was Tommy up there in heaven, telling me to stop being a rookie and go with my gut. But I never did anything crazy. Until you came along."

She lifted her head to look at him. "What do you mean?"

He smiled. "When Clayne and Danica walked out of the MPD interrogation room with you, I should have let them take you. They had the right paperwork with all the right signatures. By all rights, you belonged to them. But then Tommy started shouting at me in my head to go after them, and I forgot about every rule I'd ever followed and went."

"So you're saying Tommy is the reason we ended up together?"

Braden caught the end of her hair, curling it around

his finger. "Yeah, I guess so. I think he would have liked you. You're a lot like him. You don't care for rules, you do what you want, and you follow your instincts before all else."

She thought about that, then nodded. "Yeah, I guess I see your point. I hope you find me more attractive, though."

He lifted his head and kissed the tip of her nose. "Much more attractive."

Dreya laughed and put her head on his chest, wiggling until she was completely comfortable against his warm body. She covered the scar on his shoulder with one hand, promising herself she'd never let him get shot again. No matter what she had to do.

She was on the verge of falling asleep when she felt Braden's warm fingers gently caressing her naked shoulder. She smiled, wondering if he was thinking about making love again. She had no doubt that would wake her right up.

"Do you mind if I ask you something, Dreya?" he asked suddenly.

The hesitancy in his voice caught her off guard. "You can ask me anything you want."

There was a pause, then a deep breath, like he was getting ready to drop a doozy on her.

"Why do you steal stuff?"

Okay, she hadn't seen that coming. She pushed herself up on her elbow to frown at him. "What?"

He shrugged, looking almost uncomfortable. "I've been wondering. Humor me."

She sighed. "I don't know why I do it. Why does anyone do anything? Because they can."

The answer didn't satisfy him. "I'm serious. Why do you steal? It's not like you need the money. Do you even sell the stuff you take?"

She didn't answer, waiting to hear the punch line of a question she was sure was a joke. When it never came, she realized he wasn't going to let this go. Not that she was surprised. Not letting go of something was the reason he'd caught her in the first place, why he'd followed her into the DCO, even why she'd ended up in his bed.

She supposed this was something they needed to talk about at some point. Now was as good a time as any.

"Was it Rory?" he demanded. "Did you start stealing because of him? You said you owed him. Did he use that debt to get you to steal for him?"

Dreya should have been furious at the question. But so many people assumed Rory had been using her to steal for him that she was used to them asking. It wasn't true, but after the first few times, she hadn't bothered trying to correct them, because they didn't believe her. Braden was different, though. For some reason, she couldn't stand the idea of him thinking poorly of her old friend. In many ways, Rory was to her what Tommy was to Braden—the person who'd become the foundation for who she had become and the person who still whispered in her ear when she was doing something she shouldn't.

"Rory taught me how to steal, but only because I asked him to," she said.

Braden gave her a skeptical look.

"It's true," she insisted. "When we first became friends, he was dead set against me learning anything about the jewelry business except making the stuff. He never wanted me to be a thief. Part of me didn't want to be one either. I did it because it was what the animal inside me wanted."

Braden frowned. "The animal inside you? What does that mean?"

Dreya sighed. It was complicated, but if they were going to be partners, he should know the whole story when it came to working with a shifter.

"This is going to sound crazy, but being a shifter is more than just claws, fangs, and really good senses," she said, trying to frame her thoughts and hoping what she said would make sense to him. She'd only had this conversation one other time—with Rory—and that had been over a decade ago. But Kendra and Lucy, as well as Clayne to a certain degree, had helped her understand a lot more about herself. She only hoped she could get it out in a way Braden would understand.

"You already know I can see in the dark, pick up your scent from a hundred feet away, hear your heart beating from the other side of the room, run fast, and all those other things, right? Well, those skills are the outward expressions of what it means to be a shifter, but none of them are what makes me a shifter. Being a shifter is about what's inside that really makes me different."

He regarded her in silence for a time. "And what's inside?"

She shrugged. "It's hard to explain, but sometimes, it's like there are two people living in the same body. One half is me—Dreya, the woman who likes to make jewelry and watch Netflix. The other half is my feline shifter. That part likes to drive fast on my motorcycle, climb tall buildings, and steal things purely for the thrill of it. Both halves are equally important. If I ignore either side for too long, the whole becomes…well…cranky I suppose is the best word for it. Rory figured that out a long time ago and taught me how to be a thief to keep my feline side happy, even though he didn't want me doing it. When I said I would have gone insane without his help, I wasn't kidding. He helped find a way for both halves to be happy."

She caressed his hair-roughened jaw. "Does that make any sense at all?"

Braden didn't say anything for a long time, but then he nodded. "Yeah, I think it does."

Taking her hand, he tugged her to his chest. The position was just as warm and cozy as it had been before, but for some reason she couldn't understand, something felt different now, and she couldn't help wondering if she had told him something that put a wedge between them.

Chapter 15

Ivy didn't expect Trevor to be with anyone when she walked into the common room of the psychiatric facility to visit him. In all honesty, after the runaround Brand had given her when she'd gotten to Stillwater that morning, she half expected Trevor to be locked up in a padded room. According to Brand, her "brother" needed to get acclimated to his new surroundings without his sister's interference. She'd been afraid he was trying to cover up the fact that something had happened to Trevor when the hybrid escaped, and she wasn't leaving there until she saw that the coyote shifter was okay. Not only that, but she and Landon needed an update about what was going on inside Stillwater. When it looked like Brand wasn't going to budge, she threatened to call the Maine State Police and have them poke around. Brand hadn't been happy, but he agreed to let her see Trevor.

She eyed the dark-haired teenage girl beside Trevor on the couch as she took a seat on the matching chair.

"Who's this?" Ivy asked.

"Brooklyn," Trevor said softly. "She's a patient here and a new member of the I've-seen-weird-shit-but-kept-my-cool-when-the-doctors-questioned-me club. You can talk in front of her. She's smart enough to avoid getting herself turned into a medicated zombie in here, and she's a friend of Ian's, the hybrid you might have noticed flying out the window last night. I've told her pretty much everything else. Speaking of Ian, you and Landon caught him, right?"

Ivy wasn't quite sure what she thought about Trevor divulging classified information to a teenager in a mental institution, but if he thought it was okay to talk in front of her, then she'd go along with it, especially since it didn't look like Brooklyn was going anywhere. Besides, as Trevor pointed out, she knew Ian. Maybe she'd be able to give some insight into the kid so she and Landon could apprehend him.

"No, we didn't catch him, which is why Landon isn't here. He's out looking for him," she said, keeping her voice low even though the only other patients in the room were two elderly men, clearly hard of hearing, playing chess on the other side of it. "Ian's not like any hybrid we've ever dealt with before. He's way more clever."

She didn't miss the look of concern—or pride—on the girl's face.

"Instead of running for the hills like other hybrids would have done, he's hanging around the woods out there," Ivy added. "Landon and I haven't been able to figure out why."

"I think I might be the reason," Brooklyn said. She pulled her ponytail around to the side and played with the end of it. "Ian won't go, because I'm still here."

Ivy studied the girl. The fact that Ian refused to leave—even if it meant saving himself—said a lot about Brooklyn. It also said a lot about him. Ivy knew there was something special about the hybrid from the moment they'd started chasing him last night.

"If the bumbling orderlies were the only ones out there looking for him, we wouldn't be nearly as worried," Ivy said. "But unfortunately, Thorn's men are out there, too."

Trevor frowned. "Thorn's men? He sent backup for you?"

Ivy grimaced. "More like reinforcements. Thorn's head of security, Douglas Frasier, is the one leading these guys, which means Thorn doesn't trust us anymore."

"Crap," Trevor muttered.

"Exactly," Ivy said. "No doubt Frasier already told Thorn that Mahsood created a functional hybrid and that Ian is on the loose out here in the forests of Old Town."

"Who's Thorn, and what does he want with Ian?" Brooklyn asked, looking from Trevor to Ivy and back again.

"He's a man who makes Brand look like a saint," Trevor said. "If he gets his hands on Ian, it won't be good."

Panic flickered in the girl's eyes for a moment before being replaced with grim determination. "So how do we stop him?"

"First, we let Ivy and Landon worry about Ian," Trevor said. "They'll keep an eye on him and make sure Thorn's people don't get to him. While they're doing that, we need to work on getting me into that isolation ward so I can free that shifter and stop Mahsood from turning any more patients into hybrids."

Ivy was wondering exactly how much Trevor had told Brooklyn about all of this stuff when the girl spoke.

"Can't you go kick the crap out of all the orderlies and walk in there right now? I saw what you did to that door last night, Trevor, so don't even pretend you didn't break that knob with your bare hands. A few out of shape orderlies shouldn't be a problem for you."

Trevor's mouth tightened. "Trust me, if I could, I would. But I can't do that without causing a scene. One wrong move on my part, and we could be risking that shifter's life."

Brooklyn didn't look like she was fond of that idea, but she nodded. "So what's the plan then?"

Ivy had been going to ask the same question. Maybe they should just let the girl run the mission.

"It's simple." Trevor grinned. "I make sure Mahsood's research is destroyed and get the shifter out, then all three of us meet up with Ivy and Landon in the woods. Something tells me the moment Ian gets a whiff of you, he'll come running. Then we all get the hell out of here."

Brooklyn smiled, too, her blue eyes sparkling. "That's a good plan. I like it."

"What if something goes wrong between now and then?" Ivy asked. "What if you run into trouble? With Landon and me outside, there's no way for us to communicate with you."

Trevor thought about that. After a moment, the coyote shifter jerked his head toward the far side of the room "See that window on the far left over there?"

Ivy glanced at the window in question. It had bars on it like all the others and sheer curtains pulled back to either side. "What about it?"

"It's not in the view of any of the cameras," Trevor said. "By the time you leave, there will be a small piece of surgical tape stuck in the bottom left of the window. Four hours later, Brooklyn or I will move the tape to the right bottom corner to let you know that everything is fine. Four hours later, it goes to the left again. If you check and the tape isn't where it should be, that means we're in trouble."

"Every four hours?" Ivy frowned. "If there's a problem, that could leave you two in trouble on your own for a long time before we even know something has gone wrong."

"Nurse Ratched and the orderlies watch everyone like hawks. It will be tough enough for Brooklyn or me to get to that window every four hours," Trevor said. "Any more often than that, and it's bound to draw someone's attention. If we run into trouble, we'll make do until the cavalry comes."

Ivy didn't like it, but for now, it was the best plan they had.

As she got up to give her "brother" a hug just in case Brand was watching them on a camera somewhere, Trevor reminded her of something else.

"If things turn out the way we planned, we're going to have a shifter on our hands who's probably been experimented on for months, plus two teenagers fresh out of a mental institution, one of whom happens to be a hybrid. They can't go to the DCO with us, so I think John might want to call Adam and get him to send some of his people up here."

Ivy blinked in surprise. "You know about Adam?"

Trevor chuckled. "I'm a spy, remember? You and Landon dropped enough hints here and there along the way for me to realize that John has someone with a lot of pull helping him deal with Thorn. I sniffed around and figured out that the DCO's very first shifter probably didn't die like everyone said. I get the feeling the guy is hard to kill. It wasn't difficult figuring out what was going on after that."

Wow. Just how much did Trevor know about Adam and the shadowy organization he'd created for no other purpose than to keep the bad guys in the DCO in check? Adam and his collection of hidden shifters had been working completely off the grid for over a decade while collaborating with John the entire time. The fact that Trevor had learned about it after he'd done some digging was alarming but not surprising. Underneath all that dry wit, the coyote shifter was extremely good at his job. Ivy only hoped no one else in the DCO or on the Committee had someone as smart as Trevor digging around, or the dangerous game being played by the factions within the agency could get a lot more perilous.

Dreya frowned at the silhouette targets set up in front of her on the DCO shooting range, only partially satisfied with all the holes in them. Instead of her bullets finding the center of each, most were on the shoulders and arms. A few even took out an ear or two. If they'd been real bad guys, she would have scared the hell out of them, but she probably wouldn't have killed very many.

She was just picking up her Glock to try again when she felt a tingling along the nape of her neck, telling her someone was behind her. It wasn't the guy who ran the range, because he was still moving around in the supply building, getting more ammo, and it wasn't Braden, because he'd left a few minutes ago to grab some takeout from the cafeteria for them.

Setting her gun on the table, she turned to see John standing there. With the wind in her face, she hadn't smelled him. How long had he been standing there? More importantly, had he seen what an incredibly average shot she was?

He smiled. "I didn't mean to interrupt."

She laughed as she took off her protective hearing muffs and placed them next to her gun. "That's okay. I should take a break anyhow. Braden keeps telling me I can't do it all in one day."

John's smile disappeared to be replaced by a frown. "Have you been shooting all morning?"

She nodded. Braden had told her repeatedly that she'd done a good job in Miami, but she knew she needed to get better with her weapon. She hadn't been able to take a shot at Cabo for fear of hitting the woman he'd been holding hostage, and she didn't ever want to find herself in that situation again. She could do better—she *would* do better. She simply needed more practice.

"I'm just trying to learn as much as I can, as fast as I can," she said.

"I have no doubt you're up for the challenge," he told her. "I can't believe how fast you and Braden are melding as a team as it is. You're up there with some of the best I've ever seen."

She did a double take, as stunned by the compliment as she was about how good it made her feel. "Seriously? Wow. Thanks."

"Speaking of Braden, I ran into him on the way here," John continued. "He said that if he didn't go up to the cafeteria to get you something for lunch that you wouldn't have stopped to eat at all."

She boosted herself up with her hands to sit on the table. "We're going to run through the shoot house again this afternoon, and I wanted to make sure I got in enough practice out here before then."

He regarded her thoughtfully. "You don't have to push yourself so hard, you know. I don't expect you to learn everything in a week. This job is demanding. You and Braden need to set aside some downtime when you can."

"We will." She smiled. "In fact, we hung out together this weekend."

"That's good. Do anything fun?"

Dreya hoped she didn't blush too much as thoughts of exactly what she and Braden had done this weekend popped into her head. Yeah, she didn't see herself telling John that other than going to visit Braden's parents, they'd hung around his place naked for most of it, or that they'd only left the bed to make love in some other part of on the apartment, like the floor, the kitchen table, and the shower.

"Nothing special," she said. "We just hung out and stuff, talking and getting to know each other."

John smiled. "Sounds pretty special to me. In my experience, the partners who make the best teammates are the ones who are friends outside of work, too. If you're going to trust each other, it starts with spending time together, bonding and understanding what makes the other person tick."

Dreya had to fight to keep from laughing. After this past weekend, she could say with a certainty that she had a very good idea what made Braden tick, and they definitely had one heck of a bond. Especially in bed.

Not that making out was the only thing they'd done. They'd spent hours talking, too. She told him about how she'd built up her jewelry business and what she was going to do with it now that she was going to be working for the DCO, while he'd told her about what it was like being a cop in a family of cops. Despite coming from different worlds and the opposite side of the law, they had more in common than she'd expected.

For reasons she still didn't completely understand, she trusted Braden more than she'd ever trusted anyone in her life, even more than Rory. She never dreamed she could feel so close to any man, much less one who'd been trying to put her behind bars for years. She didn't want to push things too fast, but she was seriously starting to fall for her partner, and she got the feeling he was falling for her, too.

To think it had all started with John recruiting her into the DCO at the exact moment Braden arrested her. How was that for coincidence?

Unless it hadn't been a coincidence.

This wasn't the first time she'd wondered that over the past week. She hadn't given it much credence, though, mostly because it seemed ridiculous that anyone could manipulate events to the degree necessary to get her and Braden together.

But this was the DCO she was talking about here, and if she'd learned one thing, it was that the supersecret organization didn't leave very much up to chance.

"Can I ask you a question?" she asked.

John smiled, leaning against the table. "Of course. What's on your mind?"

"How did you find me?" she asked.

"Find you?"

She nodded. "Lucy said the DCO spends a lot of time and energy looking for shifters who might fit in here.

But in my case, it had to be more than just the fact that Braden arrested me for stealing a porcelain dog."

John chuckled. "I was wondering when you'd get around to asking me that. No, getting arrested wasn't the thing that put you on our radar, although it did accelerate my timetable about when to bring you in. In reality, I've been keeping an eye on you for a couple of months now."

She frowned. If John had been watching her for a couple of months, that meant... "You've known I was a shifter since I broke into Thomas Thorn's home, haven't you?"

"Yes," John admitted. "A team from the DCO was brought in to help with the burglary case. They confirmed you were a shifter and, in the course of the investigation, figured out who you were."

More pieces of the puzzle slowly started falling into place. "The woman who came to my apartment—the one I gave the diamond and the black box to—she works for you, doesn't she?"

"She does. Her name is Ivy Halliwell. She's been worried about you and will be very happy to hear I was finally able to bring you in to the DCO."

Dreya thought back to that day and the woman's scent, which had seemed unusual but so tantalizingly familiar at the time. Now she knew why. "Ivy...she's the one Kendra told me about—the superhero, right?"

John laughed. "I doubt she'd agree about the superhero part, but yes, Ivy is like you...in more ways than one. I think you two will get along well."

Dreya liked the idea of meeting the woman who had saved her life. Because that's what Ivy had done by getting Thorn off her trail.

"It seems like you and the DCO went to a lot of work to convince Thorn that the person who broke into his house was dead," she remarked. "Why go to so much effort to help me?"

John's brow rose. "You don't think you're worth it?"

Dreya snorted. "Of course, *I* think so. But there was no reason why you should. At that point, you didn't know anything about me beyond the fact that I was a shifter and a thief."

He considered that. "Well, I could tell you that I was intrigued by the fact that you'd never been caught and seemed to be stealing more for the fun of it than the money. Or I could say that Ivy liked you the moment she saw you and didn't want to see you get hurt any more than I did. But while all of those things are true, we also had a somewhat selfish reason for helping you."

"The black box," she concluded.

John smiled. "Exactly. We needed to know what you took that was making Thorn so reckless. He had his head of security torturing people to find you, so we knew you'd stolen something else from him besides a diamond. We didn't know what the box was at the time, but if Thorn wanted it so badly, that was a good enough reason to make sure he didn't get it."

"Okay, that makes sense. You don't have to tell me twice that the man's a douche," she said. "But why was a team from the DCO brought in to help Thorn? What does he have to do with the DCO?"

The director sighed, his brow furrowing. "Sometime, I'll tell you the entire history of the DCO, but for now, Thomas Thorn is my boss. He and several other very powerful individuals pull the strings of the DCO from behind the scenes. Some of them are good people, but others—like Thorn—are corrupt, violent, and evil. When you stole his property, he tried to use DCO assets to track you down so he could get it back."

Dreya shook her head. "What the hell is so important about that box that it's worth killing over?"

"My tech people could do a better job of explaining to you exactly what it is, but in layman's terms, it's a hard drive. A very large and very secure digital storage device."

Dreya had thought it was something like that when she'd first seen it. "I hope you looked at what was on it before you gave it to him," she muttered.

Rory was dead because of Thorn. She hated the idea that he'd gotten what he wanted after he hurt so many people.

John gave her a smile. "We never gave it back to him. Ivy and her partner Landon were able to trick Thorn into believing the black box was destroyed in the explosion that collapsed the building on the so-called thief. We gave him remnants that looked right, but we kept the real one."

That was a relief.

"What's on it?" she asked, even though she was sure John would say the information was too classified for her to hear.

"I wish we knew," he admitted. "Thorn has been doing illegal crap for decades, and we think evidence of it is all on that hard drive. Unfortunately, the box requires a special hardware key to access the data on it as well as some kind of long complex code to decrypt the data after you get to it. We don't have either of those things. Ivy broke into Thorn's mansion a little while after we convinced Thorn the storage device had been destroyed, but she couldn't find the key or the code. Which isn't surprising. I doubt he's going to keep anything of value there now."

"Or he got rid of the key after he thought the storage drive had been destroyed," Dreya pointed out.

"We thought of that, too," John said. "That's why I've had people digging through his garbage for weeks, both from his home and his Chadwick-Thorn offices. So far, they haven't found anything."

Dreya cringed at the thought of digging through the mountains of garbage a place like Thorn's defense company would produce. She hoped John never asked her to look through someone's trash. She'd have to wear a biohazard suit.

"We've also been thinking that the black box you stole was Thorn's backup drive and that he might have another matching drive at Chadwick-Thorn," John added.

"What makes you think that?"

"Because within weeks of your break-in at his home, Thorn started a major security upgrade at Chadwick-Thorn. We haven't been able to get in to look around yet, but we're working on it."

Dreya thought back to the night she'd broken into Thorn's home. She'd searched his desk in his study to see if there was anything interesting in it, and while she hadn't seen anything that looked like a hard drive key, she'd found a long, complex series of letters and numbers written in a little black book in his desk. It had been way too long to be a normal password, and all the letters and special characters meant it wasn't an account number for some offshore account.

"I think I might know the decryption code," she said.

He looked at her surprise. "You do?"

She told him about finding the book in Thorn's mansion when she'd broken in two months ago. "Except there weren't any booty call numbers listed. It was all user IDs and passwords."

"And you think the password could be our decryption code?"

She shrugged. "It was twenty-four characters long and a completely random mix of letters, numbers, and special characters. I can't imagine what else it could be."

"Did you write it down somewhere?"

Dreya shook her head. "No. Remember, I told you a couple of days ago that I memorize stuff like that? I committed every user ID and password in the book to memory in case I ever needed them."

John stared at her, clearly stunned. "You memorized a book full of numbers two months ago and still remember them?"

She almost blushed. "It's not that big of a deal."

"Trust me when I say it is." He took out a small spiral notepad and pen from the inner pocket of his suit jacket and handed them to her. "Write down the code and anything else you remember from that book."

Ten minutes and five pages later, Dreya handed the book to her boss. "That's everything, including some info on overseas accounts. If you want to go in and transfer a few of those into my bank, I won't complain."

John chuckled, opening the book and flipping through the pages. "This is absolutely amazing. I can't believe you can remember all of these passwords. I'll have my IT people look at the code. Even without the physical security key, they still might be able to tell me if these numbers are legit."

"What do we do next?" she asked.

"*We* don't do anything. You've done enough by giving us this code," John said. "I'll find a way to break into Thorn's offices and get the security key."

"I could do it," she said.

John smiled. "I appreciate the offer, Dreya, but Ivy, Landon, and I went to a lot of work to keep you off Thorn's radar, and we'd rather not put you on it. Thorn is my problem. Let me deal with him."

She was tempted to point out that there was no one in DCO better at breaking into secure locations and stealing things, but she decided not to bother. Something told her that John wasn't the kind of man to change his mind just because someone badgered him.

He glanced at his watch. "I have a meeting, so I'd better get going. Keep this conversation between the two of us, okay? Only a select few even know about Thorn and the storage device, so don't tell anyone. And whatever you do, don't ever breathe a word of this to Dick Coleman."

Dreya frowned. How could a man that high up in the organization be excluded from something as important as this? "The deputy director of the DCO doesn't know about it?"

John snorted derisively. "Oh, he knows. Because he's involved with Thorn up to his eyeballs. His sole purpose at the DCO is to keep Thomas Thorn informed of every move I make." He pocketed the notepad and took out his car keys. "I'll see you later. And remember, not a word to anyone about this."

Dreya was still thinking about everything she and John had talked about when Braden showed up with two bag lunches and a couple of bottles of water. He set the bags on the table beside her Glock, then glanced at the silhouette-shaped targets.

"Did you spend the whole time I was up at the cafeteria shooting?" he asked as he unwrapped a ham and turkey sandwich for her, then opened a bottle of water.

She desperately wanted to tell him about her conversation with John and what he'd said about Dick, the black storage device, and the security key, but she didn't. John had told her not to talk to anyone about it, emphasis on *anyone*. Dreya felt like crap about including Braden in that group, but she supposed she was going to have to get used to keeping secrets if she was going to work for the DCO.

She shook her head and forced herself to smile. "No, not the whole time."

As they ate lunch and talked about shooting techniques and what she could do to get better, Dreya's mind kept going back to the conversation she had with John. If the DCO director had that security key, Thorn would probably be looking at a long prison term, maybe even life. She couldn't help thinking Rory was laughing somewhere out there at the idea of Thorn going to prison because a thief had stolen the one thing that would put him in jail. There was something definitely *right* about that.

She might have promised herself she wouldn't go after powerful men with their own security forces, but she'd never promised John she'd stay away. Besides, the promise she'd made to herself was before she'd joined the DCO and realized how amazing it felt to do something for someone other than herself. This was her chance to make Thorn pay for what he did to Rory.

She wished again that she could tell Braden, but she knew he wouldn't approve. Not only because she'd be going against what John wanted her to do, but also because he'd be worried she was getting tangled up with a man as dangerous as Thorn again. When she went into the Chadwick-Thorn headquarters to see if she could track the physical key they needed to solve this puzzle, she'd have to go in alone.

She wouldn't be able to tell him what she was doing until after she'd done it. She only hoped he would understand.

"Can I borrow your Charger for an hour or so?" she asked when Braden came back from tossing out their garbage in the trash can.

Braden looked a little surprised but nodded. "Sure, but if you need to go somewhere, I can take you."

"Thanks, but the thing I need to do is sort of for you." She felt horrible lying to his face like this. "I don't want you to know about it until I'm ready."

Braden hesitated, and Dreya was sure he was going to call her out for lying, but then he nodded and dug his keys out of the cargo pocket on his uniform pants and handed them to her. "Text when you get back. I'll be up at the main building with Clayne and Danica, figuring out what training we're doing next."

The fact that Braden didn't give her any grief about using his car—not even a reminder to not speed or drive crazy—made her feel that much worse. She was going to have to do something special to make this up to him.

It took her a little while to get her weapon turned in to the arms room, but in thirty minutes, she was heading north on I-95 to Chadwick-Thorn's corporate offices. It was broad daylight, so she wouldn't be able to do anything other than case the place, but she'd never found a building she couldn't break into, and she doubted Thorn's office would be any different. Especially since this time, it was personal.

Chapter 16

Trevor gazed out the window of the common area, watching as the sun went down on the four Stillwater orderlies who'd been standing in the circular driveway for the past fifteen minutes, talking to Mahsood and Brand.

When the conversation was over, the group of men moved over to the large van parked near the curb. One of the men looked around as if worried there was someone watching them before opening the door. Reaching inside, he pulled out sets of night-vision goggles for him and his buddies, then short MP5 submachine guns equipped with long silencers for each of them.

Beside Trevor, Brooklyn inhaled sharply at the sight of the weapons. He didn't blame her. Obviously, Mahsood was going with a new approach when it came to Ian. One that included heavily armed men. It probably wasn't a coincidence that the four men gearing up for another go at the hybrid who'd been on the loose since late Thursday night were the biggest and most militant-looking members of Stillwater's orderly staff. No doubt they were among the new employees who'd started working at Stillwater around the same time Mahsood had shown up.

Weapons in hand, the men disappeared into the thick woods. Despite the fact that Mahsood and Brand already had other orderlies out there searching for days, things were different this time. Clearly, Mahsood was cutting his losses and was more interested in killing Ian than capturing him now.

Trevor only hoped Ivy and Landon were aware the situation had changed. Without any way to call them, he couldn't warn them that there were going to be four more people out there in those woods running around with weapons carrying bullets instead of tranquilizer darts. The possibility of this whole clusterfuck turning ugly was getting worse by the second.

"You don't think they could hurt Ian, do you?" Brooklyn asked softly, anguish clear in her voice.

On the street below, Mahsood and Brand got into a shiny BMW and drove off.

Trevor forced a smile. "I wouldn't worry about Ian too much. According to Ivy, he's been running them and everyone else in circles for the better part of three days. I don't see that changing anytime soon."

Brooklyn didn't look convinced.

"While Mahsood and Brand are away and most of the orderlies are out in the woods, we should seize the opportunity and try to get into the isolation ward," he said, both because it was the best time to try and because Brooklyn looked like she could use a distraction. "We could be in and out of there in a flash and catching up with Ian in a couple of hours."

Trevor had been looking for a chance to sneak into the isolation ward since Friday, but the opportunity had never presented itself, which had been frustrating as hell. Since their meeting with Ivy, Mahsood and Brand had that part of the Stillwater facility under constant guard by anywhere from four to eight men. He and Brooklyn had tried to go to the janitor's room several times and hadn't gotten close even once. Mahsood and his goons had just given him and Brooklyn their first—and maybe only—chance to get where they needed to go. Trevor couldn't waste this opportunity.

The thought of meeting up with Ian soon seemed to brighten Brooklyn's mood. With a small smile, she wandered casually over to move the white piece of surgical tape on the far window in the corner. The two of them had been taking turns moving that damn piece of tape every four hours since late Saturday afternoon, and it was getting old. He was ready to get into the isolation ward and get this mission over with. He just hoped he hadn't waited too long. If that shifter in there had died because he'd been too cautious, he'd never forgive himself.

He and Brooklyn headed down the same hallway they'd used a few nights ago when they'd first tried to sneak into the isolation ward. Even though it was late afternoon now, it was quiet. Since Ian had escaped, most of the patients had taken to staying in their rooms. It was like they could feel something bad coming and didn't want to have anything to do with it.

Man, he hoped they were wrong about that bad feeling.

He and Brooklyn made it to the door of the janitor's closet easily, and Trevor was relieved to see that no one had gotten around to putting a better lock on it. While it was a new one, it was as cheap as it had been before. His nose and ears told him there were four orderlies manning the recently repaired doors to the isolation ward, but they were around the corner and down the hallway from where they were, so he wasn't too worried about them. As long as he didn't make a lot of noise popping the lock, it'd be fine.

Brooklyn slipped to the corner to keep an eye on the orderlies while he went to work on the door. The lock snapped so soundlessly that Trevor couldn't help thinking this might actually work out even better than he'd hoped.

Then he picked up the scent of a man coming down the hallway behind him.

Shit.

He'd been so focused on the four orderlies by the isolation ward that he hadn't even thought about anyone sneaking up on them from behind. But the guy was already close and coming fast.

Trevor shoved the door to the janitor's closet open and turned to yank Brooklyn in with him, only to realize she was still at the far end of the hall, keeping an eye on the orderlies near the isolation ward. She had her back to him and didn't have a clue what was coming, and it wasn't like he could shout to get her attention.

Cursing silently, Trevor closed the door of the janitor's closet just as the man rounded the corner and saw them. Trevor prayed the man wouldn't notice the broken door. Maybe then, he and Brooklyn could talk themselves out of this situation.

"Hey! What are you two doing here?" the blond man demanded.

At the end of the hallway, Brooklyn spun around, her eyes wide.

Trevor cringed. No chance that the other orderlies hadn't heard that. This was getting messier by the second.

"We were just taking a walk." Trevor glanced at

Brooklyn to see her hurrying down the hallway toward him. He grinned at the blond orderly. "Getting some air, you know?"

The guy frowned, his eyes narrowing suspiciously. "Uh-huh. Step over to that wall there, and stay where I can see you."

Trevor had the urge to point out that they were standing in a wide open hallway and that there wasn't anywhere he or Brooklyn could go that the man wouldn't be able to see them. But he refrained. Pissing off the orderly any more than he had wouldn't be a good idea.

It turned out that it didn't matter.

The man walked straight over to the door on the janitor's closet and twisted the knob. Not only did the door open up easily, but the knob spun in his hand, some piece of the lock mechanism falling off and bouncing loudly across the hard floor.

The orderly immediately spun and advanced on them, his face angry. "Turn around and face the wall!" he shouted, pointing as if Trevor and Brooklyn were too mental to understand the simple instructions.

Trevor nodded at Brooklyn, then turned and faced the wall, only to have the man shove him against it. The orderly grabbed his arms, twisting them around behind his back. It grated on Trevor to let a guy four inches shorter and thirty pounds lighter manhandle him like this, but he knew he had to put up with it. Hopefully, the orderly would simply take them to their rooms, and this would be a temporary speed bump to their plans.

But then the asshole reached into the pouch at his hip and came out with a set of thick, plastic police zip ties, putting them on Trevor and cinching them tight.

Then he moved over to Brooklyn and did the same. The guy seemed to get his jollies restraining the teenager, yanking the ties so tight, he practically lifted her right off the floor.

"Ow! That hurts," Brooklyn protested.

"Come on, man. Back off," Trevor growled. "She's just a kid."

The orderly gave him a smirk as he jerked the plastic restraints even tighter, cutting them into Brooklyn's wrists. "Right, she's just a kid. Is that why the two of you were sneaking into the janitor's closet?"

Brooklyn let out another cry of pain, and Trevor decided he'd had enough. Screw this perverted a-hole.

Flexing his shoulder muscles, he twisted his wrists in opposite directions at the same time. The plastic of the zip ties held for a fraction of a second, digging into his skin, but then snapped with an audible pop.

Biting back a growl, Trevor grabbed the orderly by the shoulder, slinging him across the hall and bouncing him off the opposite wall with a loud thud.

Brooklyn was twisting her arms back and forth, trying with all her might to get the plastic bands off her wrists or at least loosen them. But all she did was chafe the hell out of herself. If she kept that up, she was going to hurt herself badly, maybe even cut off the blood flow to her fingers.

Trevor grabbed one of her arms and steadied her. "Hold still."

When she complied, he slipped one of his claws under the plastic cuff material and yanked, severing the thick restraint in a single swipe.

Trevor didn't have time to check to see if Brooklyn

was okay, because four orderlies rounded the corner to find out what all the commotion was. That's when everything went to shit.

He threw himself at the four men, but one of them already had his Taser out and tagged Trevor right in the middle of the chest before he could reach them, sending a couple of thousand volts through his body. Trevor stiffened, every muscle in his body contracting at once.

Yeah…that frigging hurt.

A shifter could manage a hit from a Taser, but that didn't mean it was fun, and it still slowed him down as he fought to reach up and jerk the barbed electrical probes out of his chest.

That gave the other three men all the time they needed to dogpile him. He growled but did everything he could to keep his claws and fangs from extending. He fought them with pure and simple muscle power and technique, shoving them away to give him room to maneuver, slamming one against the wall and another into the floor. But then one of the idiots jumped on his back and shoved a needle in his shoulder, injecting him with some clear liquid.

Assuming it was some sedative that the orderlies carried to handle unruly patients, Trevor didn't expect it to have an effect on him, but he'd barely slung one guy off his back and was reaching for another one trying to get to his feet, when the whole corridor went wobbly, and his knees when weak.

What kind of frigging drug had they just pumped into him? He never knew a shifter could be taken this easily, especially one like him, who usually shrugged off drugs like they were nothing.

Trevor took a step forward, hoping movement would

force his body to metabolize the drug faster, but his feet wouldn't work, and he saw the floor coming up to say hello to his face. Surprisingly, it didn't hurt that much when he landed.

Brooklyn tried to run, but one of the orderlies chased her down and shoved her violently to the floor. Trevor promised to find that particular man and kick the shit out of him as soon as whatever drug they'd given him had worn off.

The last thing he saw was someone getting a grip on his ankles and dragging him toward the doors of the isolation ward. If his mouth worked, he might have laughed. He had wanted to get in there, after all.

"Crap. We're in deep trouble," Ivy said over her headset microphone as a van full of men who looked like mercenaries unloaded in front of the Stillwater facility.

It had been bad enough when those four orderlies had run off into the woods with night-vision goggles and silenced automatic weapons thirty minutes ago. Now it looked like Mahsood and Brand were bringing in heavyweight backup. If her experienced eyes weren't fooling her, these new guys were military to the core. And all those bags they were toting sure as heck weren't carrying stethoscopes in them. They were weapons—lots and lots of weapons.

This mission was getting uglier by the second.

"What's wrong?" Her husband's voice came over the line.

"That member of the Committee funding Mahsood's research just sent in more muscle," she said.

"You don't know the half of it," Landon replied, his voice taking on that whisper-soft tone he used when he was worried about being overheard while out in the bush. "I think Frasier and his crew have given up on capturing Ian. They've turned around as a group and are heading to your location."

Dammit. That was all they needed. More heavily armed men converging on Stillwater.

Landon had been trailing Frasier and his group since Friday night, keeping tabs on them and making sure they never got too close to Ian. That had been a tough task, because Frasier's crew was well trained, and that tracker they had was damn good. If Landon hadn't slipped in to mess up Ian's trail a couple of times, Frasier probably would have caught the hybrid teen by now.

The one good thing was that Landon and the hybrid had crossed paths a few times. Somehow, the kid seemed to realize Landon was out there helping him. For a hybrid, Ian seemed to have it together.

While her husband had been running through the woods, keeping an eye on Ian, Ivy had been stuck watching Stillwater to make sure Trevor and Brooklyn didn't get in trouble. They hadn't yet, if the recently moved piece of surgical tape on the window was any indication.

But that could change quickly.

"What do you think Frasier will do when he gets here?" she asked, dreading the answer.

When Landon didn't answer, Ivy felt a tendril of worry creep up her spine. She hated working apart from her soulmate like this. It felt wrong the entire time they were apart, and it made thinking straight damn near impossible. But it was necessary, so she forced down her fear and pushed it into the dark hole it had crawled out of.

"If I had to guess, I'd say he's tired of chasing after Ian and decided to go to the source instead," Landon finally said. "He's probably going to break into Mahsood's lab to get his hands on the man's research. Hell, he might even go after Mahsood. Once he has what he wants, he can chase Ian at his leisure without worrying about what happens if the hybrid gets away."

Ivy swore silently. That was exactly what she'd been thinking, too. Frasier was an impatient man, and if Thorn had been lighting up his phone like he had Ivy's and Landon's, it was likely he was under pressure to make something happen sooner rather than later.

Thorn had called her and Landon a few times right after Frasier had first shown up in the area, wanting to know what they were doing to capture the hybrid in the woods and get into Stillwater for Mahsood's research. Thorn had never dropped anything to confirm Frasier was up there operating on his orders, but the fact that Thorn knew everything that seemed to be going on before they told him pretty much proved it. The scary part was that Thorn hadn't called since late yesterday. It was entirely possible that he no longer trusted Ivy and Landon and was depending on Frasier to get what he wanted.

To say that was bad was an understatement. She and Landon had twisted themselves into knots over the past couple of months to get in good with Thorn. All on the off chance it would get them close enough to find the information that would put him in prison.

If Thorn knew they were playing him, there was no telling what the man would do. He wasn't above trying to have them killed. Worse, while Thorn might think they had switched sides and were playing for another member of the Committee now, it was also possible that he'd figured out who she and Landon were really loyal to. Thorn coming after her and Landon was one thing, but the thought of him going after John scared the hell out of her.

"What's the plan?" Landon asked in her ear. "You need me to come in?"

"No, not yet," she said. "With those new guys moving your way, I want you out there watching Ian. But be ready to come in the moment I call you and say there's a problem. I'm going to get in contact with John and let him know what's happening. With all the trigger pullers showing up around here, we need backup—fast."

"Agreed," Landon said, and Ivy could practically hear her husband's tactical mind spinning as he thought out all the angles. "But what do we do when this backup arrives?"

"I think we need to go into Stillwater and get Trevor, Brooklyn, and that shifter out of there immediately. We can't wait around any longer. Hopefully, we'll catch Mahsood and destroy his research at the same time."

Landon was silent on the other end of the radio for a moment. "You realize Frasier and his crew aren't going to sit back and let us carry out that plan, right? This could turn into another shoot-out like we had over in Tajikistan and Costa Rica and Washington State. Worse, any chance of talking our way out of this with Thorn is going to be gone the second Frasier realizes what we're doing."

"I know." She sighed. "We knew it would come to

this at some point. But on the bright side, we shouldn't have to deal with too many hybrids."

"We hope," her husband said. "But in those other fights, we didn't have to deal with a whole mental institution full of innocent people hanging around either. The chances of a civilian getting hurt is pretty high with this plan."

"We'll just have to be careful."

"Uh-huh. Tell that to Frasier's crew and those other trigger pullers who just showed up."

Ivy didn't say anything. If they were lucky, they would be able to get in and out of there without ever firing a single round. Hell, maybe they'd get really lucky, and Trevor would have gotten into that isolation ward on his own before she and Landon had to go in.

~

Braden looked across the conference room table at Dreya, hoping his face didn't show how much he was freaking out on the inside.

They'd just gotten home to his apartment when the phone had rung, and John called them in to the main office in DC for a mission briefing. While Braden was extremely interested in what the new mission was—not to mention curious to finally get a look inside the secret offices under the EPA building—he had to admit he was more worried about Dreya and what the hell she was up to.

The moment Dreya had told him that she needed to borrow his car to run an errand after lunch, his BS radar had started screaming off the hook. He'd been questioning her about crimes for years and had never been able to tell when she was stringing him along, but when she looked him in the eye and said she was doing something for him, he had absolutely no doubt that she was lying her sexy little ass off.

The fact that he realized it had shocked the crap out of him almost as much as the lie itself. Had he seriously gotten to know her so well in the week they'd spent together that he could tell when she was lying to him?

He'd been so sure of it that he'd borrowed a DCO vehicle and followed her, hating himself the entire frigging time. But then she'd driven straight to the Chadwick-Thorn headquarters on I-295 near Joint Base Anacostia-Bolling. He sat there and watched for almost an hour as she cased the building, scouting along the perimeter fence and looking at the place from every angle.

Dreya was planning to break into the place and steal something. And not just any place but the frigging seat of power of the man who had nearly killed her only two short months ago.

That knowledge had been eating at Braden ever since. It was like everything Coleman had said was coming to pass. Dreya was falling into her old ways, for no other reason that he could see beyond needing to give the shifter inside her another jolt of adrenaline like some junkie. What else would explain casing the offices of the most dangerous man in Washington, DC? Then again, there was always the possibility she was there to get revenge for Rory's murder.

Neither of those things made him feel any better.

Sitting outside Chadwick-Thorn earlier, he had come damn close to calling Coleman and telling him everything so the DCO could intervene before she did something that couldn't be repaired or covered up. Breaking into Thorn's company definitely seemed to be in the irreparable damage category.

The only thing that had stopped him was Tommy's voice in his head telling him he was screwing up, that partners didn't do stuff like this to each other. But he was terrified Dreya was going to do something to break up their partnership and get her canned from the DCO, maybe even sent off to jail, or worse, killed. He couldn't deal with any of those things happening, no more than he could accept her stealing again just for the thrill of it.

Braden knew the reason he was so torn. Dreya wasn't simply his partner anymore. She was the woman he'd fallen in love with.

That was insane, of course. They'd known each other for all of a week. Even if he included all the hours he'd spent interrogating her over the past few years—which no one in their right mind would consider as quality date time—he still hadn't known her long enough to be in love with her.

Yet, he was in love with her all the same.

He had to admit, there was a lot to love about her. She was the toughest, smartest, most tenacious, most stubborn woman he'd ever dealt with. She was also the most beautiful, passionate, and alive woman he'd ever been around. She was funny and engaging, with an infectious laugh and a sparkle in her eyes that were impossible to resist.

Damn...he had it bad.

But that didn't solve the problem. He was a cop, even while he was working for the DCO. It wasn't like he could overlook the fact that she was stealing. So did he call Coleman, or did he trust the woman he'd fallen in love with to somehow not be the woman he once knew her to be? Or did he confront her?

On the other side of the conference table, Dreya was talking excitedly about the mission, wondering out loud if they would get to go to some exotic foreign country like Nepal, Fiji, or Belize. When John walked in a few minutes later, however, she immediately fell silent. Braden could understand why the moment he saw the older man's face. Something was wrong…very wrong.

John sat at the head of the conference table, a thick folder in his hands. "I don't have time for a full briefing, because you two need to be on the way to the airport in less than fifteen minutes if you're going to make the flight I chartered for you."

"What's wrong?" Dreya asked, her face suddenly as worried as John's.

"I have three DCO agents on an operation in Maine, and one of them just called in asking for emergency backup. Those operatives are some of my best, so if they are asking for backup, it's bad. I would normally have a dozen people heading up there already, but this mission is sensitive, and there aren't that many people I can trust to handle it."

Braden frowned. What kind of mission was so sensitive that the director would rather send a brand-new team than people with more experience? He opened his mouth to ask John that same question point-blank when he spoke.

"You don't know Trevor Maxwell, but you're both familiar with the other two agents—Ivy Halliwell and her partner, Landon Donovan."

Braden did a double take. "Ivy and Landon were working for you the entire time they were helping me track Dreya?"

"Ivy's in trouble?" Dreya asked, ignoring Braden's question.

"Yes, Braden. Ivy and Landon were working for me back then," John said. "And yes, Dreya. Ivy's in trouble. She's the one who called for backup."

Braden had about a million things he wanted to ask, but John held up his hand to forestall them. "I know you both have a lot of question, but we don't have time. I have to give you two the basics of what's going on up there, so you can decide if you're willing to go on this mission."

That stopped Braden cold. John wasn't telling them he had a dangerous mission he needed them to go on. He was asking them to volunteer for it.

"What the hell's going on, John?" he asked. "What kind of trouble did your agents get into up in Maine?"

John's mouth tightened. "The kind that involves Thomas Thorn."

Shit.

John opened the folder and took out pictures, placing them on the table. Braden recognized the first few. There was Thorn, then his head of security—Braden was pretty sure his name was Frasier. Next came photos of Ivy, Landon, and the man Braden assumed was the other DCO operative, Trevor. The next two people—an older dark-haired woman with sharp features and a gray-haired man in an expensive suit—were also familiar.

Then John laid out a series of disturbing photos that almost made Braden cringe—and he'd seen some terrible things on the job. The people in the pictures were dead shifters, their bodies horribly twisted and their faces bearing the grimaces of humans who had died in terrible agony. Some of the dead tortured souls were lying on the ground, while other were strapped into beds or thrown onto piles of other bodies. It was truly gruesome.

Braden looked at Dreya. Her face had gone pale, her eyes wide.

He glared at John. "What the hell are you showing us these pictures for?"

"So you have some idea about the kind of people you're going to be dealing with if you go on this mission."

The director tapped two of the photos. "You both know Thomas Thorn. This man beside him is Douglas Frasier, his chief of security. Dreya, it might interest you to know that this is likely the man who killed your friend Rory."

Braden darted a glance in her direction to see her eyes glowing green. She looked fierce—and angry.

"Frasier is up in Maine right now, leading a group of trained killers you'll probably end up facing if you go up there." John pointed out the other pictures, one by one. "Ivy, Landon, and Trevor." He took a breath. "Trevor got himself committed to a psychiatric facility undercover almost five days ago. Ivy thinks he's okay but doesn't know for sure, since she has no way to make contact with him at the moment."

John moved to the photos of the other man and woman Braden had recognized. "You might recognize these two if you follow DC politics. They're Congressional Representatives Rebecca Brannon and Xavier Danes. Along with former Senator Thorn, they're the three most powerful members of the oversight Committee that runs the DCO."

Braden wasn't sure, but he thought his jaw might be sitting on the table. He scooped it up to ask the same question he'd already asked. The one John hadn't answered.

"Okay, what the hell is going on here? What do Thorn and these congressional reps have to do with a psychiatric facility in Maine and with these tortured shifters?"

John spread the pictures of the tortured people out a little more, like he wanted to make sure Braden and Dreya could see them clearly.

"These aren't shifters," he said. "These are regular, everyday people who some very sick, power-hungry doctor experimented on in an attempt to make them into man-made shifters. We call them hybrids. The process is prone to failure, and when it fails, the results are horrible. On those occasions when it is successful, the hybrids are usually violent and uncontrollable."

"Who would do something like this?" Dreya asked softly. "Some of these people don't look any older than teenagers."

"Thorn would do it," Braden whispered.

"He would, and he has," John agreed. "Most of these people are victims of the research programs Thorn has funded all around the world. Unfortunately, he's not the only Committee member involved in this."

"Brannon and Danes?" Braden asked, having a hard time believing that two people currently in Congress would be involved in something like this.

John nodded. "To a lesser degree than Thorn, but yes, they're involved. It's why Ivy and Landon went to

Maine in the first place. To check into a possible new hybrid research lab that Thorn found. A lab probably being funded by Brannon or Danes."

Braden narrowed his eyes. "Wait a minute. Ivy and Landon were investigating a lab *for* Thorn?"

"It would take hours to explain everything to you and Dreya, but suffice it to say, Ivy and Landon have done more to stop these hybrid labs than anyone," John said. "They've also been able to insert themselves into Thorn's inner circle in the hopes of getting enough evidence to send him to jail for a long, long time. Thorn wanted them to go up to the Stillwater facility in Old Town to see if they could find any useful research he'd be able to use to jump-start his own hybrid efforts. Unfortunately, it seems that Frasier followed them and may have exposed the fact that they've been playing Thorn all along."

Dreya leaned forward. "Do you think Frasier is going to try and kill Ivy and Landon like he did Rory?"

John nodded. "That and more. Trevor is in danger, too, as well as a teenage girl who seems to be in the psychiatric facility for no other reason than because the people watching over her family's estate won't be in control of the money if she ever gets out. If the situation weren't complicated enough, there's also a hybrid who recently escaped from the facility and is now running around the woods of Old Town."

Dreya looked horrified. "You expect us to hunt down and kill a hybrid?"

"No. I expect you to earn his trust and save his life," John told her. "There will likely come a time when you run into hybrids so wild that you have no choice but to kill them, but that isn't the case here. If what Ivy says is true, the hybrid is staying in the area because he's concerned about the girl I told you about. Any hybrid willing to risk his life for another person is worth saving, as you'll learn when you get a chance to meet the other hybrids that we have here at the DCO."

Braden could tell that Dreya wanted to ask more questions—so did he, for that matter—but John was already looking at his watch. "There aren't very many people in this organization I can trust on a mission like this. I would have sent Clayne and Danica, but they left this morning with my only other trusted team to investigate a string of brutal murders in Chile that might involve a trio of rogue shifters. There isn't anyone else I can send."

"What about Lucy?" Dreya asked.

John shook his head. "I trust her, but this isn't her kind of work."

Well, that was cryptic as hell. Braden waited for John to elaborate, but instead, he looked at them expectantly.

"What's it going to be?" he asked.

Braden exchanged looks with Dreya. If this wasn't Lucy's kind of work, Braden doubted it was Dreya's either, but he could tell from the look on her face that she'd already decided to go and had assumed he would go with her.

Well, it was his fault for falling in love with such a tough, stubborn, tenacious woman.

"We'll do it," Braden told John, praying to God he didn't regret this.

John scooped all the pictures into the folder and handed it to them. "There's a car waiting outside the door. It will take you to the airport where a private charter will fly you straight to Bangor. You'll be there in less than an hour and a half after takeoff. A vehicle will be waiting for you on the ground with the Stillwater facility loaded in its GPS. It's a short twenty miles from the airport to the facility. Get in contact with Ivy and Landon as soon as you land. You'll find all the information on how to do that on the plane, as well as weapons, ammo, and tactical gear. Only take what you're comfortable using. We haven't trained you on everything yet, so if you don't know how to use it, don't bother with it. Braden, trust Dreya's eyes, nose, and instincts. Dreya, trust Braden to cover your back. This is just like Miami—times a hundred."

Before John could hurry them out, Dreya stopped him. "Don't worry. We'll get Ivy, Landon, and Trevor back here in one piece. The hybrid and his girlfriend, too."

Braden couldn't help but be moved by the conviction in her voice and think his earlier concerns about Dreya had been an overreaction. She wasn't the same woman she'd been. He knew that now.

Chapter 17

TREVOR'S HEAD HURT LIKE HE'D GONE TWELVE ROUNDS with Mike Tyson, his eyes burned like someone had poured battery acid in them, and his mouth tasted like a yak had taken a dump in it. He squinted at the bright lights overhead and tried to push himself up on his elbows, only to realize he was strapped to a metal exam table with lots of leather and canvas restraints. He flexed his sluggish muscles, straining against his bonds. They creaked but didn't budge. Apparently, these people had learned something since Ian's escape.

He supposed that meant he was in the isolation ward. That was good. On the downside, Brooklyn was here, too. He could smell her a few feet away.

He lifted his head and looked around as much as he could but didn't see her. That must mean she was somewhere behind him. He listened, hoping to pick up her heartbeat, but it was lost in the mix of whoever else was in the room. He couldn't see them either. From the scents, they were a bewildering combination of shifter, human, and hybrid, all blended together in a way that made them hard to distinguish from one another.

"Brooklyn, can you hear me?" he asked. "Talk to me, Brooklyn."

No answer.

Dammit.

According to his internal clock, he'd been out for

maybe two hours, three at the most. It would still be another hour before Ivy and Landon would realize there was a problem and ride in to save the day. He was on his own until then.

Trevor closed his eyes and tried to sort through all the scents in the room, trying to figure out if Brooklyn was bleeding, but he couldn't tell. If there was one thing that wasn't in short supply around here, it was the scent of blood. It was like this place had been used as a slaughterhouse for months. That definitely wasn't a good sign.

He lifted his head and looked around again, taking in his surroundings this time instead of looking for Brooklyn. The place looked like a medical exam room straight out of a frigging sci-fi movie. The traditional turn of the century construction had been heavily renovated, and now a big set of operating lights hung over the metal surgery bed he was strapped down on. Multiple trays of stainless steel equipment that had way too many sharp, pointy ends on them for his liking ringed the bed. They reminded him of something designed for torture—or maybe a dentist's office. He could never really tell the difference.

The walls on either side of the room were lined with makeshift holding cells, made out of heavy-gauge wire mesh partitions that had been bolted to the floor, ceiling, and walls. Two of the cells on the right and one on the left held people restrained to their beds the same way he was. Unlike him, they didn't seem very interested in getting away. They were alive, because he could hear them breathing, but the sound was labored and shallow, like they were drugged. At least he hoped that was the case. Something was off about their scents. They smelled like hybrids but not like hybrids at the same time.

He was still trying to pinpoint exactly what it was about their scents that creeped him out when Mahsood and Brand walked in. Both men started when they realized he was awake. But they recovered quickly enough and hurried over to him.

Trevor expected Brand to say something first, but beyond the fact that he looked nervous as hell, the man who ran this place seemed to be content to let Mahsood run the show.

"I'm surprised you're awake already, Miles," Mahsood remarked, his dark eyes regarding Trevor with interest. "With the heavy-duty tranquilizers the orderlies gave you, we expected you to be out for some time…days even. Peter was worried you might never wake up. He was quite concerned about what your sister would say." He smirked. "He's always worried about where his next monthly payment is coming from."

Trevor looked from one to the other. "Yeah, sorry about getting into it with those orderlies. I promise I won't do that again. So, you can let me go to the common room, right? My sister never needs to know about any of this."

For a moment, Brand looked almost hopeful.

"He's special," a female voice said softly.

Trevor craned his head around and saw a woman in her midthirties with dark, curly hair, standing in the shadows of one of the cages in the far corner of the big room.

"Special how, Ashley?" Dr. Mahsood asked curiously.

Trevor's heart began to beat faster. Oh shit, this couldn't be good.

The woman moved out of the shadows and across her cage. In some ways, her cell was much like the others with its same mesh wire construction and brass key lock on the door. But in other ways, it was unique. Unlike the other cells, this one had a window that looked out over the circular drive in the front of the building. There was also a shelf full of hardcover and paperback books, a desk covered with drawing paper and art supplies, a colorful blanket on the real bed, and even an expensive-looking music box with glittering gold paint and crystals on an armoire in the corner. The comfort of her prison stood in stark contrast to the cold and antiseptic feel of the rest of the room, especially the other cages.

As the woman moved closer to the door of her cage, Trevor got a whiff of her scent and realized she was the shifter they'd been looking for. But even from where he was strapped to the table, Trevor could tell there was something wrong with this shifter. The unfocused eyes, the semislack expression, and the slow, careful movements told him she was heavily sedated. It wasn't simply the drugs, though. There was something about the way she looked at him that was just plain creepy. This woman was flat-out scary.

But as unsettling as the woman's eyes were, Trevor couldn't help the feeling that he'd seen her somewhere before.

The shifter stopped at the door of her cage and pressed her face right up to the metal mesh, pushing until her nose was sticking out. She didn't look quite so familiar then—just freaky.

Fangs slowly extending, she began to blatantly sniff the air. She did it without even appearing to be conscious of the change or that people were watching. Maybe she didn't care. Or maybe there was a really good reason this woman was in the wacky ward.

"He smells like me, but not like me," the woman said in a slow singsong voice that made Trevor's skin crawl. "Special."

Mahsood gazed at him. "Really, Ashley?" He picked up one of the medical instruments on the tray beside him. "As special as you?"

"He's not as special as me!" The woman's tone was part petulant, part angry, and part mad as a frigging hatter. "Peter said I'm the most special."

This was the shifter he'd hung around in a mental institute for five days to rescue? He could have been binge-watching *The Walking Dead* and not be this depressed.

Mahsood gave Brand a smile. "Peter is right, Ashley. You're the most special, but this man smells like you, doesn't he?"

That seemed to satisfy Ashley, who nodded as she turned and walked over to sit at her writing desk. "Yes, he smells like me."

Both doctors turned to look at him again, Brand in a nervous way, Mahsood in a cold, calculating manner.

"Do you think that's possible?" Brand asked. "That we could get two of their kind committed to a facility this small in the middle of Maine?"

Mahsood grabbed one of Trevor's hands and dug under his nail with the sharp, pointy thing he'd taken off the tray. It didn't necessarily hurt a lot, because that part of a shifter's finger tended to get desensitized to pain from the countless times their claws came out. But he obviously couldn't let Mahsood know that, even if it might already be too late.

"Shit, man, that hurts!" he shouted.

Mahsood dropped his hand, but probably not because he cared about the pain he'd inflicted. Trevor didn't know what the man had seen, but something told him the guy had just verified that he was a shifter.

"It's likely not as impossible as it seems," Mahsood said, turning to the tray of instruments and rattling through them. "You mentioned that Miles had gotten himself in trouble for taking part in a series of adrenaline-fueled acts that demonstrated a complete lack of impulse control, didn't you? I would propose that what we see as a man living his life on the edge of control is in reality a shifter who is simply bored with a world that moves at half speed from his perspective."

Brand considered that for a moment, then nodded thoughtfully. "That's quite insightful. It makes me wonder if perhaps some of the patients that the field of psychiatry is labeling as maladjusted are in fact simply suffering from some level of this shifter condition."

Mahsood snorted. "It makes me wonder if I should be scouring the psych wards of the world for more shifter subjects to experiment on."

Trevor's stomach clenched. He yanked at the leather and canvas restraints holding him, this time not worrying about how much noise he made. But while the straps creaked and groaned, they held him fast. Oh yeah, these people had learned their lesson with Ian.

Mahsood turned around, a big syringe in his hand.

"What the fuck are you going to do to me?" Trevor growled.

He let his fangs slip out and his eyes flash, but while Brand seemed to be a little taken aback, Mahsood didn't even bat an eye. He simply slammed the syringe into Trevor's thigh, right through the material of his pajama bottoms, and pushed on it until the plastic barrel wouldn't let it go any deeper. When Trevor howled in pain, Brand shoved a leather wedge in between his teeth and strapped it into place behind his head.

"What are you going to do with these samples?" Brand asked as he reached over to the nearest tray for another syringe.

Mahsood didn't answer at first, too busy withdrawing the plunger of the syringe in his hand and filling the barrel with Trevor's blood.

"I hope to be able to use them to recreate the serum we produced from Ashley's DNA. It's helpful to have such a compliant subject as her, but it's likely the effects we see in our test subjects are a direct result of her chemical imbalance. If this subject's serum works better, we might not need Ashley any longer."

"Really?" Brand asked, handing Mahsood the other syringe. "When do you think we can test the serum?"

Mahsood shrugged and jabbed the second needle in Trevor's thigh, drawing more blood. "Not long. The process is getting more refined every time I do it. We could be trying it out on the young girl within the hour."

Trevor felt his stomach drop. Oh, hell no. He struggled again against the restraints, harder this time, his teeth trying to shred the leather wedge in his mouth while his claws extended to reach for Mahsood. But it did no good.

"Don't you think you should wait until the antipsychotic meds in the girl's system have cleared?" Brand asked. "We don't want the drugs to mess up the test results."

Mahsood laughed. "Peter, that girl hasn't been taking her meds for years, no more than the boy Ian was. Don't you have a clue what's happening in your own facility?"

Before Brand could say anything, Mahsood grabbed another syringe off the cart. This time, the needle on the syringe was shorter but as thick as pencil lead.

"Hold him still, Peter. I need a sample of cardiac tissue, and I don't want the needle to bend again like it did the last time we did this. We get this, and Ashley isn't nearly as important to us anymore."

Trevor had been shot before—several times, in fact—but none of those times had hurt as bad as when Mahsood shoved that big bore needle in his chest. His whole body went rigid in pain, and he tried to move away from it, but he couldn't. White-hot fire shooting through him, he turned his head away until he was looking at Ashley, standing at the door of her cage, her face twisted in rage.

What the fuck was she so pissed about? He was the one lying here with a metal shiv shoved in his heart.

"Okay, here's the deal," Ivy said softly, her eyes glowing green in the dark shadows of the forest where Dreya and Braden had met up with her and Landon. "You can find a way to sneak into the secure psychiatric facility, slip past the heavily armed guards in there, and find the isolation ward, so you can rescue Trevor, Brooklyn, and the shifter. Or you can stay out here and fight off Frasier and his heavily armed killers when they storm the place, which should be sometime in the next ten or fifteen minutes. Your choice."

Dreya swung her gaze to look at Stillwater and groaned as the reality of the situation hit her. This was really happening. She and Braden were about to break into a hospital full of mental patients that was protected by quasi-military guards armed with automatic weapons, who were probably much better trained than they were. Well, better than she was, for sure. Oh, and if that weren't enough, the building they were planning to sneak into was almost certainly going to be attacked by a group of extremely violent military types, with more automatic weapons, looking to get inside the isolation ward ahead of them.

This was an impossible situation that only someone insane would attempt.

She and Braden had met up with Ivy and Landon ten minutes ago. The signal that Trevor was supposed to give them letting them know he and Brooklyn were okay was forty-five minutes past due. She might be a former cat burglar and Braden a cop, but there was no time to waste worrying about how unprepared they were for this kind of scenario. This was going to happen. Now, it was just a matter of what part she and Braden were going to play in it.

If it came down to breaking into a secure facility and sneaking around or standing toe-to-toe and shooting it out with a bunch of trained killers, Dreya knew which option she'd rather take.

"Braden and I will rescue Trevor and the others," she told Ivy and Landon. "You keep Frasier and his guys off our backs."

Braden gave her a nod. "Good choice. Now we just have to find a way in there when Ivy and Landon couldn't."

That part had Dreya a little concerned, but she'd rather look for a way into a building than run through the woods fighting. She wasn't a fighter.

Neither Ivy nor Landon second-guessed Dreya's decision. They just checked their ammo pouches, then Landon slipped off into the darkness so quietly, Dreya would have thought he was a shifter if she didn't know better.

"Be careful in there," Ivy warned. "And don't try to be a hero. Just get Trevor, Brooklyn, and the shifter out of there, then get out to the woods behind the facility. When Ian smells Brooklyn, he'll find you—I'm almost sure of it."

Then Ivy disappeared into the woods, making even less noise than her partner. Dreya knew she and Braden were good together, but they weren't even in Ivy and Landon's neighborhood of talent.

"You ready for this?" Braden asked. When she nodded, he gave her a nod back. "You lead the way, and I'll back you up."

The thought of him watching her back firmed her resolve, and she took off across the dark grounds of the psychiatric facility.

While Braden was concerned about how she was planning to get them in, she already had an idea about that. It was so crazy, though, that she hadn't wanted to bring it up in front of Ivy and Landon.

She led Braden into the darkest shadows along the edge of the building, then followed it around until they got to the gardens in the rear. A big, high stone wall ran along the perimeter, and she jumped to the top, then leaned down and grabbed Braden's hand to help him up.

They dropped to the ground on the far side and ran until they saw the door that should open up onto the first floor of the isolation ward—if the quick drawing Ivy had given them was right.

"There's a camera covering the door," Braden pointed out when they stopped. "How are we going to get past it?"

Dreya pulled her canvas bag off her back and dug through it, then pulled a black cylinder about the size and shape of a Star Wars lightsaber out of her bag.

"We're going to blind it with a laser," she said as she set it up on a small tripod and pointed it straight at the camera mounted on the wall over the door.

Braden frowned. "If we blind the camera, won't whoever is watching the monitors know there's something wrong and come looking to see what's up?"

She nodded as she pushed a button on the side of the cylinder, pulsing the red laser just long enough to make sure it would hit the camera directly in the lens. "I hope so. How else do you think we're going to get in?"

He did a double take. "Wait a minute. I thought we were just going to sneak in."

"Nope," she said. "I screw up the camera, they send somebody to check it out, you beat them up, and poof… we're in."

Braden groaned. "That's the best idea you can come up with?"

"Yup."

Dreya swung her canvas pack back on, then got a firm grip on the little remote for the laser and pushed the button. There wasn't a lot to see—unless someone was dumb enough to look down the barrel of the laser, which would blind a person for life—but the 750 milliwatt high-intensity laser was currently scrambling the hell out of the camera.

"Come on," she said, running for the door.

The moment they reached it, she pushed Braden to the side, then stood right in open view of whoever stepped out.

"I'll distract them," she told him. "You take them while they're focused on me."

Braden opened his mouth to say something, but before he could, the door swung open, and a big guy stepped out. He was dressed like a hospital orderly but carried a small, scary-looking weapon strapped across his chest.

He had enough time to stare at Dreya in disbelief before Braden came at him from the side, slamming his fist into the guy's jaw and sending him flying.

Dreya would have cheered, until she saw a second orderly come out after the first. She didn't think but just launched herself at the man, her fangs and claws extending in the rush of pure adrenaline that surged through her.

The man's eyes widened in alarm as she hit him full in the chest, sending him reeling backward.

That's when she realized the situation was worse than she'd thought. There weren't two guys but four. And while she was climbing all over the second one, the third one brought up his weapon to shoot her, and the fourth guy was reaching for his radio.

She had no time to deal with problems three and four. She had her hands full with problem two—the man she'd pounced on. He'd tumbled to the floor and was trying to take her with him. Dreya knew she couldn't allow herself to get caught up in a wrestling match with a man who outweighed her by seventy pounds. She was a thief, not an MMA fighter.

She slashed her claws at the man's arms. He let go of her damn quick.

Dreya had no clue what to do next and really wished Clayne and Danica had spent a few hours teaching her to fight hand-to-hand instead of running around shooting stuff. She was pretty sure firing her 9mm right now would bring a lot more trouble down on them.

"Radio!" Braden said from behind her.

He wanted her to stop the guy with the radio before he could warn the rest of the orderlies.

Dreya clicked the button on the laser remote, praying the door alcove was clear as she turned off the laser and bounded up from the man on the floor, stomping on his face as she leaped for the guy with the small machine gun. She slashed at the hand on the trigger, feeling her claws dig in deep and tearing a grunt of pain from the guy.

Two more swipes, and he was stumbling back, dropping his weapon to let it dangle by the short straps around his neck as he tried to protect his face from her claws. She changed her attack direction, shredding the straps holding the weapon, as well as a lot of his chest and shoulder muscles.

As the weapon clattered to the floor, she shoved him aside and headed for the last orderly, sure she wouldn't get there in time. The man's hand was only inches from the radio.

Dreya growled in frustration.

The man spun around with a look of pure terror on his face, ignoring the radio and reaching for the pistol on his hip instead. She'd been okay with slashing at the other men and hurting them enough to get past them, assuming that Braden would deal with them as he came up behind her. But it sounded like Braden had his hands full, dealing with the three men she'd already left him to handle. She couldn't simply swipe at this guy's hands and face and hope to keep him busy until Braden came to her rescue. She needed to take him out herself.

And how the hell was she going to do that? She didn't know how to punch somebody without breaking her hand, and clawing him in a way that would cause serious damage—like to his throat—almost made her feel ill. She couldn't do that.

So instead, she dropped into a slide on her hip, intending to swipe the guy's leg in passing just like she'd done to Cabo in Miami. But as she slid straight at the guy standing there with his legs spread wide, another target presented itself, and she retracted her claws in time to close her hands into what she hoped was a proper fist and punch him in the balls as she slid between his legs.

The man fell forward over her with a groan as she came up on the other side.

The guy was rolling on the floor, dry heaving so violently that Dreya almost felt sorry for him. Until she remembered the pictures of tortured people that John had shown her. Then she didn't feel so bad.

She jumped on him, rolling him over to rip the pistol out of the holster on his hip. Then she moved to see if she needed to help Braden.

But Braden was handling himself just fine. In fact, he

seemed to be handling himself better than that. As she watched, he pummeled the third guard, the one she'd clawed the automatic weapon away from.

Dreya had never considered a burglary detective as needing to get down and dirty with a criminal, but apparently, Braden was a boxer. A six-foot-plus, really muscular boxer. He was jabbing and punching the man standing in front of him so fast and hard, it was like the poor guy never had a chance. The orderly's head snapped back violently as Braden connected with the tip of his jaw. The guy's legs turned to rubber, and he collapsed to the floor.

Braden moved to clock the guy she'd punched in the groin before the third guy had even reached the floor. One pop to the side of the head, and the guy was out. It was probably a mercy—at least he didn't have to worry about how badly his balls hurt anymore.

Braden turned to look her way when the radio crackled.

"Checkpoint Four, the camera is back on. What's the situation? Over."

Braden grabbed the radio from the unconscious guy's belt and calmly thumbed a button on the side. "Checkpoint Four clear. It was a damn owl sitting on the camera. Over."

"Roger, Checkpoint Four," the voice said. "Return to your patrol. Over."

"Wilco. Out."

Thumbing the button, Braden clipped the radio to his belt.

Okay, she was impressed. She'd just watched him take down four big dudes mostly on his own. Yet he'd talked on the radio as calmly as if he'd done this kind of stuff every day.

She watched him go through the pockets and equipment pouches of the four men on the floor, coming up with ammo magazines, Tasers, and monster-sized zip ties like she'd seen the police in DC use during protest arrests.

Without a word, Braden neatly trussed up the men.

"So," she said softly as she moved over to help. "You're a boxer, huh?"

He didn't stop working but nodded. "Dad bought Nate and me boxing gloves when we were kids. He thought a cop needed to be able to handle himself in any situation, and he planned on us being cops from the day we were born."

She smiled. "Well, yay, Dad. What about the military talk on the radio? Did your dad have you running around learning that, too? What the heck does 'wilco' mean anyway?"

He looked up from the last guy—the one she'd punched in the balls—and smiled. "That's all the Saturday morning G. I. Joe cartoons I used to watch. Wilco is short for 'will comply.'" Straightening up, he looked around. "We need to find a place to stash these guys. They'll be out for a little while, but I don't want someone coming out here and stumbling over them."

She moved over and grabbed his hands to check out his abraded knuckles. Those were going to bruise up pretty good before long. "You know, you're pretty good at this stuff. You sure you haven't been holding out on me?"

He moved his hands to hers, taking in the sight of her

slightly bloody fingertips. "I'm trusting your instincts and covering your back." He flashed her a grin. "Though you might want to let me know before you try anything that crazy again."

She felt heat swirl through her. In that moment, she realized she trusted—and loved—this man so completely, it made her heart ache. "Deal."

"What's the plan after we hide the bodies?" he asked, moving to check out a second door.

She tested the air with her nose, immediately picking up shifter scent and something slightly different that must be hybrid. It seemed to be coming from the far end of the corridor. But it was faint, like they might have to go up a few flights of stairs.

"We follow my nose until we find what we're looking for," she said as she reached down to drag the smallest of the four guys over to the storage room Braden had found. "After that fight, the rest of this mission should be a piece of cake."

Braden looked at her sideways.

She laughed. "What? You're doubting my instincts now?"

—

Chapter 18

"She doesn't look so special to me," Ashley said sullenly as she dragged a ragged, squared-off claw across Brooklyn's throat.

Brooklyn was still unconscious, and the claw barely left more than a welt across the teenage girl's skin, but Trevor still growled at the other shifter, trying to warn her away, even though he still had the stupid fucking leather wedge strapped into his mouth. If he made it out of this, he was going to toss out every piece of leather in his apartment, because he officially hated the stuff. Hell, he might even give up eating cows.

Okay, maybe not.

The sound of his anger seemed to get through to the psychotic woman, and she turned petulant eyes on him.

"Did you say something?" she murmured, poking him hard in the chest with a clawed fingertip that dug into his skin at least a half inch. "I couldn't hear you with that muzzle on your face."

Eyes flashing, he growled again.

Mahsood and Brand had finished taking their damn samples a while ago, leaving him writhing on the metal table until the pain receded. Trevor had been a bit concerned that poking around near his heart was going to cause damage even a shifter couldn't survive, but Mahsood obviously knew what the hell he was doing. That was clearly the case...since he wasn't dead at the moment.

Two orderlies had come in thirty minutes ago and dragged Brooklyn out of her cage and strapped her to the table beside his. He'd growled at them, but they'd acted as if he wasn't even there, then left without saying a word.

Right after that, Ashley had unlocked her cell from the inside and waltzed over for a look at the doctors' newest test subject. Any thought that the woman might have about helping them had disappeared when she'd started poking Brooklyn and accusing her of trying to steal Peter's affection.

Okay, that was seriously creepy.

Ashley leaned down and put her face close to Trevor's, her gaze full of ten kinds of crazy. Her hand came up, and for a second, he thought she was going to rake her claws across his throat. But instead, he felt them working behind his head. A moment later, she loosened the leather wedge and took it out of his mouth.

"Thank you," he said softly.

He wasn't sure how else to start the conversation, but he needed to keep her talking. His sense of time was all screwed up, but he was sure it had been at least four hours. If so, Ivy and Landon would be showing up soon. He just had to give them a little more time.

Ashley tilted her head to the side, looking at him strangely. "Your eyes look like mine," she said in a distracted way, like she wasn't actually talking to him.

"That's because I'm a shifter—like you."

Ashley seemed to consider that, but then leaned close to take a big sniff of him. Her fangs popped out again, like she had no control over them. Her curly, dark hair brushed across his face as her head moved lower, and for a moment, Trevor was sure he recognized the scent. But then the image of the strange woman sniffing the dried blood on his chest distracted him from anything that resembled rational thought.

She looked up at him sharply, confusion on her face. "Peter said there's nobody as special as me. He's told me that many times."

Trevor was about to point out that Ashley had been the first one to suggest that he smelled *special*, but then decided against saying anything so confrontational. Keep the scary shifter happy. That was his new motto.

"You are very special," he agreed. "People like us are very rare and unique. There aren't many of us in the world. We're almost like family."

Ashley winced at the word *family*, like it upset her to hear. It made him wonder if she'd been dumped in here like Brooklyn and Ian by some assholes who wanted her out of the way.

"How long have you been here, Ashley?" he asked.

The woman moved so that her face was only an inch or two from Trevor's. Crap, those sharp features were so damn familiar. Why couldn't he remember where he'd seen her?

"I've been here forever," she said softly. "Since long before Peter came and told me I was special. Long before I was given my beautiful bedroom with my window, my books, and my art supplies. Back when the rooms were all white, and I slept on the floor day and night."

Trevor stared at the woman's face, trying to understand why she was so familiar, while at the same time trying to comprehend the fact that she may have been in here her whole life. And from the sounds of it, she had it much better now than she had in the past.

"Do you remember who put you here?" he asked.

Her face darkened. "Mommy put me here when she said I couldn't live with Auntie Mel and Uncle Joe anymore. When she said she couldn't let anyone ever see me. When she hurt Auntie Mel and Uncle Joe and took me away from them." Ashley's eyes flashed, the scent of anger rolling off her. "Mommy gave me the music box and told me to be good for the doctors, but they weren't nice to me. They kept me in the white room and wouldn't let me see the sun." Her face twisted in a sneer. "But then when I was older, I became special, and the doctors who weren't nice to me were very sorry. That's when Peter came and made everything better."

Trevor opened his mouth to tell her that he was sorry for bringing up unhappy thoughts, when Ashley's head suddenly jerked up, and she looked at the door.

"Peter and the mean doctor are coming back." She looked at Brooklyn. "When they poke her with the needle, will she be special like us, or will she be angry like the boy they tried to help?"

"They're not trying to help her, Ashley," Trevor said. "They're not trying to make her special like us. They're going to hurt her and then put her in a cage. And when they're done doing that, Peter and the mean doctor won't need us anymore. They'll kill us."

Ashley jerked back like he'd struck her. Then she reached out and slashed her claws across his arms and chest. If not for the straps holding him down bearing the brunt of her fury, she would have gutted him.

"Peter would never do that!" she growled, her short,

rounded canines coming out to their full length, her eyes flashing. "He said I'm special. He said I'm his most special!"

Even though Trevor knew it was hopeless, he opened his mouth to try and convince her how horrible Peter was. But she spun and ran to her cage, clanking the door closed behind her and reaching her fingers through the mesh to snap the brass lock into place.

Seconds later, Mahsood and Brand came in. They ignored him, instead going directly over to Brooklyn's side. Brand was holding five syringes in his hand, each full of a different liquid.

"Leave her alone!" Trevor shouted, straining at the bonds. "Or I swear to God, I'm going to kill you!"

Mahsood laughed. "Clever shifter, getting the bit out of your mouth. Quiet now, or I'll be forced to drug you senseless. At least this way, you get a chance to see if your friend survives the serum. You should appreciate that."

As Trevor watched, Brand put one of the needles in Brooklyn's arm and shoved the plunger home. The girl, who finally seemed to be regaining consciousness, convulsed a little but had no other reaction. Trevor shoved against his restraints with all his might, swearing he heard something tearing.

"I'm with the DCO," he told them. "There are DCO operatives moving on this location right now. If you stop what you're doing to the girl, you might just live through this."

Brand looked at him in confusion, but Mahsood said nonchalantly, "If the DCO is coming, then I guess we need to hurry."

Taking another one of the needles, he pushed it in Brooklyn's other arm. The convulsions lasted longer this time and seemed more violent.

Trevor heaved again, feeling his bones creak with the force of his effort. He definitely heard a tearing sound this time and looked down to see that several of the straps were indeed beginning to part. But it wasn't just his effort he had to thank for them ripping. It was the swipe Ashley had thrown his way. She had damaged the restraints more than she'd damaged him.

He shoved and pushed, slowly working himself free. But it was still too damn slow. He wouldn't be able to get himself loose before they pumped more of that shit into Brooklyn's body.

"Mahsood, what are you going to do to me and Ashley when you're done?" he demanded.

"Kill you, of course," Mahsood said simply as he readied the third syringe for Brooklyn's arm.

Trevor glanced at Brand. "Are you going to let him do that, Peter? Are you going to let him kill your special Ashley?"

Brand eyed Ashley for a moment, then shrugged. "Special Brooklyn. Special Ashley. From where I'm standing, there's not a hell of a lot of difference."

Trevor fought his bonds like he was on fire as Mahsood moved the third syringe toward Brooklyn's arm.

Suddenly, a barrage of gunfire exploded outside the facility, and the sound of breaking glass and bullets thumping into brick and wood was almost enough to overwhelm the screams of the patients panicking throughout the hospital.

At the same time, Ashley tore through the door of her

cage, not even bothering with the lock. In a few incredible strides, she crossed the floor of the lab and threw herself toward the doctors. Mahsood ducked, and the insane shifter landed right on top of her dear Peter. The way she tore into him, it was likely that she was aiming for him to begin with.

Trevor strained again and felt the top few straps part. He shoved, then slithered his way out from under the rest, falling to the floor of the lab. His body was still a little sluggish from the tranquilizer he'd been given, but there was no way in hell he was letting Mahsood get out of here.

He pushed himself to his feet and charged across the lab, though charge wasn't a very good word for it. Limped was better. He was still fast enough to get to the evil doctor scrambling toward the door with the three remaining syringes of hybrid serum in his hand.

Trevor caught up to him, slashing his claws across Mahsood's right hand and sending the syringes crashing to the floor. Then he casually swiped the man across the face, opening up four deep gouges and sending him flying. Mahsood tumbled a few times, then came to a groaning, moaning pile near the exit door.

Brand was screaming bloody murder as Ashley tore him apart, but Trevor simply couldn't give a shit. A part of him felt concern that Ashley might go after Brooklyn, but something told him she wouldn't leave Peter while the man was still making noise. If the way she was playing with him was any indication, that would be for a while.

Trevor advanced on Mahsood, stomping on the liquid-filled syringes along the way. The doctor rolled over and looked at him through blood-filled eyes as he reached up to hold his face together. Trevor had never considered himself a violent man, but right then, he seriously wanted to tear this guy a new asshole…about the place Mahsood normally knotted his tie.

He was still a few feet away from the doctor when he smelled men coming. A moment later, three orderlies stepped into the room, their MP5s coming up to point right at him.

Braden and Dreya were still on the stairwell just short of the third floor when shooting started out in the gardens. Braden heard Ivy and Landon over the headset, calling out instructions and warnings to each other, then a god-awful screaming ripped through the air from upstairs.

Dreya was running that way before he could even think to tell her to stay behind him. Why the hell would he have bothered? The woman went wherever her nose and instincts told her to go. Nothing he said was going to stop that.

He hurried to catch up to her as she ran up the stairs, covering her as best he could with the MP5 he'd grabbed off one of the guards they'd taken out downstairs.

When they reached the top of the stairs, Dreya didn't even slow down as she took one of the main branches in the hallway and headed down it at nearly full speed. It turned out to be a good thing he was right there with her, because if not, she probably would have gotten shot by the armed orderly who stepped out of a side room and aimed a gun in her direction.

Braden ignored the cop instinct to shout *Police!*

Freeze! Instead, he lifted his submachine gun and got off the first burst of automatic weapon fire, stitching a line of 9mm bullets through the man from his left hip to right shoulder.

Dreya was forced to slow then, not only to avoid the man's body falling to the floor, but also from the cloud of acrid smoke that was suddenly rolling from the room the man had just come out of. But she charged through the haze and kept going. Braden took a peek in the room as he passed and saw a heavy-duty filing cabinet with smoke pouring out of every drawer, a big computer on the desk that had been shot to crap, and two young doctors in lab coats lying on the floor with holes in their heads.

Somebody's cleaning up.

Braden caught up with Dreya just as a bloody form stumbled down the stairs at that end of the building. He thought it might be Mahsood, but he didn't have time to check as Dreya ran into automatic weapon fire. Braden went after her, quickly taking in the scene of the three orderlies with MP5s chattering out rounds nonstop at a pile of metal tables across the room before turning on them.

Beside him, Dreya took aim with her Glock, shooting slowly and smoothly at the men. Two of the orderlies went down before they realized they were under attack. The third died as he was turning to engage them.

Braden ran toward the overturned tables, sure no one could be alive over there, but then a woman with long, curly hair and blood on her nightgown came charging out, screaming like an enraged banshee. Eyes wild, she ran straight for the corner of the room and into a wire cage that was set up there. She didn't slow down even then but threw herself through a big window covered with steel bars and careened out of sight, screaming like a madwoman every second of the way.

Trevor Maxwell popped his head up from behind the tables and looked at them. "I'm guessing John sent you?"

"Yeah." Braden said, looking in the direction the woman had gone. "What the hell was that?"

"That was the shifter we were after," Trevor said as he stood, carrying a young girl in his arms. She wasn't bleeding, but she wasn't conscious either.

"Do we need to go save her?" Dreya asked.

A pain-filled scream erupted from outside, followed by another, then another.

Trevor shook his head. "That would be a big nope. We might need to track her down and kill her someday, but we definitely don't need to save her." Walking over to Braden, he handed the girl to Braden. "Hold her for a second, would you?"

After Braden had her in his arms, Trevor went over to the window and looked out. Then the DCO agent turned his attention to the music box in the corner and a pile of papers on the desk. He shuffled through them, then lifted one out of the pile and stared at it.

That was when Braden realized Dreya wasn't at his side any longer. He looked over and saw her coming out of another one of the cages that lined the wall. He hadn't noticed until then, but there were people strapped to beds in three of those makeshift cells.

"Do we need to get them out too?" he asked Dreya, even though he wasn't sure how the hell they were going to be able to do it.

She shook her head. "No. It's too late for that."

Trevor came over to take the teenager from him, but not before Braden saw the pencil sketch of a woman in his hand.

"Is that Rebecca Brannon?" Braden asked.

Trevor shoved the painting into his pocket and cradled the girl in his arms. "Yeah, it's her." He glanced over his shoulder at Braden as he fell into step behind them going downstairs. "You two must be new at the DCO. First mission?"

"Second," Dreya said from in front of them.

"Oh. Well, then this is probably just another day at the office for you."

Braden thought they might actually make it all the way off the property without meeting up with any more bad guys, but when they got to the parking lot, two orderlies popped up from behind a car and opened fire on them.

Trevor immediately took cover behind a car with the girl, but before Braden or Dreya could even shoot back, a dark-haired shifter burst out of the woods with fangs and claws flashing and tore into the two orderlies.

Braden didn't realize Trevor was up and moving until he saw the DCO agent walk over to the dark-haired shifter. That's when Braden realized the shifter wasn't another agent but a teenager.

Crap, this must be the hybrid kid.

As Trevor handed the girl over to him, the hybrid's fangs and claws disappeared, concern and fear on his face.

"I stopped them before they got all the serum into her, but they hit her with two syringes full of something, so we need to get her to some people who can help her," Trevor said. "Can you carry her?"

The teen hybrid nodded, gently cradling the girl to his chest as he turned and headed off into the woods. Braden, Dreya, and Trevor followed.

They hadn't gone more than a half mile into the dark, quiet forest when the hybrid suddenly stopped at the edge of a clearing, his head cocked to one side as if he'd heard something. Dreya and Trevor stopped, too, mimicking the hybrid's gesture.

A moment later, a slender, graceful woman with long brown hair stepped out of the darkness and into the clearing. A huge mountain of a man followed at her heels. Surprisingly, he was as quiet as she was.

Beside Braden, Dreya's breath hitched.

"I can't smell them," she said softly. "They're upwind, so I should be able to."

Trevor looked perplexed by that. "Did John and Adam send you?" he asked the newcomers.

The slim girl smiled. "Yes. They said you'd need our help."

Braden listened in disbelief as Trevor explained what had happened in the psychiatric facility, horrified not only by the situations that had put these two kids in a mental institution for life, but by the experiments that had been conducted on them. The worst thing was, it was likely that no one would ever be punished for it. Mahsood had escaped, and no one would ever be able to pin this on Thorn or the other Committee members. They were too powerful.

"Ian, I want you to go with these two people," Trevor said to the kid. "They'll make sure you're safe and taken care of."

The hybrid looked at the girl in his arms questioningly. "What will happen to Brooklyn?"

"I don't know," Trevor admitted. "But I do know that no one will ever try to separate the two of you again."

Giving Trevor a nod, the slim woman and huge bull of a man turned and walked away with Ian and Brooklyn.

"What do we do now?" Dreya asked.

"We head to the airport, get out of here, and hope that Ivy and Landon are able to resolve their side."

"Frasier?" Landon asked. "What the hell are you doing here?"

Thorn's head of security turned to give Ivy and Landon a glare that could have melted the paint off a car as they walked into Mahsood's research lab. When they'd met up with Dreya thirty minutes ago, she'd given them a rundown on what had happened up here, but Ivy still couldn't help shuddering a little at the sight of the exam tables, medical instruments, and metal cages.

The local cops and feds had arrived a little while after everything had gone down and were trying to make sense of what had gone on at Stillwater. Ivy and Landon hadn't filled them in, and she assumed Frasier hadn't either.

Frasier walked over to them, a pissed-off look on his face. "Where have you two been?"

"We were out hunting the hybrid that escaped, like your boss Thorn wanted us to do," Landon said. "We would have had him, too, if you and your goons hadn't started World War III. It spooked the creature so much, he bolted and headed north. He'll probably be in Canada by morning because of your dumb ass."

Frasier sneered. "You expect me to believe that

you've been hunting a hybrid since Friday and only now got close to him?"

Landon's eyes narrowed, making Ivy wonder if he really was pissed or just pretending. Regardless, time for her to tag in.

"How did you know exactly when the hybrid escaped? We never told Thorn that," she said. "Unless you've been up here the whole time. And if you were up here, why the hell didn't you try to help us catch the hybrid?"

"Unless you were just more interested in shooting up a mental institution full of patients?" Landon jabbed. "How'd that work out for you, Frasier? You got anything to show for all the dead people we saw downstairs?"

Frasier looked like he wanted to punch Landon right there in front of the whole room full of cops. But then he swallowed his anger and glowered at them in disgust. "We got nothing. Mahsood is gone, the guards destroyed all his research when our attack stalled, and the test subjects in here," he said, pointing at the three body bags lined up on the floor, "were obvious failures. Without that hybrid, this whole thing was a waste."

Landon shrugged. "Feel free to head north. Canada is a big country. But if you work hard, you might find him in thirty or forty years."

Frasier didn't reply, but the look of hatred he gave them said all it needed to say. If Ivy and Landon didn't have to watch their backs around him before, they almost certainly would now.

Chapter 19

DREYA RODE SLOWLY UP AND DOWN ON BRADEN'S COCK, refusing to move any faster, even though she was oh so close to coming. Pleasure this good couldn't be rushed. The waiting just made it better. Braden lay underneath her on their bed—she definitely thought of it as their bed now—holding her hips to help guide her in a perfect rhythm. He wasn't in a rush, either—even if his teeth were grinding together audibly in an effort to hold back his own release.

It was after three thirty in the morning, and they'd only gotten home from the airport fifteen minutes ago. By rights, they should be sleeping, but the moment they'd gotten to his apartment, he'd pulled her into his arms for a kiss, and what had started out as a sweet display of affection had turned into something more, and their clothes had hit the floor.

Maybe it was the fact that they'd just made it through something so insane, or maybe it was simply because they needed to show each other how much they cared. Either way, there was no putting their passion off until later.

Leaning forward, she moved her hands from where they'd been on her thighs and placed them on his chest, her claws gliding gently across his pec muscles. Braden let out a husky sound of approval, and she scratched harder.

Dreya picked up on the sudden increase in Braden's

heart rate, felt his shaft stiffen even more than it already had been, saw those gorgeous abs clenching tighter, and she knew he was close to coming.

She stopped teasing and sat down hard on him, gasping as he buried himself deep inside her. She'd been on the edge of climax for the past five minutes, and this one single thrust was enough to tip her over the edge. Braden's hands on her hip tightened, and she let him take over, following his lead and riding him to orgasm. When she scratched him a little harder as she came, he thrust up into her even deeper, coming with her in a long, loud groan that made her pleasure more intense.

Once she was spent, she collapsed forward on his chest, her breathing and heart rate matching his. His hands slipped to her ass, and he moved her gently against him, coaxing yet more pleasure from her body. A woman could really get used to this. And she planned on doing exactly that.

After, she slowly slid off him to curl up at his side and drape her leg over his.

"Do you know how perfect you are?" she whispered. "My true partner in every way possible."

He slid his fingers into her hair, caressing her face with his warm hand. "We're perfect together."

"I never expected any of this," she said, tears welling and threatening to roll down her cheeks. Braden's gentle thumb came to wipe them away, but more replaced them. "I knew we were a good team, and when we became lovers, that was even better. But at some point, even before any of that, I felt there was something between us. That I had found my soulmate. The love of my life."

He smiled, and it made her heart squeeze in her chest.

Then he started to chuckle, and even though she had no idea why he was laughing in the first place, she couldn't help but join him.

"What's so funny?" she asked.

"I was just imagining what my dad is going to say when I tell him I'm going to marry my partner, a former thief who breaks into places and steals things for the federal government."

Her heart started thudding harder than it had during her orgasm. "Marry?"

He grinned. "Yeah. Isn't that what two people do when they love each other and can't stand the idea of ever spending a moment apart?"

She nodded like an idiot, grinning from ear to ear. "Yes, that's definitely what two people who love each other do. Was that just a proposal?"

"Not a very good one, no. But it's what's in my heart, and I think that's important to say. I love you, Dreya. I have almost since the moment I slapped those cuffs on you. I promise to do this properly when I get a ring, but for now, I need you to know how incredibly important you are to me. You know that, right?"

She nodded, giving into the euphoria and climbing on top of him to kiss him. "I love you too, Braden. Maybe not from the moment you arrested me, but close. And I don't need a ring to make this official. Saying the words is enough."

Braden shook his head. "No. There has to be a ring. Rings are very important in my family. So we're going to do this all over again once I find a ring worthy of you."

She kissed him again, loving his silly, traditional ways of doing things. Then she smiled. "If rings are that big of a deal for you, we could run down to one of my storage units. I have about a hundred diamond rings you can sort through. That way, we can make it official tonight."

When he gave her a look, she settled down beside him with a sigh, her cheek against his chest. "Okay. We can do this your way. The old-fashioned, expensive way."

"You're worth it," he whispered as he pulled the blanket up over both of them.

She sighed again and snuggled into his warmth. She couldn't believe how lucky she was. Finding Braden, this job, this life. It was almost perfect.

There was just one small thing she needed to do.

Braden barely felt Dreya move as she lifted the covers and ghosted out of the room, but the moment she slipped out of bed, his eyes snapped wide open. He glanced at the clock on the nightstand and saw that it was barely after five in the morning. They'd only been asleep a little over an hour.

Out in the kitchen, he heard her pick up her keys from the counter where she'd left them the other day. All at once, his heart began to thud in his chest. He had his clothes on in a flash and was just grabbing the keys to his car when he heard the soft purr of Dreya's motorcycle on the street below.

He cursed and hurried out of the apartment. He knew exactly where she was heading.

The roads were relatively empty at this time of the morning, so he hung back, not wanting Dreya's kitty cat senses to pick up on the fact that he was behind her. He caught up with her as she merged onto I-295, following her to the exit for Chadwick-Thorn.

Even though he'd known that this was where she was heading, it still hurt like hell to find out he was right. By the time he pulled up to the curb, Dreya was already off her bike and over the security fence that surrounded the building. He opened the door and started to get out of the car when he realized he was wasting his time. He knew how good she was. He'd never be able to catch up to her in time to stop her. More likely, he'd get the both of them caught.

So he got in his car and waited, his guts churning at the thought that she was in there alone, that she hadn't said a word to him, and that she was doing something so damn stupid in the first place.

Braden felt like punching something. He thought he and Dreya had something real, something good enough to keep her from doing stuff like this, but apparently, Dick was right. Dreya was so addicted to the rush of doing something dangerous that she was willing to walk into Thorn's heavily guarded facility. Even after they'd had to deal with a crap storm of the ex-senator's making only hours ago.

He swore out loud, calling himself every kind of stupid. He'd been going with his gut a lot lately, but if he kept letting his gut lead the way, it was going to get Dreya killed. Just like it had gotten Tommy killed.

There was no fucking way he was going to let that happen again, no matter what he had to do.

He had his phone out and was punching Coleman's number before he remembered how early it was. But the deputy director answered on the second ring.

"I think Dreya is about to do something stupid," Braden said, wishing he didn't have to do this.

"How stupid?" Coleman asked.

"She just broke into..."

Braden hesitated as Tommy's voice echoed in his head. *Trust your partner. Trust the woman you love... or it's all over.*

"Braden?" Coleman prompted. "Where did Dreya break into?"

Braden ground his jaw, ready to rip the bandage off and just get it over with, but then he saw Dreya dart across an open space between the nearest buildings and race for a part of the fence where two lengths met at a ninety-degree angle. She jumped up, her foot hitting the chain link mesh halfway up before she caught it with her hands. A yank and a somersault, and she was over, hitting the ground lightly and sprinting for her bike.

Damn. She'd been in and out of the place in ten minutes.

On the other end of the line, Coleman was asking if he was okay, if Dreya was okay. But Braden couldn't answer. He was too focused on Dreya. She wasn't carrying anything in her hands that he could see, but that didn't mean anything.

As Dreya started her bike and sped away, Braden knew he couldn't finish the conversation he'd started with the deputy director. Even though his gut was the thing that had gotten him into this situation, he still felt the overwhelming need to trust Dreya, to ride this out and see where it ended. It was probably going to end up exactly where he thought it would, but he had to know for sure.

"I'll call you as soon as I know more," he told Coleman, then hung up.

Braden turned his car around and followed Dreya as the sun began to crest the horizon. It was a short trip, across the river to Alexandria. Then she zipped through the small, quaint streets of one of the older parts of DC until she reached a warehouse near the river. He pulled over three blocks down the street.

He held his breath as Dreya climbed off her Ninja and walked toward the door. She had to be meeting with the buyer.

But when the warehouse door opened, Braden was stunned to see John. Dreya held out something small and rectangular. A flash drive, maybe?

John smiled, and she smiled back. Then they both went inside the building and closed the door.

Braden sagged with relief. Dreya hadn't gone out to steal something from Thorn for the thrill of it. She'd gone after something for John and the DCO.

He was still pissed about her going without him, and they sure as hell would be having a long conversation about that particular subject. But as he cranked his car and headed to their place, he was grinning like an idiot. They were going to talk, but it wouldn't be with her on the wrong side of a set of prison bars.

Coleman had been wrong about her—and so had he. Dreya wasn't stealing again. He could trust her.

Digging out his phone, he dialed the deputy director's number. When Coleman answered, he told him about Dreya sneaking into Chadwick-Thorn to swipe what looked like a flash drive for John, and that they could trust her.

When he got to his place, he took a quick shower, then made a fresh pot of coffee and sat on the couch to wait for Dreya to come home.

Home. Yeah, that had a pretty nice frigging sound to it.

Dreya walked in the door twenty minutes later. She froze when she saw him, a dozen different emotions flitting across her face. Fear, worry, regret, pain, doubt.

"Why didn't you tell me that John sent you to Chadwick-Thorn to steal something?" he asked.

She frowned. "You followed me?"

He nodded.

Would she be upset that he hadn't trusted her? He'd have nothing to say to that, because he hadn't trusted her. That hurt like hell to admit, even in the privacy of his own mind. He couldn't imagine it would be any better saying it out loud.

But Dreya didn't go there. Instead, she came over and perched on the corner of the coffee table in front of him.

"John didn't send me," she said quietly. "Not directly."

He listened in amazement as she explained about a hard drive she'd stolen from Thorn along with his honking big diamond, the encryption/decryption code, the security key, and everything John had thought might be on the drive.

"John didn't want me going in there, but after what we saw up in Maine, I knew I couldn't just let Thorn walk away," she added. "Not if there was something I could do to help put him away."

Braden had left the apartment a few hours ago fearing that Dreya was going back to stealing, but it turned out she'd risked her life to get evidence that would put a monster in prison. He couldn't think of anything that justified theft more.

"Did the key open the hard drive?" he asked.

Dreya nodded. "I didn't get a chance to see much of it, but what I did see was enough to convince me that what we saw tonight is just the tip of the iceberg. Thorn is responsible for hundreds of crimes, not to mention hundreds of deaths."

Braden was off the couch and pulling her into his arms. Thank God that when he was on the phone with Coleman, about to tell him everything, he had done the right thing and trusted her.

Somewhere, Tommy was smiling his ass off. Then Braden started laughing as a crazy thought struck him.

Dreya pulled back to look at him. "What's so funny?"

"I think I finally figured out what Tommy meant when he said, 'don't be scared,'" Braden said. "He was trying to tell me not to be scared of trusting with my gut instead of my head. It was the one thing he'd tried to teach me from the moment we met, but it was the first thing I stopped doing after he died. Everything changed when I met you, though. You didn't give me a choice. I had to learn to go with my instincts and trust you." He grinned. "I admit, it was hard for a while. I thought you were going to start stealing stuff again to satisfy the animal in you."

Dreya smiled. "Don't get a big head about this, but my inner kitty hasn't been interested in stealing for the thrill of it ever since I met you. I think she found something else to keep her occupied."

Braden pushed her hair from her face. "I can trust you, and so can Coleman."

Dreya gave him a confused look. "What do you mean?"

He felt like crap telling her about the conversations he'd had with Coleman and the man's concerns about her. "He was worried that you wouldn't be able to live without the adrenaline rush that comes with climbing high-rise buildings and stealing. We'd been talking about setting up an intervention in case I saw anything suspicious. At least he knows that's not an issue now."

Her face drained of color. "You didn't tell him where I was tonight, did you?"

"Yeah. I told him you slipped into Chadwick-Thorn and swiped something for John and that you dropped it off a while ago at a warehouse in east Alexandria."

Dreya lifted a hand to cover her mouth, a look of pure terror in her eyes.

Braden suddenly felt like he was swimming in Jell-O. He couldn't seem to figure out which direction was up and which was down. "What's wrong? Is there a reason I shouldn't have told Coleman?"

Dreya didn't answer. She took her phone out of her pocket and pulled up her contacts.

"Who are you calling?" he asked.

"John."

When no one answered, Dreya ran for the door. Braden caught her arm.

"Dammit, Dreya. You're scaring me. What the hell is wrong?"

Her eyes flashed green, and for a moment, he thought she was going to push him away, but then the glow disappeared.

"Dick didn't know anything about any of this because he's Thorn's personal spy in the DCO," she said. "By telling Dick what you saw, you told Thorn that John has enough information to put him in prison for the rest of his life."

Braden's heart stopped. There was no way Coleman could have played him like that. He would have seen it coming from a mile away. But Coleman had played him, and the reason he hadn't seen it coming was because the deputy director recognized how much Braden cared about Dreya and had used that against him.

"I didn't know," he said softly.

Dreya shook her head. "It doesn't matter now. When we left the warehouse, John was heading to the DCO complex to set up a meeting with a prosecutor who would be willing to go after someone as big as Thorn. I need to get there and warn him that Thorn knows everything."

"*We* need to get there," Braden said. "I screwed this up; I have to help fix it. I have a light and a siren in my car. I can get us there faster. You keep trying him on the phone."

Chapter 20

THE FLASHING LIGHTS IN THE GRILL DID A GOOD JOB OF getting most of the traffic out of the way. Braden even managed to get a police cruiser to pull ahead of him and help them make better time. But with all that and the worst of the traffic thinning after they got outside the belt loop, it still took forever to get to the complex.

Dreya's heart raced as fast as the engine on Braden's Charger as she dialed John's cell number again and left yet another message. Why the hell wasn't he answering his phone? It was like something was sending her calls straight to voice mail.

She'd called Ivy, Kendra, and Lucy, but Ivy and Landon were still cleaning up the mess in Maine, while Kendra and Lucy were fighting morning traffic as they headed to the complex themselves. Kendra said she'd try to get a warning to a few other people, but none of them could get to John any faster than Dreya and Braden.

While Dreya was mad at Braden, she was smart enough to realize Dick was a manipulative son of a bitch who'd started working Braden the second they'd met. Plus, she was honest enough to admit that she'd given her partner plenty of reason to doubt her. Hell, she'd doubted herself for a while there.

Braden hit the exit ramp for the complex so fast that his car almost went up on two wheels. He blazed through the front gate, barely giving the guards a chance to check their IDs.

They pulled into the first spot they found in the main parking lot and bolted out of the car just in time to see John walking into the building. Dreya shouted at him to wait, but he must not have heard her before the door closed behind him, because he never even turned around.

They were twenty feet from the building when it exploded.

She and Braden were thrown to the ground as the corner of the building where John's office was disappeared in a cloud of fire, smoke, and rubble.

Ears ringing, Dreya scrambled to her feet and ran for the big glass doors. A part of her mind numbly noted that there wasn't any glass in the doorframes any longer. Funny—she'd never even heard them break.

Braden beat her to the doors, climbing through ahead of her, then reaching back for her hand. There was so much black smoke rolling out the opening, she could barely see anything.

That's when she realized the place was on fire. Oh, God. John was still in there, and the place was burning.

She ran down the main corridor, letting her memories of the layout of the building guide her through the acrid, throat-burning smoke. There were other people inside, scrambling for the exit. She heard Braden shouting behind her, grabbing the dazed and confused people, shoving them in the right direction.

Dreya focused all her attention on getting to John's office, avoiding the pieces of the ceiling and walls that had fallen into the corridor, the sections of ventilation ductwork, and the hanging wires that were probably live. The sprinklers that weren't missing dumped water everywhere, but if the amount of smoke rolling across the ceiling was any indication, the sprinklers were losing the battle with the fire. She tried not to cough, knowing that would make her suck in more smoke, but that soon became impossible as she got closer to the source of the explosion.

Behind her, Braden shouted her name, warning her not to go too far. She didn't listen to him. She had to keep going. She had to get to John and save him. After everything he'd done for her, she had to.

Dreya wasn't sure how he did it, but Braden caught up to her as she was making her way toward John's office.

Braden put his hand on her shoulder. "You can't stay in here. The smoke is too thick. We have to leave—now!"

"We can't!" she shouted. "John's office is right down there. We can get him out."

Just then, a gust of wind whipped through the space, and the smoke momentarily cleared. She was stunned to see that John's office wasn't there anymore. It was gone.

Then the smell hit her. Through all the smoke and fire, one scent cut into her like a knife—blood. Thick, metallic, and overpowering.

It was everywhere.

Dreya's eyes had already been watering from the stinging smoke, but now the tears started to flow.

"We're too late," Braden said, but she could barely hear him over the roar of the flames and the pounding of her heart. "We can't stay here. We have to go."

She let him lead her out of the building, tears making everything around her a blur. They'd been too late, and now John was dead. She wasn't sure how he'd done it so fast, but somehow, Thorn had murdered him.

Dreya sat on the curb in the parking lot across from the main building, watching firefighters move in and out of the rubble that used to be John's office. There wasn't much smoke coming out now, but the entire area still reeked to high heaven of flames, burned wood, and melted plastic.

Braden sat beside her, his arm around her as he tried to get her to drink some water to clear her throat. If she drank one more sip, she was going to drown.

The scene had been chaos right after the explosion as the DCO security force had moved in and tried to make sure there was no one else in the building. It was still early morning, and the guards on the gate had just changed out, so no one was sure who had come into work already, who had been in the building during the blast and subsequent fire, or who might still be in there. Jaxson had stopped by a while ago and told them that they might not know for a while how many people had died.

Order was slowly being restored, but not by the person who should be here to lead them—John. Instead, Dick Coleman—with Thorn at his side, of all people—was acting like he gave a crap about all the people scattered around the area, receiving medical attention.

Dreya felt her fangs and claws extending every time she looked at the two men. They had murdered John, and they were walking around like they were the heroes. She'd never wanted to kill a person before, but right then, she wanted them dead. And she wanted to be the one to make it happen.

Two people suddenly blocked her view, and Dreya looked up to see Kendra and Lucy standing there. Their eyes were as red from crying as hers.

When she and Braden got to their feet, Lucy wrapped her arms around Dreya, pulling her in for a hug.

"You both need to leave town and disappear," Kendra said.

Dreya frowned. "Why?"

"Because John is dead, and Dick is making his move," Lucy said. "A dozen of Thorn's security people are already on the complex, and more are on the way. He knows there are people at the DCO who were more loyal to John than they ever were to the organization, and he's going to fire them. He's also going to get rid of everyone who knew he was involved in John's death, and in a far more permanent way. You two will be on the top of that list."

Dreya didn't say anything. She was still too busy trying to wrap her head around the idea that she and Braden had been targeted for murder.

"Dreya was a thief," Braden said. "She knows how to make us disappear."

She glanced at him. "What about your family?"

"I'll get a message to them somehow," he said. "That doesn't matter right now. The only thing I care about is getting you somewhere safe and keeping you that way. I assume you already have fake IDs, but I'm going to need one."

Dreya felt tears start in her eyes again. After all the crying she'd done for John, she didn't think she had any left. But knowing that Braden was willing to give up everything to be with her, even if that meant going on the run, was enough to make her heart ache.

She nodded. "I can take care of that."

Braden looked at Kendra and Lucy. "Are you going on the run, too?"

Kendra nodded. "We all are."

"How will we stay in contact?" he asked.

Dreya was a little shocked at how calmly he was taking all this.

"That will be up to Ivy and Landon," Kendra said. "They'll find you. Until then, stay off the grid."

Giving both women a nod, Braden took Dreya's hand and led her across the complex. She expected him to take her to his car, but they walked right by it and kept going all the way to the gate and out to the visitor's parking lot where a sedan was parked. Braden opened the back door on the passenger side, then climbed in after her.

Dreya blinked when she saw Mick in the driver's seat. He didn't say anything but simply cranked the engine and drove out of the parking lot.

She glanced at Braden.

"I knew we were in trouble before Kendra and Lucy came over to talk to us," he said before she could ask. "I realized that you knew too much and that Thorn couldn't let you live. Our vehicles would be too easy to trace, so I called Mick. He's going to get us to a place on the Canadian border that we should be able to get across without leaving a trail, but we're going to need those fake IDs first."

Dreya looked over her shoulder as the gate to the

DCO complex disappeared in the distance. This was the second time Thorn had chased her away from DC, but this time, it was different. She wasn't running just to protect herself but the man she loved, too. She had no doubt the former senator would come after both of them, and she'd do anything to keep Braden safe.

Turning around, she grabbed Braden's hand and squeezed it. He squeezed back, then leaned over to kiss her. Something told her that they were going to have to go deep underground to escape Thorn's reach, but as long as she and Braden were together, that was all that mattered.

Epilogue

FRASIER STOOD TO ONE SIDE OF THE BIG DCO CONFERENCE room as Thorn briefed the other members of the Committee and brought them up to speed on the people he thought were responsible for the bomb that killed John Loughlin.

Almost everyone on the Committee seemed uncomfortable with where the organization was heading, but no one said anything, not even that ballbuster Rebecca Brannon. That surprised him. Thorn had already appointed Coleman the new director without consulting them, going with the whole "we must act decisively in this time of danger and uncertainty" bullshit. Frasier never would have thought Brannon was the kind of woman who'd go along with someone else running the show, but she merely sat at the table alongside her fellow Committee members with a calculating look on her face.

"We're sure it was an inside job," Thorn said. "Initial indications are that the explosives used came straight out of the DCO bunkers."

Frasier almost laughed. Of course it was an inside job.

He'd just gotten back into town from that fiasco in Maine when Thorn had called him and said that Loughlin needed to die—ASAP. Less than an hour later, one of Frasier's most trusted friends at the DCO had dropped off a copier paper box full of C-4 plastic explosives to Loughlin's office, then remotely triggered the device the moment the director had shown up for work.

At the front of the room, Coleman gestured to the projection screen. "The investigation is still ongoing, but we've already positively identified these people as part of the assassination plot. There may be others, but these twelve are the ringleaders."

Xavier Danes frowned. "You're sure of that?"

Frasier wondered for about the hundredth time what Danes's deal was. In all the time Frasier had worked for Thorn, he'd never been able to get a handle on whether Danes was a saint, a demon, or something in between. The guy was a consummate politician. He never gave anything away.

Coleman smiled, clearly enjoying his rapid rise to power. "Within two hours of the explosion, all twelve vanished off the radar. I think that's conclusive evidence of guilt."

Xavier considered that, his expression once again unreadable. "I see."

"Since we need to move quickly, I've already authorized the assassination of all twelve former DCO members," Thorn continued. "They are to be eliminated immediately, on sight."

Several Committee members shifted in their seats and exchanged looks, obviously stunned Thorn was going to kill the *rogue* DCO agents. But again, none of them said anything. That was how the Committee worked. If Thorn suggested something and Danes and Brannon didn't object, none of the other five would even open their mouths.

"John Loughlin was a good man," Thorn added. "He did a lot of good things for this organization, but he also let in a lot of bad apples. We need to clean house before we can move forward as an organization. To that end, I've put a team together under the control of my head of security, former DCO agent Douglas Frasier, to move out and quickly deal with these rogue agents...unless there are any objections?"

Of course, there weren't any. The whole fancy Committee had turned into a bunch of church mice. Now it was all on Frasier to make all their problems go away.

As he studied the photos displayed on the screen, he realized the hardest issue would be deciding which one to kill first—Landon Donovan, Ivy Halliwell, Kendra and Declan MacBride, Clayne and Danica Buchanan, Angelo Rios, Minka Pajari, Jayson Harmon, Layla Halliwell, Braden Hayes, or Dreya Clark.

Decisions, decisions, decisions.

Here's a sneak peek at the next book in Paige Tyler's sizzling X-Ops series

HER DARK HALF

Quantico, Virginia

"THE DIRECTOR WANTS YOU IN HIS OFFICE ASAP."

Trevor Maxwell glanced up from the hot dog he was eating to look at the guy standing in front of his table. Short and stocky, the man was regarding him like something to be scraped off the bottom of his shoe. Trevor resisted the urge to bare his teeth in a snarl and took another bite of his hot dog. He wasn't really hungry, but at least lunch was a pleasant break from the monotony of an otherwise miserable day. And the cafeteria served damn good hot dogs.

Unfortunately, he'd had a lot of miserable days at the Department of Covert Operations, the secret government organization where he worked. It came with being labeled a traitorous freak.

"You have a problem understanding what ASAP means?" the man asked, a buttload of attitude lacing his words.

Gaze never leaving the man, Trevor slowly finished chewing, then swallowed. "It means Dick Coleman wants me in his office *as soon as possible*. I'll go just as soon as I finish eating. Because I couldn't *possibly* leave before that."

The man looked like he wanted to say something snide in reply, but when Trevor let his eyes glow coyote-yellow and his upper canines slide out far enough to extend over his lower lip, the guy quickly changed his mind.

"Whatever," the man muttered. "Your funeral."

The comment probably would have come across as more ominous if the asshat hadn't shuddered before walking away. But hey, most of the guys that had been brought into the DCO lately didn't have a lot of experience with shifters, and seeing a man sprout claws and fangs—not to mention flashing gold eyes—was a bit much for most of them to deal with. Most of the other people around the cafeteria were regarding him with the same mix of hatred and revulsion. It wasn't only the muscle-headed thugs Dick—or rather Thomas Thorn, the man Dick answered to—had hired lately. The agents who'd worked alongside shifters like Trevor for years were throwing him dirty looks, too.

Trevor supposed hating shifters was sociably acceptable now that John Loughlin, the former director of the DCO and de facto champion of the organization's shifter program, had been killed when a bomb had exploded in his office.

The day John had died everything had changed. Now the covert intelligence organization the man had spent more than a decade building from the ground up was quickly falling apart from the inside out.

One look around the cafeteria proved that. It was lunchtime, yet you'd never know it from the handful of people scattered around the room shoving food in their faces as if they couldn't wait to be somewhere else. The place used to be filled with agents, analysts, and other support personnel at this time of day. While there'd always been some who were anti-shifter in the DCO, their numbers had been more than offset by those who realized the good that people like Trevor and his kind brought to the organization.

Somehow, John had perfected the concept of pairing shifters with highly trained covert operatives. People had said it would never work, that shifters were little more than animals and couldn't be trusted to work in a team environment, much less be given missions critical to national defense. John had proven the doubters wrong, fielding teams that had accomplished things that should have been impossible.

But John's death had led to a complete change at the top of the organization, and the new regime was blatant in their opposition to all things shifter. These days there were probably half as many people working for the DCO as there had been a month ago. Trevor couldn't blame them. Why stay when Dick's very first act had been to announce that the very shifters John had trusted had conspired to murder him? There hadn't been any proof of course, but then again, when had that bastard Dick ever let something like proof get in the way of what he wanted? Hell, he'd barely let John's seat get cold before sitting in it.

Lots of good agents had read the writing on the wall and bailed. The moment they were gone, Dick had filled their positions with trigger-pullers who spent most of their time chasing the rogue shifters or sitting on their asses.

It made Trevor wonder what the hell he was still doing here.

COMING SEPTEMBER 2017

Check out this teaser of the next book in Paige Tyler's heart-pounding SWAT series

WOLF HUNT

Remy didn't realize how much he'd missed New Orleans, but as he walked down Bourbon Street basking in the ambience of the city he called home, he remembered why he loved it so much. To make it even better, he was getting the chance to show it off to the most important people in his life—his pack mates. SWAT officers-slash-werewolves Max Lowry, Jayden Brooks, and Zane Kendrick took in the bright lights, crowds of partying people, various music coming from nightclubs on either side of the street, and the unique combination of scents hanging in the air with a mix of curiosity and excitement.

His mouth twitched. Yeah, New Orleans had that kind of effect on people.

Gage Dixon, their boss, pack alpha, and commander of the Dallas SWAT team, had sent the four of them to New Orleans to cross-train with the city's SWAT teams. At the same time, four officers from NOPD SWAT would take part in a weeklong exercise in Dallas. Cross-training with cops who weren't werewolves meant hiding their abilities, so Gage had made his expectations extremely clear.

"Don't run too fast, lift anything you shouldn't be able to, let your tempers get away from you, and whatever you do, no claws, fangs, or frigging glowing eyes," Gage reminded them before they'd left.

Remy let Zane and Max lead the way as the four of them headed down Bourbon Street.

"Is it always this wild here?" Zane asked as a group of attractive women passing by gave them long, lingering looks and dazzling smiles.

"Yeah, it's always like this," Remy confirmed. "New Orleans is a city that takes the concept of having a good time to a whole different level."

Remy whipped his head around and sniffed the air when an unusual but extremely tantalizing scent caught his attention. His nose was okay, certainly nothing special. It made him wonder why he was picking up this particular smell so clearly.

There were a lot of scents on Bourbon Street. Sweat, booze, perfume, cigarette and cigar smoke, moldy wood, drugs, sex—you name it. This particular scent stuck out like a rose in the middle of all that other stuff, demanding his attention.

"Hey, you okay?" Brooks asked.

Brooks was one of his pack mates blessed with a good nose. Remy turned to the big guy.

"Do you smell that?" he asked.

Brooks sniffed. "I smell a lot of things. Which one are you talking about?"

"That flowery, spicy scent."

Brooks sniffed again. Beside him, Max did the same. They both looked at him and shook their heads.

"I don't smell anything like that," Brooks said.

Remy breathed deeply through his nose and almost got weak-kneed. What was more, he actually started getting a boner. What the hell?

He glanced at Brooks and Max. "You guys are screwing with me, aren't you? You seriously can't smell that?"

He didn't have a clue what the hell he was smelling, but he damn well knew he needed to figure out what it was. He'd go nuts if he didn't.

"I'm going for a walk," he said.

Zane and the other guys followed as he moved down the street.

He realized he was following a woman. He tried to tell himself that was insane. He'd smelled thousands of women since becoming a werewolf. None of them had ever possessed a spicy flowery scent this delectable. Not even close.

Remy walked faster. The curiosity was killing him. What kind of woman could generate a scent so powerful it gave him a hard-on the moment he caught a whiff?

He wasn't sure how long he followed the scent, but the next thing he knew, he was walking into a nightclub with a throbbing dance beat. In bloodhound mode, he headed straight to the second floor, moving like an arrow shot through the crowded, noisy room until he was standing in the middle of the dance floor full of gyrating bodies.

Right there, dancing with her back to him in a group of four other women, was the source of the scent that had dragged him across the French Quarter. This close, the scent was damn near overwhelming. If he wasn't such a gentleman, he probably would have leaned forward and licked the small portion of her neck that was exposed every time her long black hair swung aside. If she smelled this good, he could only imagine how she tasted.

He was trying to figure out the best way to initiate a conversation—tapping her on the shoulder and saying he'd been tracking her scent for blocks might come off a bit stalkerish—when the woman turned to face him.

Maybe she'd sensed him behind her, or perhaps it was because her friends had stopped dancing to stare over her shoulder at him. Either way, when she spun around, Remy swore his heart stopped beating for a second.

It was dark on the dance floor and the flashing strobes were bright enough to practically blind him, but it didn't matter. The light brown–skinned beauty would have stood out in any light. Hell, she would have stood out in complete darkness, too.

He was still taking in the smoking hot curves, perfect skin, and exotic amber eyes when a realization struck him so hard he almost stumbled backward.

He *knew* her. Not in the biblical sense, though that was obviously one hell of a shame. He'd known her back in high school when she'd been a skinny, awkward teenager who never seemed to look anywhere but at the ground.

She was a lot different now—understatement there—and easily the most beautiful woman he'd ever seen. Now she possessed a confidence that made it hard to look at anything but her. Even with all the changes, he would have known her anywhere. He hadn't talked to her since high school graduation, but they'd been friends, and probably would have been more if he hadn't been such a chickenshit back then.

"Triana?"

Remy didn't expect her to recognize him. While she'd grown from a girl into a woman, he'd grown from a boy into a werewolf. He looked a lot different than he had in high school.

Triana's eyes widened. "Remy, is that seriously you?"

Coming June 2017

Acknowledgments

I hope you enjoyed Dreya and Braden's story. When we first met the "cat" burglar, we knew a by-the-book detective would be perfect for her—even if she didn't! Now, with everyone on the run, it's up to Trevor Maxwell to catch the people responsible for setting that bomb, something that will be even more difficult because the new DCO director, Dick Coleman, is pairing him up with a partner he's not sure he can trust.

This whole series would not be possible without some very incredible people. In addition to another big thank-you to my hubby for all his help with the action scenes and military and tactical jargon, I'd like to thank my agent, Bob Mecoy, for believing in us and encouraging us and being there when we need to talk; my editor and go-to person at Sourcebooks, Cat Clyne (who loves this series as much as I do and is always a phone call, text, or email away whenever I need something); and all the other amazing people at Sourcebooks, including my fantastic publicist, and their crazy-talented art department. The covers they make for me are seriously droolworthy!

Because I could never leave out my readers, a huge thank-you to everyone who has read my books and Snoopy danced right along with me with every new release. That includes the fantastic people on my amazing street team, as well as my assistant, Janet. You rock!

I also want to give a big thank-you to the men, women, and working dogs serving in our military, as well as their families.

And a very special shout-out to our favorite restaurant, P.F. Chang's, where hubby and I bat story lines back and forth and come up with all of our best ideas, as well as a thank-you to our fantastic waiter, Andrew, who sends our order to the kitchen the moment we walk in the door!

I hope you'll enjoy the seventh book in the X-Ops series, coming soon from Sourcebooks, and look forward to reading the rest of the series as much as I look forward to sharing it with you.

If you love a man in uniform as much as I do, make sure you check out my other action-packed paranormal/romantic-suspense series from Sourcebooks called SWAT (Special Wolf Alpha Team)!

Happy Reading!

About the Author

Paige Tyler is a *New York Times* and *USA Today* bestselling author of sexy, romantic suspense and paranormal romance. She and her very own military hero (also known as her husband) live on the beautiful Florida coast with their adorable fur baby (also known as their dog). Paige graduated with a degree in education but decided to pursue her passion and write books about hunky alpha males and the kick-butt heroines who fall in love with them.

Visit Paige at her website at www.paigetylertheauthor.com and be sure to sign up for her newsletter to receive a free ebook.

She's also on Facebook, Twitter, Tumblr, Instagram, tsu, Wattpad, Google+, and Pinterest.